The Wallflower & The Running Back

by USA TODAY bestselling author

GINGER SCOTT

For all us nerdy, curvy girls!

Diffusion: *the movement of molecules from areas of high concentration to areas of low concentration.*

Wallflower: *a person who typically prefers areas of low concentration over areas of high concentration.*

prologue

Rachel Edwards

I DON'T KNOW why I thought having my big brother tag along with me at freshman orientation instead of my parents was a good idea, but it's too late to rehash that idea now. He's already called me Squirt twice in front of people I hoped to impress. And now he's inviting the tall, blonde, senior sociology student running the future alumni booth to his football game at state, three hours away.

Great. She just said yes.

"You're gonna love it here, Squirt." That makes three. And this time he actually ruffles my hair.

I glance around and sigh in relief that nobody seems to have heard him. I love my brother Casey. And I know his doting over me comes from a well-meaning place. But as much as the both of us would like to see me blossom into an amazing social butterfly during my college years, I'm not cut from the same outgoing fabric that my brother is. He's charismatic. Like a magnet, people cling to him. They seek him out at parties simply to be around him. They throw parties simply to invite him in hopes that he'll come.

I am the flip side of the magnet. The side that pushes

people away. I am in constant diffusion, drifting from the action—from people. I survive on the perimeter. It's where I'm comfortable. It doesn't mean I like it.

"Something wrong, Squirt?"

Four.

I plaster on a tightlipped smile and push my glasses up my nose, shaking my head. "I'm good. A little overwhelmed, but . . . good."

The crowd of freshmen is filing into the arena, where we'll break into groups and be forced to get to know one another. I'm dreading this, but also, I know it's something I have to push through. A hand lands on my shoulder as I start to spin—both physically and metaphorically. My brother nudges me to face him and drops his chin to meet my eyes.

"I can stick around longer if you want. We can grab dinner?" His brow lifts. He's giving me an out. And as much as I want to leap at him with a hug and beg him to transfer to Tiff for his senior year and rent an apartment with me, I know that's not practical.

I give him a tepid shake of my head.

"I got it. Thank you so much for coming today." I push up on my toes and hug my brother tight. He chuckles, probably because I'm shaking like a leaf.

"You're gonna do great, Rachel. I promise."

He kisses the top of my head and I break our hug first, trying not to cling to him.

"Call me after your game Saturday. You know I like hearing about it, even if it's on TV." I grin at Casey with pride and memorize his comforting wink as he backs away then turns to leave me on my own. He's a senior tight end at Southern Iowa State, which is about thirty minutes away from our parents' home, and he plans on opening a second family hardware store with our father after he graduates.

I've been watching Casey play football since I was old enough to handle three hours in a bleacher seat. I'm going to miss seeing him play this year. It was always part of my routine. How I spent every Friday and Saturday night with my parents for most of my life. I'm going to miss a lot of those routine comforts of home. But that's what growth is, right? Pushing through personal boundaries and stepping into the sunlight.

"Hey, first-year! This way!"

I spin to my right at the sound of someone shouting and immediately smash my face into an incredibly hard, very immoveable chest.

"Oh, shit!" The guy attached to the chest steadies me as his massive hands land on my shoulders. My nose burns with a sensation that makes me feel as though it's bleeding. *Oh, God! Is it bleeding?* I blot at it with the back of my hand to check.

"I'll be right there!" the guy shouts. I blink to focus on his face and stem the watering. Hair the color of an old penny piles into waves on top of his head, the sides shaved into a fade the way my brother wears his hair. Faint freckles dot his cheeks, and his mouth pushes into a crooked smile. His green eyes are hugged by the crinkles formed from his grin.

"He was calling me. Sorry you got caught in that crossfire, Shortcake." He breathes out a short laugh, and I'm not sure if he's being friendly or smug. He's wearing a Tiff U jersey, and I note the number to look up later—thirty-four.

"Shortcake?" I wriggle my arms out of the sling backpack we all were given at the orientation fair. It tightened around my body when we collided and was cutting into my shoulders' circulation.

"Yeah, you know—cuz they're red?" He picks up one of my strawberry blonde braids then drops it back to my shoulder.

My mouth forms the shape to say *Oh* but nothing comes out.

"See ya 'round, Shortcake." He winks before he jogs off toward another guy in a jersey, and as annoyed as our brief exchange left me, it also left me feeling something else. Not quite flushed, but definitely not like I'm *going to do great* here.

Three years later

rachel edwards

I **FELT** my phone buzz in my back pocket an hour ago. I was finishing up inventory when the call came in, which made for a convenient excuse to put off listening. I'm out of excuses now, however. And I am terrified.

I applied for the fall semester abroad scholarship three months ago, and I haven't stopped thinking about it the entire first half of summer. I recognized the university's number on my missed calls list. I could push a button to read a transcript of the message someone left. But I can't seem to get myself to do that either.

What if I didn't get it?

Of course I have a contingency. The classes are already reserved for me to swap in should I need to take my final labs instead this fall. But I've already let my mind wander to the adventure of studying in Germany. Of learning from the best. Exploring Berlin on my own, living out an adventure, and writing for scientific publications with scientists I've looked up to my entire life on hand to review my work. If I don't get this scholarship and I have to wait and apply again for

Spring, I'm not sure my soul will be able to handle it, let alone my heart.

Pacing through my brother's store isn't doing me any good. And since he took the day off to get in some fishing with his buddies, he won't be back anytime soon to help me rip off the proverbial Band-Aid. My parents are busy with the main store's redesign, and truth be told, neither of them are hip to the idea of me venturing over the Atlantic alone. I don't want their negative energy putting a curse on my news.

I flip the sign in the store window to closed, not that we have had a customer in the last two hours. I drag my way to the back office and hang my apron on the hook behind the door. Pushing a stack of invoices to one side, I take a seat on my brother's desktop and palm my phone.

Deep breath.

Rather than pressing play and holding my phone to my ear, I text my best friend Stella for reassurance.

ME: *I got the scholarship message. I'm afraid to listen.*

I wait for her to write back, but when my message sits on delivered for nearly two minutes without any sign that she's reading or responding, I figure she's probably still working in the lab. She took an internship this summer near Tiff, working with a start-up supplement company running toxicology tests. I lucked out rooming with her sophomore year after a terrible dorm experience my very first semester.

My first-year roommates were sorority pledges who both rushed and moved out within weeks of the school year beginning. They managed to pack a lifetime of partying into our time together, though, usually bringing elements of the parties back to our shared and tiny dorm room. The amount of times I slept in the rec room that first month should have earned me a break in my room fee. Stella had a similar experience, and when she posted in the roommate search group for the Tiff science department, I was the first to respond.

We clicked instantly. Two introverts who preferred spending our weekends watching period dramas and having frozen yogurt for lunch rather than actual meals. We have had every lab together since we became roommates, and made plans to apply to the same grad programs. When I started dating Dalton, she fit in as the three of us had been friends for years.

Despite how alike we are, though, Stella brims with confidence. While she prefers to hang out on the fringes, she's quite comfortable basking in the spotlight. And she's fearless about the future. She'd rip this scholarship Band-Aid off in a blink and demand it deliver me good news. Crazy part is, the universe would listen and heed her wish.

I'm going to have to do this on my own. If I'm so confident I'm ready to travel abroad alone, I should be able to handle the simple act of bracing myself for acceptance or rejection via voicemail.

"Dear universe, you know what Stella would want. Make it so." I smirk at my weird, mystical voodoo wish then press play on the message.

"Hello, Miss Edwards. This is Patricia Sewald. I'm the executive director of the Midwest Region Studies Abroad program, and I am calling to let you know that unfortunately . . ."

The message went on for another twenty-seven seconds. It played. I have no idea what words she said after that devastating one—*unfortunately*.

My phone is ringing with the call I made to Dalton. I don't remember swiping to his contact info. I don't remember how I got outside the store. I hope I locked up, but I can't recall actually pushing a key into the lock. I'm not sure I should drive, but I don't know what else to do.

His voice filters through my speakers as my phone syncs with my Bluetooth.

"This is Dalton. I'm pre-law. I don't do phone calls. Do what you will." It beeps and I hang up, no longer amused by what I once thought was such a clever and witty voicemail greeting. Right now it feels cold. That message is meant for other people. Not me.

I press call again, the patter of summer rain dotting the sheen of dust on my windshield. I flip the wipers on and they smudge muddy streaks across the glass.

"This is Dalton. I'm pre-law. I don't—"

I end the call quicker this time.

He must be in the library.

My pulse thrums throughout my body; even my fingertips are pulsing with the rapid beat of my heart. It takes my jittering hands a few attempts to send Dalton a text to let him know I'm going to be invading his study room in a matter of minutes. He's been studying for his LSATs for weeks. He stayed on campus to take part in Tiff's special eight-week prep course. He's applying to Harvard, and the score is everything. While he was toiling away over legal precedents and practicing his analytical reasoning skills, I was earning twenty bucks an hour helping my brother set up the new family hardware store. I figured I could use the extra money for my time in Europe.

What a waste.

The sun set, and I passed through three separate pop-up storms during the two-hour drive up to Tiff. The trip somehow took forever yet happened in a blink. I never turned the radio on, a strange fact that only now hits me as I pull into a visitor spot just outside the main campus library. I don't think I've ever driven without music.

Where have my thoughts been? Unfortunately. *That's where.*

I hit the lock button on my key fob and shove my phone in the back pocket of my jeans as I march across the well-manicured lawn. The hum of sprinklers echoes in the distance, filling the air with the scent of wet grass. I take the library steps two at a time, my pulse now booming against my eardrums. I have yet to cry, but only because I'm holding on to delusional hope that when I see Dalton he'll magically make it better. As if he could say *just kidding* and make it all right.

I spot the back of his head through the glass door of the farthest study room and make a beeline toward him. His hands are on either side of the table, palms flat on the surface and head locked in place, staring at his computer screen. For a moment, I wonder if he's fallen asleep. But then I slip through the last row of tables near the reference section, and get a full view of how my nightmare of a day ends.

Stella is on the floor. Between his knees. I grind to a halt and puff out a silent laugh that stings my chest like a hot knife. I'm frozen in place for several seconds. I can't even blink. Mentally rewinding my route through the library, I try to remember if I passed anyone who would have been able to see what my best friend and boyfriend are up to. As if that's the biggest concern—someone catching them.

What the fuck!

I swallow down the bile threatening to creep up my esophagus and ball my hands into fists, my right one clasping around the key fob so tightly that I inadvertently press the panic button. The honking shrills in the distance, but rather than turn it off, I let it ring out as a test. *Exactly how sound-proof is that study room?*

Dalton doesn't flinch. And Stella . . . well, the only movements I see from her are the obvious bobbing of her head and a sudden shift of her blonde hair from her right shoulder to her left. If he were a gentleman, he'd hold it back for her. *Like he does for me.*

My eyes narrow, and my chest explodes. I'm not sure which hurts more, betrayal or rejection. In a way, I've been rejected twice tonight, so I guess that wins.

I take a step toward the study room, my molars gnashing together, but suddenly spin on my heels and head back to the parking lot, toward my blaring car horn. Rather than confronting the two people I thought were my circle, my found family, in the act of the ultimate form of treachery, I decide to deal with this moment as I would an experiment. For more than two years, I worked under the hypothesis that good things could happen to a wallflower like me. The evidence, however, seems to have proven that theory false.

Well, maybe one small note for my files.

I pull to a stop in the Tiff library lot before pulling onto the main road and type out a short and not-so-sweet text to my former boyfriend and bestie.

ME: You guys can go fuck yourselves. Oh wait. You already are.

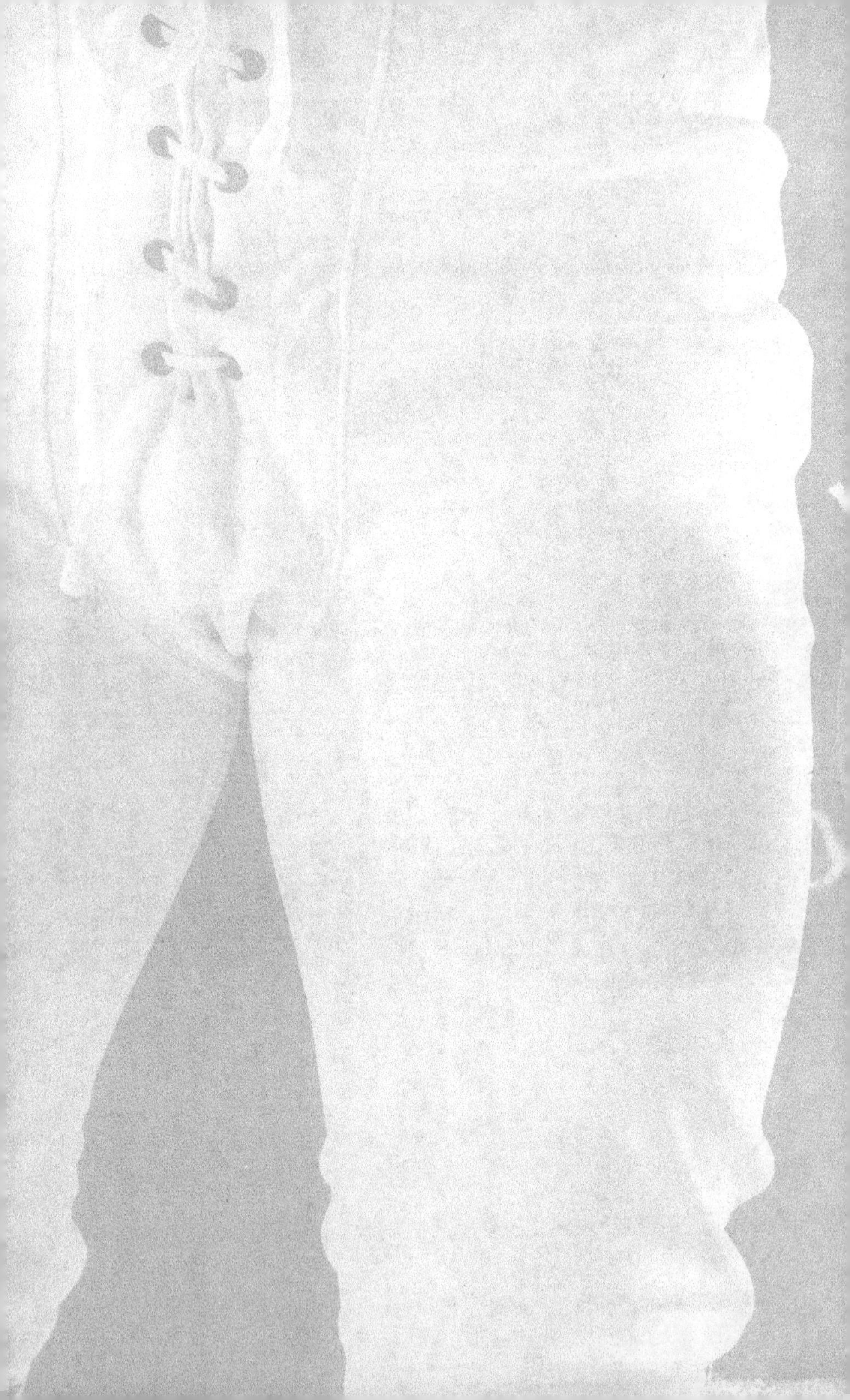

logan ford

PALMING the football in a way I never would on the field, I hold it straight out from my body and scowl.

"Maybe growl a little too," the photographer prompts.

I roll my eyes and adjust my grip, then do as she asks, gritting my teeth and pushing out a guttural animal noise that forces me to snarl my upper lip.

"Perfect," she coos.

Media. My final media day. I should probably be nostalgic about this and commit every moment to some special mental memory trove, but I'm simply not feeling it today. It might have something to do with the photo shoot that I had to watch before my time slot, the one where my junior backup, Cam Ledger, insisted on taking his photos with his cheerleader girlfriend. My *ex*-girlfriend.

Amy and I broke up this past spring, and I'm not exactly pining after her. Time apart was good for my perspective, and it turns out that Amy is a massive narcissist. I learned all about those in my psych class. I've had that term thrown my way a time or two, but now that I know what one really is, I'm pretty sure I'm unworthy of the label.

Now, *asshole? Jerk face?* Maybe even *creep?* I'll own up to those. But narcissists love themselves way more than I ever could. I'm all too aware of my shortcomings. I'm habitually on the cusp, which is a nice way of saying second place. It's not only coming in second with my ex, either. When pundits talk about the draft, I'm what they refer to as a *Hail Mary pick.* I came to Tiff because I knew I would get great playing time. I also knew I'd get a full ride despite my shitty GPA. And I've lived up to my end of the bargain. I'm on the verge of breaking the Tiff U rushing yards record this season as the team looks to squeak into the playoffs for the first time in years.

A bubble team.

A bubble player.

On the bubble of eligibility thanks to my absolute lack of math and science skills.

"Are we good?" I drop my sneer into the bored expression that reflects my mood. The photographer looks at her camera screen and flips through a few of the shots.

"Yeah, we got it. Thanks, Ford. Send in the next." I nod at her and wonder if she thinks Ford is my first or last name. I don't think she has a clue about Tiff football. Not many people do. But this year . . . *this* is our year. I feel it. Everyone feels it. No more mediocre for us. It was slow and go building the right pieces, but we have a real shot to take the conference this year.

I spot my friend Jax, our best wide receiver, near the edge of the stage set up at the east end of the arena and head toward him. There are more members of the press here than in the past, so that's a good sign. Could also be that sports at Tiff is under a spotlight this year thanks to a huge grade scandal for last season's men's basketball team.

"You think Coach is ready for this?" Jax nods in Coach Mack's direction. He pulls a hand towel from his back pocket and runs it over his forehead, then plops his hat back in place.

"Not in the least." I chuckle and Jax shakes his head as we make our way to the front row of seats.

Coach steps up to the podium and taps the hot mic, sending a thumping alert throughout the arena.

"If you could all take your seats, we'll get this thing started," he says, backing off the mic to cough into his fist. He makes brief eye contact with me and I give him a thumbs up. He rolls his eyes in return. He hates this stuff.

About two dozen reporters file into the front row of seats while several cameras go live behind them. I've counted four photographers so far, and then there are the influencer guys all clustered in the back on laptops with cellphones propped on tripods. The hockey guy from Tiff is here too. We must be a hot story if he's willing to step away from covering the ice for our media day.

Coach goes through the usual introductions, handing out our schedule and highlighting the link where the press can download our media guide and video from last season. The photos we just took are already being uploaded, so I should be sneering online and in print by the end of the day.

The first reporter to nail us on the grades issue stands up, holding his pen like a pointer and bouncing it between our coaching staff and the athletic director. It's obnoxious. Almost as obnoxious as his bed-head hair that corkscrews in all directions and the twisted collar of his short-sleeved button-down.

Coach hands the mic off to our athletic director, Rolland James, when he sees the question coming.

"Rolland, what can you tell us about the university's plan to deal with what has been labeled as a complete dismissal of academic obligations in athletics?" It's such a pompous way to ask about how our team plans to deal with classroom cheating. I'm sure we'll have some arbitrary new system that will ensure integrity, blah, blah, blah.

"I'm glad you asked that. I want to make one thing abundantly clear—Tiff University is not for the weak, academically. The automatic passing grades given to some of our basketball athletes last season was a massive stain on this institution that will not be tolerated. So, moving forward, grade checks will be updated in real-time. Instructors have all signed updated code of conduct contracts that allow for their immediate dismissal for any grade impropriety. And the instructors and coaches involved with last year's incident have all been terminated. We have every bit of confidence that our athletes will not only succeed on their court or field of play, but in the classrooms as well. And with that, I hand the mic back to Coach Mack."

That was not the blanket statement I was expecting. And I'm not positive, but I swear Mr. James made eye contact with me as he handed over the mic. I slink down a few inches in my seat and Jax shifts his foot to the right, tapping it into the edge of mine. He leans toward me and cups his mouth.

"Dude, I'm pretty sure that message was for you and your fucking chem grade," he grumbles.

His confirmation of my suspicion lands like a boot to my chest. I give him a sideways glance and quirk a brow.

"You think?"

He shakes with a quiet laugh and covers his mouth again, which is so obvious and makes me want to punch him.

"Yeah, bro. I think."

The full picture fills in for me the second the press conference wraps and Coach pulls me into his office for a special one-on-one meeting.

"Take a seat, Logan." He taps the back of the wooden armchair opposite his desk before rounding it to take his seat.

I plop down as realization hits me. My plan to take the same instructor that slid other guys on the team through their science requirements is probably not going to pan out. I've already failed chemistry once—I had one of those teachers with integrity. And now that I've taken it, my only option this time around is to stick with it and pass.

I swallow down the bile creeping up my esophagus and fold my hands in my lap.

"Son, I'm not going to dance around the point with you. This whole grades scandal puts a lot of you guys in a pickle, and I know it. But the difference between you and, say, Michael Woods or Danny Conrad on the D-line is that I can't simply replace you. You're key, you understand?"

I meet his tired gaze and nod silently as the invisible boot kicks my chest again.

"We have expectations on us this season. There are some big contracts waiting in the wings for this program—partnerships that could pay for upgrades. Hell, a new stadium maybe. And I'm sure you've been following your own numbers. A good year is a big deal for you, too. Personally. I know that. But the tools we've had in the past to help with academic struggles—"

"I get it," I say, lifting a palm. What he means is he can't simply make a phone call and put pressure on an instructor.

"Every grade entry is going to be monitored and record-ed," he continues. "Christ, I don't even know why the faculty stuck around through this. Every professor and adjunct in this place is being watched for every little move if there's an athlete in their classroom. And you know how they love to make an example of football players."

I'm not sure that part is totally true. We get away with a lot of bad shit compared to other teams—especially the women's teams. Hell, I bet if Laney Price and her volleyball team heard him say that they'd laugh him out of his office. But still, he's not wrong that we're all being watched. And any mistake we make is going to be newsworthy.

"I've arranged for a tutor," Coach says, and my head falls back as I blow out a heavy breath.

"Is that really necessary?" I stare at the dotted tiles on his office ceiling, knowing in my gut it probably is.

"Logan, you finished with a thirty-two percent last time. If I could finagle an entire team of tutors for you to pass this fucking class, I would." His voice is caught between frustration and his typical humor, and when I drop my chin to my chest and meet his gaze, I realize he's probably annoyed with me rather than the system.

"I understand," I say, swallowing my pride. It's not that I mind getting help or that I'm above it, it's just that I know the tutors in the science department. I tried three of them last year and to say we didn't gel is an understatement. They each grew impatient with me within two or three sessions and then passed me along to the next one.

"Good, so we're in agreement. Let's get this done and focus on football, yeah?" Coach stands and knocks on the wood of his desk as if that seals my fate.

I nod and stand, then reach out to shake his hand. A family portrait sitting on his filing cabinet behind him catches my eye and I pause our shake as the girl in the frame, who I assume is his daughter, sparks an idea. She's dressed up for Halloween, a puffy pink hat and fake red braids dangling on either side of her head. I tip my head to the side and squint my eyes at Coach.

"One small request, if I may?"

He drops my hand at my question and immediately crosses his arms over his chest, taking in a deep breath. I'm testing his patience. I hold up both palms and chuckle.

"It's a good request, I promise."

He grimaces but quirks a brow and grumbles, "Go on."

"I'd like to request a specific tutor. Her name—"

"Oh, hell, Logan. Do not turn this into some excuse to meet girls," he gripes.

I shake my head and press a palm flat against my chest.

"No, I swear. That's not what this is. It's only that I've gone the tutor route before, and I think I need someone with, well . . . gumption, I guess?" I stare into his hazed eyes, his head askew as he studies me, probably trying to read whether I'm bullshitting him or not.

"I agree gumption might be called for with you," he relents.

I breathe out a laughing sigh in relief.

"There's a chemistry major, she's my year. Her name is Rachel, and I don't know what her last name is but I've seen her working with other students as a teacher's aide. She's smart. And to be honest, I probably learned more from eavesdropping on her conversations with other students than I did from the instructor."

Coach chews at the inside of his cheek for a moment, then nods once.

"I'll see what I can do," he agrees. "Now, get your ass in

the weight room. You're two-tenths of a second off your usual sixty."

He's being nice. I was three-tenths off in camp. And now that I'm carrying the pressure of a season and passing a subject I absolutely don't understand at all, I'm afraid my time is only going to go up. But speed is something I can control. That and winning over Shortcake and getting her to do whatever it takes to make sure I pass.

3 /
rachel

"TUTORING?"

I have said the word a dozen times, each recital with a different inflection. Never a positive tone. Because I don't have positive bone in me in response to my professor's request that I personally shepherd Logan Ford, Tiff's biggest meathead, through Chem 101.

I'm still reeling from discovering that my best friend has been hooking up with my boyfriend—correction, ex-boyfriend—all summer. Then she hit me with the toxic icing on the garbage cake—she applied for the abroad scholarship, too, and got it.

"Rachel, I know you're too advanced for this, but this is a request from the school president. It's really an honor when you look at it that way. The school *needs* you." Professor Combs is doing his best to sell me on this prospect, but under zero circumstances will I find fulfillment in swapping out a semester with brilliant minds for one where I'll be walking a football player through the equivalent of coloring.

"You should probably work on your poker face," Professor Combs says with a wry grin.

"I don't have one. Because I don't lie. And I will not accept this assignment without at least exploring every alternative possible." I already have my laptop out and open on the edge of his desk and am searching for the president's email and phone number.

I click the email address but before the window fully opens, Professor Combs pushes my laptop shut then raps his fingertips on the surface to make his point. I slump back in the chair and drop my shoulders and my chin.

"Fine. But I'm not responsible if he simply can't keep up. I don't have time to hold his hand through everything. I have my own labs." I snap my gaze up in time to see his pursed lips, his arms folded across his chest.

"Try to be a *little* patient. That's all I ask."

My mouth pulls in on one side and I mentally imagine my first session with Logan.

"What's up, Shortcake?" he'll say.

And then I'll break his nose with his chemistry book.

"I'll be patient." I hold my mouth in a tight line as my professor nods, sending me on my way.

There isn't much time to prepare before our first session, so I gather my computer and notebooks, then clean up my lab and rush across the street to the library. Logan Ford's back is to me when I walk in. He's sitting at one of the large tables near the reference desk, books spread out in front of him and his feet propped up on the table. His hoodie is pulled up over his head, so his last name is on full display across his back.

I bet his eyes are closed.

I clear my throat as I step up behind him. He cranes his neck and pushes his hoodie back from his messy yet admittedly cute hair. With one eyebrow arched, his mouth ticks up into a half grin just before he says, "Shortcake."

My groan is audible. I can't help it.

"Are these your books?" I glance at the open texts on the table, a variety of subjects, and determine pretty quickly that these are simply books left behind. Logan leans forward and flips one of the books closed, revealing the cover.

"*Religious Themes in American Literature from Eighteen-Seventy to Present Day*." He huffs out a quick laugh then peers back at me as he nudges the book away from him as if it's poison. "No, these aren't mine."

"I figured," I mumble, dropping my backpack on the table and closing the rest of the books. I stack them and push them to the opposite end of the table to give us room. Taking the seat adjacent to him, I flip open the Chem 101 textbook I brought with me for reference. I assumed he wouldn't be prepared, and from the looks of things, I assumed right.

"Alright. Well, the first thing you should know is that this course begins with a lot of the basics. If you can ace those first two or three exams, you will be in a much better position when the more advanced topics kick in." I flip through the first three chapters and stop at chapter four, which is when covalent bonds come into play. But while I'm pulling out my notebook and pencil, Logan flips the pages back to the very beginning of the book.

He tilts his head and gives me a bashful expression, his eye contact brief.

"If those first exams count for that much, maybe we should start there."

I hold his gaze for a moment but he quickly averts his eyes, pulling the book closer and scanning the introduction.

"I'm sorry. I thought you took this class once already." From what Professor Combs said, Logan was repeating to improve his grade.

"I did." He flips the page halfway, toying with it for a second or two before turning it completely. "I failed the first three tests."

His gaze zips up and catches mine for a breath, diving back down to stare at the periodic table printed across two pages.

"Oh." I push my tongue into my cheek and recalibrate my already low expectations.

This is going to be more work than I bargained for, and I didn't even bargain for this gig. I tap my pencil tip in the margin of my notepad a few times, forming a small trail of dots. I write the word MATTER at the top of the page and draw a line under it, then exhale.

"Thank you," Logan says, his fingertips resting on the top edge of my paper. "I know you're busy. So thank you . . . for this."

I glance up and catch him wincing with a guilty expression, his mouth pulled in tight on one side, and my stomach tightens. I'm not a patient person, and my inability to bluff has been well established. My attitude about this shouldn't bleed onto his plate.

"It's fine," I say, my shoddy attempt at, "You're welcome."

He gives me a short nod and leans in with his hands folded together, his focus immediately dropping to my notepad. It's quintessential model student posture. I fear it's going to take a lot more than sitting up straight to get him where he needs with this class, however.

We spend an hour going through the first unit, reviewing

the properties of solids, liquids, and gas, along with measurements and notations. It seems as if he has a decent grasp of the concepts so I give him a short practice test. It takes him almost forty minutes to get through twenty-five questions, his hands grabbing at his hair the entire time. He pushes the pages across the table in a rush the second he finishes the final question, flattening the pencil in front of him before pulling his hood over his now wild head of hair.

"You all right?" I give him a crooked grin, and he waves his hand at the test, almost as if he's shooing it away from him in disgust.

"Just check it." He tugs the strings of his hoodie tight then flops back in his chair, stuffing his hands in the front pocket. His behavior reminds me of when my father tried to teach me to drive a stick shift. Defeated.

"I'm sure it's not as bad as you think."

His lip ticks up and he breathes out a short laugh. It's endearing in a way, to see someone like him so uncertain of himself. I've watched him walk around this campus for three years with his head always held high and his chest full. Ironic that chemistry is his kryptonite.

I go to work on his sample test, grinning to myself as he flies through the first page of questions. I glance up with a reassuring smile as I flip the page.

"See? So far so good," I say.

He remains silent, though, and his eyes are devoid of any reaction whatsoever. I bite my tongue, deciding to grade the second page before teasing him with an, "I told you so." It's good that I did, too, because of the twelve questions on the second page, only three of them are marked correctly. He might have done better simply guessing and playing the odds. By the time I get to the final page—the test on measurements—I'm unable to find a single correct answer. Answers seem flipped, numbers in the wrong place. He finishes with a thirty-eight percent, and that doomed sense I had going into this whole thing weighs heavy over both of us.

"It's pointless," he huffs out, standing from his seat and pushing it in until the wooden back cracks against the table's edge.

I'm apt to agree with him, but my professor's voice rings in my mind, echoing *patience*.

"It's not pointless, Logan. That was our baseline, is all. Now we know where to start." I do my best to sell the positivity, but he's not buying it. I can tell.

"We didn't need a test to get a baseline, Shortcake. Zero. That's my baseline." His gaze rests on mine for a beat, mouth pinched and resolute. I was almost slipping into sympathy, but—

I gather up his test and rip it in half, plopping the torn pages into a stack on the table in front of me.

"So, here's the deal. My name? It's Rachel. It's not Shortcake. Never has been. And I don't particularly like being called that. Got it?" I pause for a moment, expecting him to nod at my scolding. He doesn't. But he's also dead silent, not even breathing, so I think I frightened him, or at least surprised him.

"Good. Next, yes we needed a baseline. I have to know what I'm working with. And fine, you win. There's a lot about this that feels pointless. I gather you have no intention of working in a field remotely close to chemistry, right?"

He nods, the movement slight enough I'd have missed it if I weren't staring at him with laser beam intensity.

"I concede that makes this feel pointless. But the university is requiring you to pass this course. And apparently, you're good at throwing or catching or whatever, so here we are, Logan. This whole thing has a point. It's to get you to pass. To stay eligible so an entire team of men who also like to throw and catch balls can do so in front of a few thousand people every Saturday for the next four months. And then our school can make gobs of money off of the whole thing. And the administration can pat themselves on the back for force feeding you a science curriculum that you will forget the moment you turn in your final. And that is the point. It's an incredibly pointless point, but there it is. And it's my responsibility. So, how about you take a seat and we review things one more time before we call it a day and pick up where we left off tomorrow?"

His mouth hangs open. A hint of a curve plays at the corners, showing his amusement. I'm not sure whether he's about to laugh at me or praise me for being tough.

"Rachel." He lets my name hang in the air, closing his mouth into a tight line and holding my gaze. He has nice eyes. Green, which is my favorite color.

"Rachel," I repeat.

He nods again, this time taking his seat and scooting in, every bit the good pupil. I flip the book back to the beginning of the measurements section, which is where things seem to have gone awry, and write a few examples on my notepad for us to work through together. His brow pinches as I talk him through the first sample problem, but when I quiz him on the answer, he gets it right, sitting back in his seat and holding his arms up to celebrate.

"All right!" he shouts, earning a *shh* from the main desk librarian. He mouths an apology then reaches his palm forward for me to slap, and I give him a high-five that doesn't quite land center and causes him to spit out a laugh.

The librarian hushes us again, and I can't help it. I smile.

"Sorry, it's just that I suck at this." He holds up my notebook the way they do picture books at story time. The librarian isn't amused, and simply glares at him over the dark frame of her glasses.

Logan gives up on trying to appease her, turning his attention back to me. He flops the notebook back on the table and taps the problem he got right with his finger.

"Hit me with another." He rubs his hands together, suddenly turning chemistry into a sport, and my grin inches a tad higher. I think maybe I'm a little proud.

"Okay, try this—"

"Rachel?"

I literally snap the tip of my pencil on the page at the sound of Dalton's voice. I've avoided the library since our breakup. I figured I'd be able to slip in and out unnoticed today because, as I have his schedule memorized, I knew he'd be in his study group at the café. Of course, now I doubt the existence of the study group at all. I bet that was yet another code word for *fucking your bestie*.

Words fail me, and my emotions are still raw and undealt with, so I slip on the invisible mask and twist in my chair to meet him with a hard glare. His eyes dance from me to Logan, that tiny dent he always gets when he's perplexed forming over his left brow. If I were certain Logan would play along with me, I'd introduce him as my friend. My tongue is still refusing to work, however, so I stick with the glare, letting it linger until Logan's the first to break the harsh silence.

"What's up, man? Logan." He stands and reaches across the table—across my chest—to shake Dalton's hand.

My ex chuckles, taking his palm and nodding.

"I'm Dalton," he says, glancing down and catching enough of my notebook to piece things together because his eyes flutter shut as he smiles. "Oh, right. Tutoring. Of course."

"What do you mean *of course*?" Now my mouth works? Those are the words I choose as my first since he stomped on my integrity and heart at the same time?

"Oh, nothing. I mean, you're probably a great tutor. And it makes sense. I'm sure Logan can use your help, and you're probably saving up for . . . you know." His sure smile falters a bit when he realizes the corner he's back himself into.

"This isn't a paid thing, so no. I'm not saving up for . . . *you know*." The corners of my mouth pinch and I swallow down the bile bubbling up.

"How do you know I'm not the tutor?" Logan pipes in.

Dalton laughs, probably assuming he's making a joke. Neither Logan nor I laugh.

"Oh, I assumed . . . I mean . . . what subject is it?" His forehead squiggles up, and I figure Logan will let him off the hook in a few seconds.

"Physical education," he says, instead of the, "I'm just messing with you" I anticipated.

His tone is dead serious, and before I have time to react, Logan hooks his foot in the leg of my chair, dragging it, *and me*, closer to him. The chair squeals along the wood floor. Without looking up at Dalton, he focuses instead on my face, leaning forward and brushing a loose wave of hair behind my right ear. His thumb grazes my cheek along the way, and my body peppers with goose bumps underneath my sweatshirt and jeans. If I could muster saliva, I'd swallow. Instead, I lose myself in the clover green of Logan's eyes.

A nervous laugh slips out of Dalton's mouth, this time earning him a "Quiet, sir," from our favorite librarian. I glance his direction in time to see his ears turn red, a tic he's had since he was a kid, a vasovagal response to unwanted attention. I used to feel bad for him when it happened. It's his biggest fear about arguing in court one day. Right now, however, I enjoy every cherry red moment.

Dalton's gaze lingers on me for a few quiet seconds, and as much as I want to hate him forever—and plan to—it also hurts having him pin me with those intense blue eyes. I should maybe step outside with him and explain. Or offer to talk later, for closure. It's been weeks since I walked out of this very building, leaving his betrayal behind me, at least literally. Maybe I owe it to myself to get the words I've been practicing ever since off my chest.

Suddenly, the gentle touch of a finger tips my chin to my left, and blue eyes are traded for green.

"You ready, Rach?" Logan's soft smile feels genuine, and the way his fingertips are suddenly scratching at the denim over my knees pulls me in even deeper. I'm not sure how many seconds pass. Two, five, six? But eventually Logan's gaze drifts over my shoulder and I follow his lead to see Dalton walking away. My palms are sweaty. And my heart is hopscotching around my sternum.

"You forgot running," Logan says, bringing my attention back to him.

I scrunch my face and pull in my brow.

"Throwing, catching . . . and running."

He scoots his chair back, returning the space that existed

between us before Dalton showed up. My pulse still hasn't slowed, but the air suddenly feels about ten degrees cooler.

"I take it you're good at the running part?"

He's pulled my notepad close and is drawing endless circles in the margin. His mouth tugs up a half second before his eyes flit up to me, and I'm instantly reminded of all the reasons I dreaded taking on this assignment .

"I'm good at a lot of things, Shortcake."

4 /
logan

I'M NOT sure who that guy was, but he's a dick. Dalton, I think? I forgot his name the second he uttered it. All I know is he made Rachel uncomfortable. She didn't even scold me for calling her Shortcake again, which I did as a distraction. I may also like how her face scrunches when she gets mad. It's cute. *She's* cute. Too cute for Dalton the dick. That's for sure.

He walked out of here five minutes ago and Rachel has been distracted ever since, constantly checking the main doors behind her and manically flipping her phone over to check the screen.

"I assume he's an ex?" I scoot into the table and lean forward, my head to one side as I try to force her to look me in the eyes. When she does, it's brief. And while Dalton might be an asshole, I sense by the slight flinch I note when our gazes meet that the hurt he left behind is still very much an open wound.

I lick my lips and fold my hands together, looking down at the table.

"Let me guess," I say.

"Don't," she responds.

I chew at the inside of my cheek and ignore my inner voice, which is currently egging me to needle her about it just a little. Not to tease her or anything. I simply want to know. I'm not sure why, but I do.

"Okay." I nod and pull the chemistry book close again, reading over the same portion we reviewed a minute ago. Reading it now, it's as if someone gave me an answer key. What read like gibberish yesterday suddenly makes a whole lot of sense.

"You know, I never understood what that meant—significant figure. I don't know that my professor last year explained it really. He expected us, well, me at least, to just know what it meant. But how am I supposed to know?" I write out a few of the number examples and chuckle at how obvious it seems.

"I always thought they should call them *obvious* numbers. Makes more sense that it's a number I'm certain is right rather than a measurement I'm guessing at," Rachel says, breaking down the definition the way she has everything we've worked on today. I knew she was the one I needed.

I glance her way and our eyes meet for a second. Her mouth ticks up on one side, the swell of her cheek lifting her glasses up a hair on one side of her face. It's cute. She has a lot of cute habits. Like the way she stacks her feet under the table, heel balancing on toe. Or sometimes, she folds herself up in her seat and rests her elbows on her knees. I would kill for that flexibility. It also makes me think about *her* flexibility. And that wakes up other thoughts.

I shake my head to clear it and refocus on the fact Dalton the dick just left her feeling pretty shitty. She can do better.

"I was dating this girl, Amy, for, well, for way too long,

honestly. And she would do this thing whenever we were out with friends or in front of others."

Rachel turns in her seat, resting her right arm on the table. Her eyes haze, suspicious, so I keep talking.

"You know those people who have to constantly point out when you say something wrong? Like, maybe it's using the word irregardless—"

"It's regardless," Rachel interjects. I sigh but when she winks at me, I get her joke.

"Funny, but also . . . not funny. And I know it's regardless. That was the example. It could be anything really. Like mispronouncing an actor's name, or getting the city wrong when recanting some travel story, or mentally flipping a word and saying the wrong thing. Freudian slip and all that."

Her brow is pulled in tight, and I realize Freudian might not have been the right term, though maybe me saying it in front of her is its own Freudian slip. Her slight nod tells me she's following me so far. *Phew.*

"Well, Amy, my ex, she would do that to me all the time. If I said San Diego instead of San Francisco, she would point it out and then laugh about how I mixed things up all the time. Even if it had zero bearing on the story. Or if I was giving an example that she didn't think was good enough, she would immediately butt in and improve it, making sure to tell everyone that she always has to do that for me."

"That's . . . annoying," Rachel says, her lips curling into a tiny sneer. She gets it.

"Right? It was so annoying. And it always made me feel stupid, sometimes in front of people I really wanted to impress." I glance down briefly and mentally riffle through the dozens of examples that really left a mark. She corrected me in front of my coach at least twice I can think of, and once in front of an NFL scout.

"I'm sorry she did that to you. It sounds awful. I hope *you* were the one to break up?"

I wince and my cheeks heat up with a rush of guilt.

"She dumped you?" Rachel slaps her palms on either side of her face with shock, then moves one of them to cup her mouth, muffling her words. "I'm sorry. That came out harsh."

I laugh it off, mostly because I'm over it. Also, I took it as a compliment. She's right. It's amazing that I am the one who got dumped. I was a damn good boyfriend. And Amy isn't exactly a rocket scientist. *Shit, is Rachel a rocket scientist? She might be.*

"Yeah, I know. I should have seen the writing on that wall for sure. We were—*are*—two totally different people. But the point I'm making is this: I know that a basic science class isn't a challenge for a lot of people. I know I'm slow when it comes to math, and it takes me a few times to get concepts. But you don't make me feel bad about it. I know when we started today you weren't really hip on this whole thing."

She begins to object, shaking her head, but I wave her off and chuckle.

"Don't pretend. It's okay. I get it. I mean, if I was assigned to teach you football, I'd probably be just as frustrated."

She shakes with a short, silent laugh. I like that I amuse her.

"I guess I'm saying thanks, is all. And I want you to know that you're a nice person. A lot nicer than some people deserve. If you get what I'm saying."

Our gazes lock for a handful of seconds, and I revel in the tightness in my chest when we stare at one another. I like tension. Some people call it butterflies, but it's more about the rules of attraction. And about the rush of dopamine. It's the best part of being with someone new.

"I get what you're saying," she finally utters, her voice caught between a whisper and her normal soft voice.

The quiet comes in again, but rather than looking me in the eyes, Rachel begins to pack up. I guess I've taken up a good amount of her afternoon. I still need to get to the weight room. And it's my night to cook for my roommates, so I'll need to pick up beef for tacos.

I gather the notes from our review sessions and fold them together in thirds to slip them in the back pocket of my jeans. Rachel catches me doing it and chuckles to herself.

"I promise I'm taking this seriously. I will get a folder for our sessions. A hole punch, even. You'll see. I'm keeping everything, and I will have the study guide of all study guides by the time I pass this class."

She straightens her spine and crosses her arms over her chest, her backpack weighing down her shoulders and a smug grin tugging her mouth more to one side.

"What?"

"You said 'by the time I pass this class.'"

I blink a few times, recalling my own words, then break into a wide smile.

"You're right. I did," I say with a shrug. I've come a long way from pointless, I suppose. All in less than two hours.

I follow her to the main door and hold it open for her and her enormous backpack.

"Can I walk you home?" I gesture to her bag, a silent offer to carry it. She shakes her head.

"I'm going back to the lab." We pause at the top of the library steps. I wonder how many hours she spends in that building. Then another thought strikes me—perhaps she's faking it to get out of walking together.

"Right." I nod. "Well, when should we meet again? I'm not sure what the test schedule is yet, but—"

"Wednesday. We should meet Mondays, Wednesdays, and Fridays."

My shoulders drop when she says Friday.

"Not long on Fridays," she's quick to add. "And we can make that a morning session if you want. It will be review for any tests you get back. But I know the schedules for everything in your section. If you think we need more, we can add sessions in. Or if you turn into an instant chemistry genius, we can cut back."

My head falls back and I belt out a heavy laugh.

"I doubt I'll be signing up for a second major in chem anytime soon. If you can get me to tolerate this subject it will be a huge win."

I drop my chin and my gaze rests on her soft lips. The hair I pushed behind her ear has come loose again and is twisting in the breeze, cutting across her face. I reach forward and put it back where it belongs, careful not to touch her face this time as I tuck it behind her ear. There's a difference when I'm doing something for show. Right now, I just want to be nice. I want her to *think* of me as nice. And I want her to swallow hard, just . . . like . . . that.

"So, Wednesday," I confirm, dropping my hands into my front pockets.

"Same place, same time?"

I nod as I take a step backward, pulling my study notes from my pocket and rolling them tight. I do it to show her I plan to take good care of them, not that forming them into a paper telescope is much better than leaving them in my pocket. Once my back is to her, I squeeze my eyes shut and scold myself for acting like a fool. I don't know why I'm so eager to impress her. Maybe I simply don't want her to consider me a massive fuckup.

"Hey, Logan?"

I spin on my heels at the sound of my name, biting my lip and raising a brow.

"Yeah?" Part of me is braced for a joke at my expense. I left her with plenty of material.

"I would never need tutoring for football. I'd pretty much ace everything." She shrugs and bunches her lips. It's that cocky sort of smug look one gets after they've thrown down a royal flush.

"Is that right, Rachel?" I'm careful not to let another *Shortcake* slip out, and I think she notices. Her eyes flicker and her smirk evens out as she nods.

"Perhaps I'll teach you other things then." This time, I'm the one throwing down pocket aces. And she's the one whose cheeks are bright red.

"I'll see you Wednesday," I say, turning around and slapping my palm with my paper tube of notes, and feeling like a smooth motherfucker.

5 /
rachel

I SHOULD BE WORKING on a new hypothesis for my final experiment, given that my last several attempts proved to be negative and, thus, boring. I know that a failed hypothesis is a complete experiment, but the chemistry majors who come out of Tiff with interesting findings end up with much better internships and placements for grad school. I want one of those *cool* findings. That means I should probably be searching for a cooler topic than color reactions as a result of magnesium and random secondary elements.

Instead, I'm making flash cards. For basic chemistry. For a guy I had zero interest in helping twelve hours ago but now . . . I don't know. I want him to do well. And maybe I'm a bit grateful for how he handled Dalton on my behalf.

It doesn't hurt that his biceps completely fill his T-shirt sleeves.

I'm on the floor amid piles of note cards when my new roommate, Claire, enters. She's a biology major, and was the only single on the honors track in need of a roommate. She also never liked Stella, which given the frame of mind I was in at the housing office a few weeks ago, was a huge plus for me. We get along fine, which will do, well, just fine. I'm done forming bestie friendships.

"Mail for you," Claire says, dropping a light purple envelope into my lap. I recognize the abroad program logo near the return address and stare at it without blinking.

"Something wrong?" my roommate asks as she flops onto her bed and tears into a padded envelope. She jerks out a small package of what appears to be saltwater taffy and wastes no time ripping it open and popping a piece into her mouth. She glances my way and holds out the bag.

"Want one?" Her words are mangled by the tacky bright yellow candy now stuck to her teeth, which she's picking at with her index finger.

I shake my head and look back down to my envelope, turning it over a few times in my lap.

"It's probably a letter from the abroad program telling me I somehow owe them money for not going this semester," I say. Claire punches out a laugh, which also somehow is muffled by the candy glued to her teeth.

"Maybe they found extra scholarships." *Her positivity would be cute if it didn't remind me of Stella's rosy look on life.*

I poke my finger into the envelope's side and tear across the top. It's a single piece of paper, and from a quick glance, I don't get a sense that this will be good news.

Dear past applicant.

(Already starting off with a bang.)

We regret to inform you that the Midwest Region Studies Abroad program is discontinuing the scholarship application process due to budget cuts. Please do not let this deter you from applying for the spring semester. The portal opens to applicants on September 28th. While our scholarship program is no longer available, we do offer many other financial aid resources, including outside funding resources and loan options. Remember, a semester spent abroad is priceless.

Sincerely,

Patricia Sewald

Executive Director

"You look like you want to throw up," Claire says.

Probably because I do. My mouth hangs open as I drop the letter into my lap. My last shred of hope just went up in smoke. I glance up as Claire flips onto her stomach, her black bobbed hair swinging around to cup her chin. Again, she holds out the bag of taffy.

"Yeah, fine," I relent, leaning toward her and picking out a blue piece. *Is blue even a flavor?*

I unwrap the candy and tear it in half with my teeth, my plan being that half is easier to pick out of your teeth. I seem to have come up with another failed hypothesis, however, as my mouth instantly becomes coated in sticky goo.

I scrunch up my face and smack my lips as I work out chewing.

"Why do you like this stuff?" I grumble.

Claire shrugs.

"I'm not sure I do. But it's what my mom sends me in the mail, so I eat it. Can't reject a gift, ya know?"

"Can't you?" I pick out the bits I haven't swallowed with my fingernail then wrap up the remaining half and toss it on top of my backpack with every intention of throwing it away later.

"What's the deal with the letter?" Claire asks, leaning

over the edge of the bed and wiggling her fingers toward me. I hand her the letter.

"Oh, you know, turns out the scholarship Stella stole from me was also the last one ever. So that's fun." My mouth pinches on the sides, my wry expression accompanied by a few slow blinks.

"Stella, *tsk*," Claire says as her eyes scan the brief letter. She tosses it back to me then rests her chin on her stacked fists.

"I'm sorry, Rachel. That really sucks. Maybe you can save enough?" Her mouth tugs up with hope, which is kind but unrealistic.

"Maybe if I had a year, but I can't take a job while I'm finishing my labs."

We both nod at the reality.

Claire rolls onto her back and rests her feet on the brick wall, which she's covered with posters of Darwin and Einstein. I quite like her taste in role models. I turn my attention back to the flash cards and have filled out a dozen or so more when there's a knock at our door.

I snap up as Claire mumbles, having started to fall asleep. She rubs two fists in her eyes, the dark circles around them more prominent after a nap. Claire very much looks like the girl from *Beetlejuice*.

"I'll get it," I say, wondering who the hell it could be. Claire isn't as much of a hermit as I am, but she's not exactly taking callers often, or ever.

A quick glance through the peephole reveals Logan standing on the other side, a red folder gripped in his hands. I open the door enough to wedge myself in the opening.

"Uh, hi?" I glance to the right then left, waiting for more football players to leap out and yell whatever people yell during practical jokes. Logan seems to be alone, though.

"Hey, sorry. I asked the girl downstairs for your room number. I hope that's okay?" His shoulders rise an inch or two, likely the coy way he gets away with murder.

"It's totally not okay, but I guess I'm glad you aren't a murderer. Unless . . . *you aren't secretly a murderer, are you?*" I'm actually only half kidding. I watch a lot of true crime, and guys like Logan make for great surprise suspects. *Shit, is he a murderer?*

He leans in a few inches and I flinch.

"If I told you, then it wouldn't be a secret, would it?" He holds my gaze hostage for a few quiet seconds before he winks and his mouth morphs into that damn charming smile. The same smile I'm sure he used on the front desk girl to get her to give up my room number.

"Sorry to bother you. Truly," he continues. I lean my weight into the door jamb just as Claire pulls the door from my grip and widens the opening enough for two.

"Hi. I'm Claire." She reaches over my shoulder and holds out her hand. Logan tucks the folder under his arm then gives her a firm shake, which she compliments him on.

"Logan Ford. Nice to meet you, Claire."

She studies him for a second then points at his folder.

"What you got there, Logan Ford?" Claire is a bit sassy. Normally, that would intimidate me, but I've started to appreciate her blunt approach. It got us a slightly bigger room on move-in day, and two windows instead of one.

"That's why I'm here, actually." His gaze shifts to me. "I snagged a folder from Coach after weights and I realized I'm missing one of the study sheets. I wanted to see if you still had it in your notebook. I was going to study."

My skeptical side kicks in and my head tilts a hint. Logan chuckles then opens the folder, holding it out for me as proof.

"I told you I would take this seriously. I'm afraid I'll forget everything we did today, so I thought I'd review one more time."

I'm a little awestruck at his response. Maybe a little shook by him standing here, too, in front of my door. This isn't a building Logan Ford visits. We don't party here. This is the dorm for people who take seven a.m. classes and who go to bed at nine, maybe ten on a weekend.

"Wait here. I'll check my backpack and notepad." I leave my space in the doorway and Claire instantly fills it with herself.

"You can come in, too. If you prefer," she says. What is this flirty side? I don't know her well, but we had a lot of core classes together, and this feels out of character for her. I think she's boy crazy or something. Is Logan really *that* good looking?

He chuckles, and the warm timbre sinks into my chest like the perfect bass line. Perhaps there is something infectious about him.

"I'm all right. I'll wait here," he says, and an odd sensation kicks in my diaphragm, not quite a punch but not quite a sting either. I think I wanted him to accept Claire's invitation to enter my space.

As I expected, my notebook has nothing but blank pages left and my backpack shows no trace of a torn-out page he could have left behind.

"Do you know what was on it?" I glance over my shoulder and Claire pops the door open wider a foot or so to give Logan a clear view of my ass as I squat in front of my bag.

Cool air dances across my spine where my waistband should be and I silently pray that I'm not giving him a plumber's crack view. I twist around and hop up to stand just in case.

"If I knew what was on it, I probably wouldn't need it," he says through a soft laugh.

"Good point. Well, let me see where what you have ends. I can probably figure out what cut off." I move back to the door. I have to physically squeeze myself into the slight space Claire gives me, and I glare at her profile when she finally moves her hip enough to allow me room. She's staring at Logan the way a cartoon dog stares at a steak. I reach over and nudge her chin to close her mouth. She shoots me a hot glare, but quickly shakes her head, ripped out of her trance.

"Thanks for snapping me out of that," she mumbles, patting my shoulder and retreating into our room.

When I look back to Logan, he's tucked the folder back under his arm. I glance at it and he shakes his head.

"It's fine. We can figure it out next time. I was here late for weights and figured I'd stop by on the off chance. You know, I bet we left it at the library. I'll stop by on my way to the lot. I'm sure the librarian has it waiting for me at the front desk. She's a big fan."

His playful smirk makes me smile back at him.

"She'll probably want your autograph," I say as he takes a few steps back.

"Yeah, I'm sure she will . . . on some form that bans me from ever setting foot in her library again. *Shhh!*" He holds his finger to his lips, his smile subtle, crooked, and forming a single dimple. He does that winking thing, and I catch myself leaning against the door jamb like a lovestruck teenager.

"I'll see you Wednesday," he tosses over his shoulder before disappearing through the stairwell door. I linger in my doorway for a few extra seconds, practically feeling the heat of Claire's knowing gaze on my back. There's zero chance she doesn't tease me about any of this.

I step back into our room and shut and lock the door. Claire's sitting with her legs folded up in the center of her bed, and she's watching a video on her phone. I pad my way back to the empty space between my piles of notecards and sit down.

"You know, if you need money you should consider entering the Science Ball pool."

My head snaps up, but Claire's eyes are still masked by her phone, the video she's watching flashing in her pupils.

"I always thought that thing was a bit insipid. And honestly, it feels cheap," I say, quickly dismissing her idea.

The Science Ball happens every winter, usually in early November. It's an awards ceremony on one level, but also a nice excuse to dress up in formal wear and eat a fancy meal someplace ritzy. The pool part started about a decade ago in response to the freshmen athlete thing that happens here at Tiff where all the male first years make bets on hooking up with girls who are *way* out of their league. Not to be outdone by a bunch of jocks, the students on honor council decided to mix it up and create a pool. Whoever shows up to the ball with the hottest date wins. Entry is fifty bucks, and the winner is decided by secret vote during the first dance. Oh, and one more caveat—there must be proof of intimacy.

"You know people cheat at it anyhow," I throw in. Claire finally moves her phone from her face and meets my gaze, her mouth quirked with disappointment.

"Last year's winner was one of my teaching assistants. He split the pot with some girl on the bowling team. They made a sex tape for proof. Offered to screen it in the ballroom and everything."

Our eyes are locked as we stare at one another with seasick expressions. I skipped the ball last year. Dalton didn't want to go. A part of me wonders if that's when he began fooling around with Stella and that was the reason why.

"Yeah, definitely not for me," I say, moving my attention to my note card stacks. I bind them with rubber bands before tucking them into my backpack for Wednesday.

"Six thousand dollars *is* a lot of money," Claire says, halting me mid band stretch. I let go of the end and it snaps against my fingertips.

"Six grand?" I figured the pool got up to a thousand, maybe two. But *six*?

"Oh, yeah, and last year was low. I heard the highest was close to eight."

I swallow hard. Forty-five hundred bucks would secure my spot in the abroad program this spring.

"Anyhow, you should totally consider it. Moral compass be damned. You walk in with Logan Ford and you'll totally win." She offers a quick shrug then lifts her phone back up, covering her face.

It's an impossible idea, and the thought of bargaining with Logan to split the money makes my stomach turn. Not because I dislike money, or dislike the idea of walking into a ball on his arm. I just don't think I have the audacity. Besides, if we went to the ball I'd have to be up way past nine. And I'm almost certain I turn into a pumpkin at 9:01.

6 /
logan

I'M HONESTLY excited to tell Rachel how my first day of chem went. I wasn't completely lost. Granted, the first day is mostly going over the syllabus and assignment expectations, but the professor finished the first class talking about significant figures. When I raised my hand to answer one of the sample questions, the teacher actually sighed. Audibly. He probably expected me to ask some dumb shit about his bathroom policy or to make a *significant* joke instead of providing an actual response.

Showed him! I got the answer right and followed it up with a *Boom!* Probably a little cocky for a basic chem class, but the rest of the students in there were pretty excited about my reaction. I don't even care that they laughed. I'm used to making my classmates laugh, though historically, it's been more in the realm of smart-ass comments and bullshit answers.

Then I did it again. And this time, the teacher walked over to my desk and held out a fist for me to bump. And *Boom!* we both went.

I'm on cloud nine. No, ten! Eleven!

Of course, I'm also fucking late. And I forgot to get Rachel's cell number, so there's no way to text her.

Coach asked me to stick around for some extra routes, and I guess I could have told him I couldn't miss tutoring and checked out, but no way was I letting Cam sub in for me. I don't feel threatened by him, but I also don't feel so confident that I can give him an edge and time in my spotlight. It has nothing to do with my ex and him dating, either. My priority is on earning draft attention. I couldn't care less who Amy dates. I'm also pretty sure the only reason she's with Cam is to get at me. She may have done the dumping, but I get the impression she still very much wants me to pine after her. Or maybe her narcissism rubbed off on me.

But now I'm busting my ass toward the library, the clouds that hovered above us most of the day finally opening up and dumping rain on me. It's an hour past the time we were supposed to meet, and my stomach is twisting in on itself with every step I take. The library is open until midnight, so I'm sure I'll be able to study, but Rachel was expecting me an hour ago.

I scan the main area through the glass doors before I enter, and every table is empty. There are a few groups meeting in the study rooms to the right, and a handful of students are parked in the chairs by the stacks. I take a deep breath as I step inside and dry the bottoms of my shoes on the rubber floor mat. The lobby smells like iron and mildew, and I'd swear there's a leak somewhere in here.

I push my hoodie back and work my way toward the study rooms just in case, peeking through windows on the off chance Rachel is waiting in one. When that turns up nothing, I head to the stairs, climbing them two at a time and pacing down every aisle of the stacks, all the way to the sixth floor. There's no reason she would be waiting for me period, let alone waiting for me in the computer lab down in the basement, but I cross that off my list. It takes me twenty minutes to scope out the entire library only to confirm what I assumed—she left because I was a no-show.

I pause just inside the main doors to pull my hoodie back over my head and tug my backpack straps tight. Staring through the wet glass, I mull over my options. I'm not so much worried about reviewing the first class materials as I am nervous that Rachel is going to bail on me. She had to know I made up that whole bit about missing a page in my notes the other night. I wanted to reassure her that I would work hard. This grade crackdown really has me freaked out. I didn't realize how much it looked like I was flirting with her until my walk back to the parking lot. And now today, I blow her off completely.

She probably thinks I'm an asshole.

The rain eases a bit, so I step outside and rush down the steps and onto the main campus mall. Spinning slowly in the center of campus, I consider my options. The edge of the chemistry building catches my eye, and something nags me to give the labs a check. I jog down the puddled walkway, doing my best to skip over the larger pools of water, and tug open the large metal door. The modern building feels as cold as it looks with its walls made of corrugated metal, concrete, and glass. The private labs are on the second floor, and when I see lights on inside at least two of them as I scale the steps, I mutter, "Please, please, please," to myself.

The first lab is taken by two dudes so I rush to the only

other lab that's lit and yank the door open. The pale pink braid hanging down the center of the white lab coat fills me with relief—which is quickly dashed the second a clearly startled Rachel turns around. Both her safety glasses and the regular glasses underneath fog up with her breath about a second before she drops a large piece of glassware with a bright yellow liquid onto the floor.

"What the ever-loving flip!" She clutches her chest, and I suck in my top lip, working hard not to laugh at her fake swear word.

"I'm so sorry," I profess, pulling my backpack from my arms and dropping it by the door so I can rush to the cleaning station and arm myself with towels.

"It's acid. Let me get it," she says, holding up a palm and flashing me a short scowl. I'm not sure whether that was meant for the scaring her part or the massively late and no-showing thing I did.

"If you could just . . ." She nudges me closer to the door, pushing my shoulder with her gloved fingers.

"Yeah, right. Sorry." I stumble back a step or two while she drapes some sort of industrial type paper towels across the floor, then sprays some blue liquid on top.

"What is that, like a special neutralizer?" I lean over my toes for a closer look.

"It's soap."

I fall back on my heels.

"Oh."

It takes her about five minutes to clean up the acid and shards of glass. She snaps her gloves off and folds them into one another before depositing them into a yellow hazard bin. She spins to face me, immediately crossing her arms over her chest and leaning her weight against the edge of the counter she was facing when I walked in.

"Well?"

Her lips purse, her eyes laser-focused on mine, and I swear she isn't saying *flip off* behind them. She's going full F word.

"I'm really sorry I was late," I say, going for affable, doing my best to force my eyes into full puppy dog.

"You weren't late. You missed it completely," she corrects.

And apparently I failed on the puppy dog thing.

"I did. I know. But it was a practice thing, and I didn't have your number, which we should remedy, by the way."

"Right," she hums, tone suspicious, her eyes narrowing on me even more somehow, literally piercing my pupils.

"I'm sorry, do you mean right as in *right, here's my number. Now let's get started.* Or do you mean it as in *right, you're full of shit?*"

"That second one has a certain ring to it," she deadpans.

I draw in a heavy breath and look down at my shoes, my laces still untied. I kick my right foot out and point at it.

"Look, straight from practice. I'm barely changed. My compression shirt is still on." I lift my hoodie and pat my stomach, which is bound in the tight blue football undershirt.

"I'm sorry, Logan. What exactly are you saying? That you forgot to build in time to get dressed? That you don't know how to tie your shoes yet?"

My mouth falls into a hard line.

"You're the one who stood me up. You don't get to make the pissy face." She pushes off from the counter and walks around me, pulling the lab door open and gesturing for me to leave.

I don't move. Instead, I hold her stare and mentally prepare the best apology I can muster.

"I understand. I insulted your time. And practicing chemistry is equally as important as football. I made a choice, and you're right. I should have made a better one. But I meant what I said. I am taking this seriously. I even answered questions in class today. And I got them right."

Her stoic face breaks ever so slightly, a tiny crease by her eye as her mouth sneaks up with a tiny twitch.

"You banking on class participation points?" Her tone sounds teasing.

"I'm banking on any points I can get. Are snack points still a thing?" I quirk a brow and Rachel rolls her eyes.

"Snack points have never been a thing, Logan." She lets go of the door, letting it fall shut again. I'm still in the room, so this is good.

She leans against it, dropping her hands into the pockets of her lab coat. With her purple-rimmed glasses on, she looks every bit the comic book scientist . . . who usually turns out to be evil and is secretly developing a toxic formula to put the entire world to sleep, but that last part is extra. Her smart look is cute.

"I don't talk in class. I mean, in my coaching theory class, sure. But let's be honest, that's not really an academic course. In real classes, I've never talked. I don't even think I raised my hand in grade school unless it was to go to the bathroom. But today—this morning—I raised my hand. I answered a question in front of people and I got it right. I'm not sure you know how big of a deal that is, but Rachel . . . it's a pretty big flipping deal."

Her eyes snap to mine when I repeat her word, her lids dimming as she studies me for a beat. I hold out my palms.

"What do I have to do? How can I make it up to you?"

She blinks slowly, twisting her lips as she seems to consider her options.

"There has to be something," I plead.

Her head tilts.

"The Science Ball," she utters, nodding slowly as if I'm supposed to follow what that means. It sounds made up.

"Sure. Science Ball. You got it." I shrug and step forward with a palm out to seal the deal. What deal? I have no clue. But if it gets me back in her good graces and means I'll pass chem and stay eligible, *Science Ball ahoy!*

"It's a formal, and an awards ceremony," she explains, hesitating, her hand still not reaching for mine. Things are mildly clearer to me, not that it matters.

"Ah, got it. And that guy the other day . . . I'm guessing he was supposed to be your date?"

She's still nodding, slowly, and not shaking my hand.

"Something like that, yeah."

Her ex seems like an arrogant asshole. I try not to make kneejerk assumptions about people, but I think I'll make an exception for that guy. I didn't like the smug way he assumed Rachel had less appeal than he did. Like he's some prize. Honestly? She was dating down with that dude. I don't care *what* his major and future earning potential is. Money ain't worth diminishing self-worth.

"Done." I step in closer, flexing my fingers with a touch of flare, like that somehow makes shaking on our deal more attractive. She finally gives in and takes my hand, and on some sort of instinct I cover the back of her hand with my other palm when I feel how cold her skin is.

Her eyes drop to our touch and I rub my hands over hers a few times before letting go.

"You were cold," I say, now feeling the heat of her confused stare.

"I was," she croaks, quickly hiding both of her hands back in her coat pockets.

Feeling awkward, I tuck mine into the pocket of my hoodie.

"So—" My shoulders lift to my ears.

She quakes with short laugh.

"So, I suppose you'd like to go over the next lesson?"

I exhale, relief pouring out of my chest like a balloon deflating. I can't hide my grin, either. I can't pass this class without her.

"That would be amazing, Rachel. Thank you," I say, picking my backpack up and moving to the empty table in the center of the room.

Rachel rolls a stool over and I grab one from the corner, nestling it next to her—close but not *too* close. I unzip my backpack and let my notes folder and chem book slide onto the table. Rachel snags the folder with her fingertip, her nails a light blue color, the polish chipped. There's something sweet about her lack of material perfection. Or maybe I dated a cheerleader for too long.

"You find those missing notes?"

I flinch at her question.

"I uh . . .yeah. I found them." I swallow and pull the folder away from her, feeling as if my entire face is flashing *LIAR*.

I flip open the book and pull the syllabus out, which I'm sure Rachel probably wrote for every Chem 101 professor in the department. When I realize she's still staring at me, I pause and lift my head to meet her gaze. Everything feels tenuous. I'm off my game with her. She's hard to read, and

I'm pretty sure she's unimpressed with most of the things I consider my best characteristics.

"You know what we agreed to, with the Science Ball?" she finally asks. Her lips pull tight, corners pinched. I hold her gaze for a moment, leaning on my elbow while I study her. I think she's afraid I'm the one going to back out of things.

My eyes squint as I give her a one-sided smile.

"I think I got it, yeah."

Her brow pulls in and her chin lowers.

"Are you sure?"

A nervous laugh slips from my mouth but I quickly shut it under the weight of her intense stare. I find myself sitting up taller as I clear my throat.

"Your ex. You want to make him jealous. Right?"

Her head shifts to the side a hair, her eyes remaining on mine, her mouth this slight and perhaps devious grin. Maybe she is one of the toxic poison types of scientists.

"Yeah, I want to make him jealous," she finally confirms. "And you're all right with that?"

That nervous laugh I ate before comes back up, a harsh *ha!* blasting at her. I lean into it and recall the way her ex looked at her, then down on me.

"Yeah, Rachel. I'm one-hundred-percent here for making him regret *flipping* things up with you," I say, my smirk undeniable. It stretches high into my cheek, forcing my right eye to squint. I may suck at chemistry, but I can handle making a cute girl feel pretty in front of the jerk who let her go. Especially if it's the girl who's going to get me through this semester.

"You don't need to watch your tongue when it comes to Dalton," she says. "He fucked up. No need to make it sound nicer than it was."

Her gaze lingers on mine for a breath, and I wait for her to say more about this ex who clearly hurt her. But she holds her tongue, leaving it at that. And maybe that's enough. Perhaps Dalton doesn't deserve an explanation. And really, it's not my business. But the weight in her eyes, the way the blue somehow deepens the longer she looks at me, causes me to hold my breath and believe her at her word.

7 /
rachel

"FIFTY BUCKS IS A LOT OF MONEY."

It's the excuse I'm sticking with for now on why I haven't bought in for this year's pool, but it's wearing thin with Claire. I shouldn't have told her that I talked Logan into going to the ball with me. She lit up with the joy of a child meeting Santa for the first time. (Important to note that I cried the first time I met Santa. We aren't all built the same.)

It's been a week since Logan and I made our deal, and I've thought about letting him off the hook every time we've met for tutoring. Not that he's asked to be unhooked. In fact, he's embraced the whole *make Dalton jealous* thing with massive zeal, even slinging an arm around my shoulder and pulling me close the one time Dalton passed our table in the library. The issue is, making Dalton jealous is a by-product of me winning thousands of dollars, and I can't seem to get myself to own up to the real reason I asked Logan to the ball.

"Is it the consummating part that has you hung up?" Claire says this at normal volume as we enter the science building and has me turtling my head into the collar of my sweatshirt. She pokes my arm and laughs.

"Look how red your cheeks are!"

My eyes widen as I make that face my mom is accustomed to seeing me make, the one usually accompanied by, "Mom, stop!"

"Do you have to use that word? Consummate? It sounds so . . . arranged marriage-y." It actually sounds like *Game of Thrones*, and my virtues are for sale.

"Fine. I won't use that word," she says, and I relax my shoulders a hint. "Is it the fucking part?"

And . . . shoulders back at ear-level.

I slap her arm and flash her a warning of bulging-wide eyes and gritted teeth, which only makes her laugh. This is why she can't be a best friend. No more best friends. Ever.

She tags along with me to my lab room, follows me inside, and I've never wished for a trap door more in my life. I prop my backpack on the side table and dig out my lab results book. I'm close to abandoning this experiment altogether, but the thought of starting from scratch feels daunting. I'm not sure my psyche can handle one more academic letdown this year.

"Seriously, Rachel. If it's the fucking thing, just tell Logan about it. Split the money with him, or better yet—sleep with him!" She waggles her brows.

I let my face fall into my palms, and actually *feel* the heat of my cheeks against my fingertips. I shift my index fingers to rub my temples.

"Splitting the money with him would be pointless. I need nearly a full five grand. And besides, how do I even explain this entire stupid concept?" I lift my head to meet her gaze, her lips caught in a knowing smirk.

"It's the fucking part."

"Gah! I wish you would quit saying that!" I turn my

attention back to my work station, her words ringing in my ear. So blunt. So, I don't know . . . dirty? Not that I'm a virgin. She's not wrong, though. Maybe if this whole thing were predicated on showing up with him as my date I could live with it. But the other part? Now I'm just locked into bringing him with me to a formal dance he likely has zero interest in, and there is no way I can win the pool because there is no way I'm going to broach the topic of, well, fucking.

"I'm not a brave person. That's what I get for being bold out of the blue. You know?"

I flatten my hands on the table top and spin around, my gaze flashing by Claire and landing on Logan, who I pray only heard the tail end of our conversation.

"Sure," Logan says, his head tilted in such a way I think he missed the embarrassing part.

"Experiment gone wrong," I blurt out.

He nods slowly, a hint of a grin on his face as his eyes shift to Claire. If he's looking to her for confirmation of my lie, I have no idea if she'll have my back. For all I know, she'll lay the terms out on my behalf and drum up a quickie contract.

I want to die.

"And I was just leaving." She shifts her gaze to me as she shakes Logan's hand. Why must she make it seem so suspicious. I don't think my throat is working. And my lungs. Yeah, my lungs are definitely broken.

"Nice to see you, Claire," Logan says over his shoulder, turning his attention back to me. I do my best to shake off everything that happened and was said in the moments before he was in the room, or that I *knew* he was here.

I straighten my spine and tilt my head.

"Were we meeting today?" I check my phone for a missed text, but there's nothing. He's here unannounced. And it's making my heart juggle around my chest cavity.

His gaze rakes over me for a second, his tongue caught in his front teeth. His expression gives me the sense that he's still working out exactly what he walked in on. I gesture to the paper rolled up in his hand, redirecting his focus.

"Oh, this?" He's suddenly coy and now I'm genuinely curious. "Just a quiz that I . . . *cough, cough* . . . did not fail."

He unfurls the page and holds it out in presentation. A red 71 is circled at the top. I take the paper from him and scan the questions he missed, making mental notes for myself. He should have gotten those right.

"Logan!" I sweep the errors to the side and focus on his pride. "While I think you should aim higher than not failing, I'm very proud of you."

His smile stretches his lips and dents his cheeks. It's one of his best attributes. His lips . . . that smile.

"Thank you. I couldn't have pulled this off without you," he says, taking his quiz back and moving toward my work-space as he pulls his backpack from his shoulders. He tucks his test into the growing folder he started.

"Come on. Lunch is on me," he says, zipping up his bag and slinging it over one shoulder.

I glance to our right, and he follows my gaze to where my notebook is open and sample materials arranged.

"Unless you're in the middle of—"

"Just finishing, actually." The lie comes out so smoothly it startles me. I shift gears and pack up my things, mostly so I can hide my panicked expression for a few seconds. I'm still working off the jolt of adrenaline from Logan showing up.

Before I'm able to swing my bag over my shoulder, Logan

tugs it from my hand and slings it over his shoulder, carrying both his and mine.

"Oh, you don't have to—"

Before I can finish my words, his elbow juts out and he nudges mine, urging me to take his arm. I warm instantly, before even touching him.

"Wow, how formal. For lunch at the student union," I joke.

"Only the best for my tutor," he says as I link my arm through his. His reminder of our roles in this relationship dampens the electricity, but there's still a tiny spark when we touch. Like shocking myself with a balloon rubbed on shag carpet. Not quite electric, but I feel it.

We garner a bit of attention as Logan leads me down the main walk toward the union. Or maybe I simply perceive it that way. My gaze darts from one cluster of people to the next, and I swear I catch sideways glances and whispers along the way.

Logan releases our linked arms and holds the door open for me, leaving me to follow behind him a step or two as we slip into the line starting to build for lunch. He hands me a tray and a plate when we reach the register and swipes his card twice before leaning in close. His mouth warms my ear.

"Football gets the gold level so go nuts. Anything you want. Sky's the limit!" He waves his hand over the bread station, and I pick up a roll.

"Maybe I'll get *two* butters," I joke, dropping the roll on my plate.

Logan laughs, then snags four rolls along with a fistful of butter packets.

"I'm not sharing, so if you're a bread person you better get the extra one now." He moves on toward the main buffet and I gnaw at the inside of my cheek for a second, then take his advice and grab one more piece of bread.

I've never had so much fun eating on campus before. We spend ten minutes evaluating our options, and Logan piles up so many scoops and slices of various meats and pastas that he has to take on a second plate. I end up building myself a salad that could barely be considered a salad. The lettuce gives it legitimacy but the pepperoni, croutons, and piles of mozzarella feel counter leafy green.

Logan grabs a can of some type of energy drink and I get a cup to fill with water. I cap it with a lid and poke a straw through before turning to head toward the table he's parked at near the windows. I pause when I catch a tall, smoking hot blonde step up behind him and suddenly wrap her arms around him.

The hard edge of someone's tray slams into my back and I stumble to my right.

"Sorry, sorry," I say, my words blending in with what I'm pretty sure is, "Fucking move."

I'm so rattled by the whole encounter that I don't see Logan walking up until he's a few steps away from me and reaching for my tray.

"People much?" he bites in the direction of the short-haired brunette who nearly took me out with her lunch. She holds her tray in one hand so she can gesture my direction, her hand splaying in the air the way my brother's does when he gets behind a slow driver.

"Sorry, I didn't realize you were that far behind me," Logan says, taking my tray and marching back to the table. The mystery blonde seems to have disappeared.

"You don't eat in here much, do you?" Logan asks, setting

my tray across from his. I slip into the bench seat and slide to the end, close to the window.

Shaking my head I say, "No." I rarely venture beyond the honors cafeteria and the food truck outside the chem labs.

I split my bread open and tear open the butter packet, dropping the entire pallet onto the roll then smooshing it between the two halves.

"I'm sorry, but did you just make a butter sandwich?" Logan's eyes are puzzled.

I bite into the roll and smile through my closed-mouth chew, nodding.

His shoulders lift with a short laugh and he shakes his head, spreading butter on his own roll, albeit at a much thinner ratio.

"I wish I could have a body like that and eat all the butter I wanted," he mutters. I pause mid-chew and my eyes freeze open a tad wider than normal. He's talking about my body. *My* body. I swallow down the doughy lump and it goes down hard.

"I'm sorry. You want to look like a curvy woman?"

His head bops up and our eyes meet, his also wide now. He glances to his right and his lips move slightly; I think he's replaying his words. Finally, he laughs.

"I see. Yeah, no. I mean, I'm not sure how you eat butter sandwiches and look like, well . . . . that." He gestures toward me with his roll, then promptly takes a bite.

I take a smaller nibble of mine, not because I feel butter shamed but because he thinks there's something noteworthy about my body. My mom has always praised my hourglass figure but it's made me frustrated for most of my adolescent and young adult life. Designers don't cut fancy dresses for curves, and tight-fitting pants and shirts don't feel like hugs on my curves, they feel like compression bandages there to remind me that I'm not a stick. Add to that my size nine feet and five-nine height, and I've basically felt like a slug hiding inside sweatpants for most of my life. Stella used to say it's why I loved my lab coat, because it was oversized and drapey. Upon reflection, I think Stella was taking a dig at me and my curves. Curves that, it seems, Tiff's star football player finds appealing.

"So, who was the blonde?" I blurt out, clearly lost in my thoughts and losing my inhabitations thanks to his compliment. I cram the rest of my bread in my mouth to keep my face from contorting into some sorry expression.

"Ah," Logan says, twisting the plate loaded with three types of chicken tenders around his tray. He stops at the plain one and picks it up, holding it hostage above a pool of ranch dressing. His eyes flit up to mine.

"That would be *my* ex. And we aren't as friendly as she tried to make that look. She's . . . I don't know, vain? Self-centered? Self-important?"

"So, she's a thesaurus entry for conceited?"

He chuckles, then dips his chicken in the sauce.

"Basically. Yes." He pops the entire tender in his mouth, and I laugh. Half because of his response and half because—

"And you judged my butter sandwich."

He smirks on one side as he chews.

"Fair point." He bunches up one of his napkins to clean the grease off his hands before pushing his tray to the side and folding his hands together.

"Amy and I went out for six months, but we'd hooked up a lot before that."

My expression must look sour because Logan's head falls to the side a touch and he shrugs.

"Sorry, I'm not judging," I say. *I was totally judging. But now I feel bad.*

"It's fine. You're probably a lot more mature than me."

I smile at his summation but the truth is I'm a hermit, and meeting new people isn't in my skillset. I only met Dalton because we both spent so much time in the library and he approached me. *I guess the library is his territory.*

"What happened to end you and Amy?" She seems ideal. I noticed her cheer T-shirt and her long, toned legs, and Logan is, well, Logan is a beautiful man. Somehow everything he wears fits him like he's a Ken doll, and his jaw is literally superhero squared. His lips seem strong, and his smile is disarming. He mentioned before that Amy dumped him, but honestly? Looking at the two of them together, I can't think of two people more built for one another.

"Apparently, I'm unambitious or boring or, I don't remember the other words she used. I think she found out I was on the bubble so she turned her attention to another guy on our team." He's about to take another bite of chicken but stops abruptly. "Sorry, being on the bubble means—"

"I know what bubble is. Remember? Football class and me equals honors student." I give him a wry look and he quickly apologies.

"You're going to have to explain that to me at some point, your in-depth football knowledge. And you might need to tutor me in two subjects, to, you know, get me off the bubble." His cheek dimples with the one-sided smile.

I chuckle.

"I might know a thing or two about that, yeah," I say. My brother was a bubble player. He was fine with that, though, because football was his means to a different end. I think Logan has bigger goals with the game.

"Right, well, Amy is the kind of girl who likes shiny new toys, and this guy Cam, he was a transfer. He's good, but not *that* good. What he has going for him, though, is a name. His dad's Bolten Ledger."

I spit out the olive-pepperoni bite I just constructed from my salad and quickly wipe my mouth.

"As in the guy who calls the NFL playoff games and sometimes the Super Bowl? On TV? And who has like four . . . or is it five rings?" Football is a thing in our house. And so are the Bears.

Logan rolls his eyes and laughs.

"He has three rings, and only one was with Chicago. But yeah, that guy."

"And she left you for his son? Not for him, but the son?" I'm kinda being serious, but it seems to amuse Logan because he leans back and cackles.

"That's a really good point," he says, leaning forward again with both palms on the table. I lean in to meet him, sensing he's about to share a secret.

"I'm not totally sure that isn't her end game."

Our eyes lock for a breath, and it's both heated and somehow comfortable. We break into hard laughter at the same time, and that, too, feels nice.

We both dive into our food for a few quiet minutes, and when Logan discards half of the spicy chicken tender he decided to try, I pick it up and plop it on my salad. He sits back and folds his arms over his chest, his mouth an oddly proud type of smile.

"What?" I mutter, covering my mouth to hide the full bite I'd just taken.

"You are so interesting. You play like you're this big

brainy introvert but you have no problem stealing right from a man's plate."

I shrug and begin cutting his chicken piece into small cubes to mix in with the rest of my salad.

"You abandoned it."

I glance up to catch him blink a few times before his eyes meet mine.

"I guess I did."

I form another perfect salad bite, one mixed with chicken and cheese, then pop it into my mouth a second before Logan hits me with a dose of my own medicine.

"What went down with you and Dalton?"

I cough, choking on the lettuce. I work it out and finish chewing, staring at my still piled-high garbage salad while I take a short trip through the worst day of my life. I decide to sum everything up into an easy one-liner.

"He cheated on me with my best friend and roommate." My eyes flit to his and he doesn't look smug, only sorry. I'm not sure I appreciate it so I look down at my tray.

"It's fine," I say.

"That's not fine," he corrects. I'm sure his face still reads sympathy, so I keep my focus on the prongs of my fork. I push my food around a little then abandon the fork completely. "I think I'm going to box this and take it home."

When I look up again, Logan's moved his tray to the side and he's sitting with his elbows propped on the table, his hands folded together and covering his mouth and chin. His eyes meet mine and in that instant, everything else around us disappears.

"If he shows up to this formal dance thing with someone, he's going to be sorry."

My toes flex inside my shoes buried under the table. It's

the only way I can rid myself of the instant nervous energy I am filled with due to his sudden verve for revenge on my behalf.

I haven't really thought about the fact Stella will be back by then, and she'll probably want to attend the ball with Dalton. She'll get an award for her abroad studies and whatever amazing paper she penned overseas. Maybe having Logan there simply as my date without all of that extra stuff is the way to go. It certainly soothes the pangs of jealousy raging through my chest.

"Did you know that people have sex in the library?" Why the hell I decide that is the next topic to bring up beats me. Maybe it's because talking about Dalton and thinking about him and Stella always puts me back in that space, staring at the study room and his back. *My former best-friend's bobbing head.*

"Uh, yeah. I've done it," Logan says, his comment so matter-of-fact. What have I been missing about college?

"I'm sorry, you've . . . what? Where?" I lean in again, the image of Dalton now superimposed with a new one of Logan's bare ass pumping against a stack of books. My body rushes with heat in the brief moment I imagine it's me being pushed against said stack. *What is happening?*

"You've never had a library tryst, Shortcake?" His voice has taken on that flirty tone, which is growing on me.

"I'm sorry, but *tryst?* Who are you, Mr. Darcy?" I blow right past the whole Shortcake thing. It's also growing on me. He doesn't need to know that, though.

"Hey, Mr. Darcy would never besmirch a woman's honor with a tryst. It's far more the kind of thing, say, Heathcliff would say." He leans back and blows on his fingernails before fake polishing them on the front of his Tiff football sweat-shirt, his cocky lopsided grin making an appearance.

"Wait, wait, wait," I blubber, waving my hands over the table as if somehow I'm pausing the universe to allow me time to understand how Mr. Football, *whom I'm tutoring to pass a class*, knows these obscure details about English lit.

"I have a romantic side, Shortcake," he coos, clearly understanding my surprise.

"Clearly," I cough out.

His shoulder lifts as his lips curl, a bragging expression sticking around his face.

"My mom is obsessed with Jane Austen novels, so when-ever I had to read a book for a report in high school, I picked one of her favorites. Turns out I kinda like 'em, too. I mean, the dated language is tough, but I got better with it. I took both courses they offer here for my English requirements. And not to brag, but I got two As."

I stare at him with my mouth open for a few seconds before finally letting out a single breathy laugh. "Well, damn."

He chuckles and hops up from our table, jogging to the utensils station where he snags a to-go carton for me. When he sits back down to box up my salad I question whether I've blinked at all in the last thirty seconds.

"Who are you?" My head falls to the side.

He smirks but doesn't look up.

"I'm a mama's boy. But don't let that fool you." He tucks the cardboard tab in and pushes the box toward me.

"Fool me how? Into thinking you're a gentleman?"

His lips settle into a soft line that teases me somehow, like he's hiding a secret, one that gives him pleasure.

"Maybe I'll share my other side with you sometime in the library."

And if the undeniable suggestion in his words, spoken deep and sultry, didn't send a rush of tingles straight between my thighs, the dimple and wink definitely do the trick.

Maybe a fifty-dollar buy-in isn't so expensive after all.

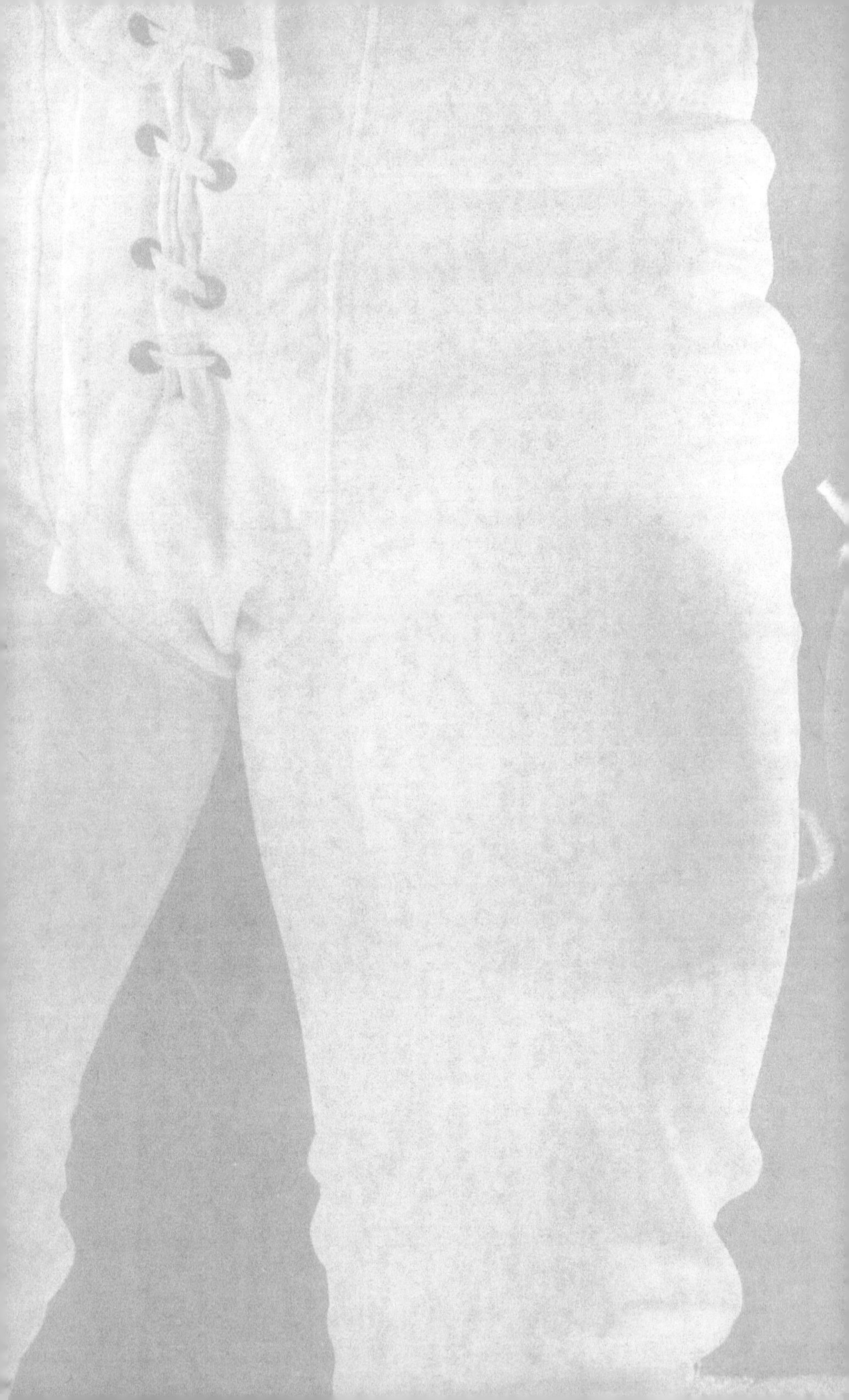

8 /
logan

I THINK I've dreamt about bending Rachel over the library study table no less than five times since our little conversation about library hookups. It definitely made this week's study sessions a challenge in the focus department.

The more time we spend together, the more I want to overstep my boundaries. I'm all for making her ex jealous, mostly because he seems like a real prick. But I don't know where the line is for when I should turn it on and off. Are we playing at being a couple all the time or just when he's around? Because I'm down for practicing whenever.

There was a moment last Friday when we were leaving the library and I held the door open for her. She passed by me, her ass brushing against my thigh, and I swear my dick swelled up and pointed at her as if it were a dog on a hunt. Her curves are like art. I imagine her face on all the damn classical paintings hanging in the library mezzanine whenever we meet. Fuck, to see her spread out on some velvet sofa while eating grapes, her perfect tits arched toward the sky, my tongue on those nipples. She wore this purple sweater Friday, the dick-pointing day, and her hard nipples taunted me through most of the lesson on chemical bonds.

But today? Today, I think she's trying to torture me.

It's Tuesday. Not our usual meeting day. We had to bump our lesson back a day because Coach wanted to break down our preseason game play after practice. I was in the team lecture hall until midnight last night with Jax and our quarterback, Dante, going through specific plays that require the three of us to be perfectly in sync. Thank God I remembered to text Rachel that morning. I don't want to ever stand her up again. At this point, I'm not sure I could take a chem quiz without her prepping me. I'm three for three on passing grades. Plus, I've gotten used to our routine. I like seeing her throughout my week. And I find I'm constantly looking for excuses to see her more.

I asked her to meet me after practice so we could study at my place. I wasn't sure she'd go for it but she said she was dying to see this place everyone calls the football house. It's not anything special. Just a two-story me and four other guys share about a block or two from campus. But Rachel? She seems to be treating the invitation as something special.

I saw her walk up the first few rows of stadium seats at the start of practice, her hair blowing around in these wild red waves, her white cotton dress swishing around her hips and tickling her knees. It's a brisk fall sunset, but warm enough I guess for her to dress like a virgin who fell from heaven. For a while, she covered her shoulders in this pink sweater that she clutched at her chest. But the wind died down, and now she's all sun-kissed shoulders and tempting breasts. Fucking beautiful. I have to know what they look like, her breasts.

"Ford! Earth to Ford!" The slap at the back of my helmet

snaps me from my most recent stare fest. I turn to meet Jax's wide grin.

"You hot for Teacher?" he teases.

"Ha, ha," I say with the snarkiest tone I can drum up. It's all a cover, and Jax sees right through it.

"Girl is fine as hell. And smart! She's out of your league," he says through a sharp laugh, slapping my shoulder pad then taking off toward the middle of the field. I jog behind him, ruminating on his assessment and feeling a whole lot less confident about seducing her over our study session.

We huddle up and take knees so the coaching staff can review the game plan for this week. Our first division game is Saturday, and we're favored to win. But in true Tiff U football tradition, being favored doesn't mean jack shit. This year is going to be different, though. Expectations will be met and then left in the dust.

After we break, I head toward the seats, stopping Jax before he takes off for the locker room.

"Hey, Rachel is coming over to study tonight, by the way. Maybe try not to walk around in your boxers and shit. Class it up some?" I'm having second thoughts about taking her to the football house. We're gross, and I'm not sure who was on cleaning duty last week, but they failed miserably. I know it wasn't me. When it's my turn, our pad smells like lemon zest and sparkles floor to ceiling. I have a feeling it was Dante's turn this round, and while he can throw a pass on a dime, the dude can't seem to work a mop.

"Yeah, I got you, bro. No boxers. Just shirtless flexing. Maybe I can do a few push-ups for her in the living room? You know, so she knows her options." He plays it serious for a few seconds so I call him a dick and leave him to laugh at his own lame jokes.

"You want me and Dante to leave the lights on and crack our doors open so she doesn't try any funny business with you?" He's shouting at my back now. I hope like hell Rachel can't hear any of this bullshit. I lift up my hand and flash him a middle finger over my shoulder, and a second later I hear his laugh bellow in the distance.

As I walk up, Rachel gets up from her seat and skips down to the first level where she can lean over the bar and meet my gaze. I shade my eyes with my hand, the sun lighting up strands of her hair. She must have her contacts in today. Either that or she can't see a damn thing. I tried her glasses on for fun a few sessions ago and the girl's basically blind.

"Every practice like that?" she says, leaning over the railing. My gaze snaps right to the curves of her tits, the loose tie binding the top of her dress. *I'm in trouble.*

"Like what?" I don't even care if she can see my gawking. I can't help it.

She shifts her sweater, which she's holding, into a folded-up mess in one hand, and it blocks my view. Probably for the best.

"Like you all don't have a clue what the fuck you're doing."

She went full F word, and her crass analysis pushes me back a step or two and leaves my mouth agape. Also, I'm impressed.

"I'm kidding," she finally gives, winking the way I do at her. Which means she's maybe teasing, maybe not.

"That"—I huff out a short, relieved laugh and point at her, waggling my finger—"Not nice, Rachel Edwards. Not nice at all."

She looks up and moves her head side to side.

"Embracing my evil scientist side."

I knew I shouldn't have told her about that whole science villain scenario I had going in my head. She caught me staring at her last week while she was finishing up her lab, and my panicky mouth spilled it. Seemed a better thing to say than *just fantasizing about sitting you on that table and spreading your legs.*

"Not sure what evil scientists have to do with football pundits, but you make the rules," I say, twisting my lips and shrugging.

Her head falls back with the sweetest laugh, and she kicks her foot up behind her, sockless and white-sneakered. Adorable. *My mom would love this girl.*

What is that thought?

"Wait for me by my truck if you want, or the benches by the lot. I'll shower fast and be out in five," I say, skipping back a few steps and taking all of her in.

I know our roles, tutor and student. It's obvious that at the very least, though, we're friends now too. In this exact moment, however? Right now, she seems like my girl. I like the idea of her waiting for me, of coming home to her after a game. Of looking up in the stands and finding her smile, catching her gaze. I'm one step away from driving her around on the back of a tractor with this infatuation.

I rush through my shower, partly because I want to get out of here before my roommates do, and also because I don't want to make Rachel wait. I overshoot my five-minute promise by another ten, so I fire off a text as I zip up my gym bag to let her know I'm heading out. I pause in front of Dante's locker and glance over my shoulder to make sure I'm alone before I grab his cologne and spray my neck with a half dose. I rub it into my skin as I walk away, diffusing it as much as I can so it doesn't seem like I'm trying so hard.

I'm trying really hard.

I laugh to myself as I make my way through the stadium corridor and out toward the lot. I just stole my friend's body spray to impress a girl. To be fair to myself, Dante does smell great. It's actually the first thing nearly every girl says to him when he hits on them at the bars. Of course, he moves right into leading them onto the dance floor where his moves get them more drunk than any cocktail or shot he could offer to buy them. My dance moves are more on the beer-can-crushing level. Not impressive at all. But maybe Dante's scent will be enough to convince Rachel to stick around for the night. And morning.

My phone buzzes in my back pocket, so I pull it out to read the incoming text as I walk.

RACHEL: *I don't think Amy likes me.*

Shit. I shove my phone back into my pocket and jog until I round the corner of the main exit. I stride into the parking lot in time to see Amy pulling open the driver's side door of her Mustang. She's wearing those super short shorts and a cropped sweatshirt, probably having just finished rehearsal with the dance team for Saturday's game. She'll stick around and wait for Cam, I'm sure. I don't like the thought that she said something to Rachel, though.

Rachel's sitting on my open tailgate, her ankles crossed and feet swinging back and forth. She seems at home there, content to be alone. Her eyes light up when she spots me.

"Did she find out you're secretly an evil scientist?" I joke when I near her. I toss my bag in the truck bed and plant a foot on the tire as I lean into the side.

"*Hmm*, I think it's more of the I'm a female and she wants to cover you in cat pee to mark her territory thing."

I bunch my brow.

"That's a . . . colorful way to put it." I glance to the right, where Amy is lounging in her car with the door open and her music turned up just loud enough to draw attention. Cat pee, huh?

"Do you trust me?" I say, shifting my gaze back to Rachel, a devious and slightly selfish idea noodling in my head.

Her head tilts to the side and her eyes narrow.

"I'm pretty sure I don't," she concludes, her answer not requiring much thought. I laugh out, assuming it's a joke, but when her lips mash together and her eyes squint with a guilty-looking wince, I pause.

"Oh." My chest deflates. I suppose we don't know each other very well, and I probably haven't given her many reasons to trust me blindly.

"But I'm willing to give you some slack. Very little, but . . . slack." She shifts her feet, crossing her ankles the other way, and my not-so-pure idea rekindles with renewed hope.

"Okay, I'll take an inch," I say, moving closer until I'm standing directly in front of her.

Her body stiffens, which tells me my slack is running out. I drop my chin and catch her gaze, her wide eyes showing how nervous she is.

"One more inch? For show?" I tilt my head a tick in Amy's direction, and Rachel's gaze follows. Her lips tick up.

"She really doesn't like that you're standing this close."

I dance my fingertips along her right knee and she twitches but doesn't leap off the truck.

"You can have more slack," she croaks, her eyes still locked on Amy, who I have no doubt is staring right at us.

I flatten my palm against Rachel's thigh then match my touch on her other leg, gliding my hands up her body, careful not to pull her dress up. At least not out here. When my hands meet her hips, her head swivels and our eyes meet.

"She watching this?" I know she is.

"Oh, yeah," Rachel hums, her words slow and almost drawled. Her gaze flits to my mouth but instantly flashes back to my eyes, as if she feels guilty she got caught.

Don't feel guilty, Shortcake. I want to kiss you, too.

I lean in until we're inches apart, then move my mouth close to her ear.

"Mind if I pick you up and take you to the passenger seat?" My fingers practically vibrate against her hips as I hold back the urge to grab.

I hear Rachel swallow.

"You may," she says, her voice cracking.

"Hold on," I say, sliding my hands under her ass and scooping her up into me. Her arms swing around my neck and her legs wrap around my waist, my hands covering the cotton of her dress along with some very smooth bare skin.

Rachel clings to me, her muscles working to squeeze my body as if she's clinging to a tree to avoid a bear. Her hands shift behind my neck and her face tucks into the space along my jawline, which feels oddly erotic yet also tickles. She's also close to choking me with her shoulder pressing into my throat.

"You know I lift four hundred pounds a few times a week. I'm pretty sure I won't drop you." I chuckle. Her grip loosens, but only a little.

"You said *pretty sure*," she responds, and I laugh harder.

"I meant to say I'm sure. I got you, Rachel. I won't drop you."

She peels back, her arms adjusting along my shoulders, hands still threaded behind my neck, but her face coming into view. A soft seriousness plays at her lips. It's not quite a smile, but it's also clear in her expression that she's not hating this.

I walk slowly with her in my arms, reaching with one hand to open the truck door before quickly returning to her body. My palm is on full skin now. The edge of her panties teases the tips of my fingers, and I so badly want to explore more. But I'm fairly certain I've used up my inch and then some. No more slack in this rope.

As I step toward the seat, her legs loosen and she slides from my hold into the cab of the truck. For some reason, I can't hear anything but her breath. Which is weird because I know there is traffic all around us. Before I back away, her hand runs down the center of my chest, her finger hooking a fold in my white T-shirt. Her eyes trace her movement as she moves to the buttons on my open flannel, giving the panel a slight tug. Her eyes flit up to mine.

"I like this," she says, flattening the button side of my shirt against my chest. Her flat palm lingers over my left pectoral for a beat, and her touch is warm.

"Me too," I say, forcing my lips to close and not allow anything stupid to follow those words. There's a double meaning there, and I'd prefer to leave it subtle.

I back away and close the door gently, feeling it click shut. When I turn around I let out the breath I've been holding and shove my hands into my pockets so I can squeeze them into fists without anyone seeing. That was some serious self-discipline I just displayed.

When I climb in next to Rachel, she's biting her lip and holding back what I hope is a growing smile.

"You like making people jealous, Shortcake?" I'm sure Amy is fuming.

Her lip comes loose from her grip and she glances to the side in thought.

"Let's just say I trust you a little more."

I nod and again, somehow, keep my mouth shut.

More slack.

Noted.

9 /
rachel

SO THIS IS the football house. Huh.

I thought it would be bigger.

Two stories, yes, but there isn't some grand staircase and a corridor of rooms like the frat houses in movies. There's a big screen and a decent entertainment center loaded up with speakers and various game consoles. The sectional in the living room is well-worn but clean, which is also somehow surprising, and the place doesn't smell like a locker room.

I have, however, noticed an inordinate amount of empty beer cans. Most in stacks, like mini challenges or sculptures. I pause at one on a small table along the wall between the entrance and the archway that leads to the kitchen.

"Did someone try to make this spell Tiff?" I crouch to view it from tabletop level, and yes, it in fact sort of spells Tiff.

"That one's Dante's. He's very proud of it. Don't poke fun," Logan says.

His expression doesn't seem like he's kidding, so I form an *oh* with my mouth and stand up tall again, then follow him into the kitchen. My eyes dart all over the place, so much stimulation around me, so many clues to lock in about this secret lifestyle I've always been curious about. And then there's Logan's ass in those jeans, his shoulders stretching the blue and red plaid flannel across his back, the slight ripples made with the movement of his arms.

And then there's my ass under this dress. I swear it's on fire. I feel as if a werewolf scratched my skin and left me raw, which is insane because I know his touch was definitely guarded. But holy hell! I'm glad I wore my hipster underwear instead of the boy shorts I usually go for when I wear a dress. I would have missed out on all of that.

"We can work in here. Can I get you something to drink?"

I snap out of my daze at the sound of his voice and retrace what I *think* I heard him say.

"Water?" *Please let that be the right answer.*

"You got it," he says, opening the fridge while I pull out one of the wooden chairs.

Logan slides a water bottle toward me as he drops his backpack on the table. He turns his back to me again to grab a jar of peanut butter from the cupboard. He unscrews the lid on a shaker bottle and dumps in scoops of peanut butter along with ice, milk, and protein powder before recovering it.

"Is that really any good?" It looks clumpy, even after he shakes it rigorously.

He shrugs and flips half the lid up before taking a big swallow.

"It's worse when I put egg in it."

I shiver at the thought and he laughs, pulling out the chair closest to me and sitting with his legs stretched out, one under my chair and the other under the table. My eyes go right to his crotch.

"So, should we review or work ahead?"

I blink up and his smirk tells me he probably saw me staring, well, at his penis.

"Review. Yeah, uh . . ." I clear my throat and tug his backpack closer. I pull out the familiar folders and his notebook, my nerdy side singing a little when I notice he's kept the tabs on the pages I marked for him the last time we studied.

"This helped?" I flick the pink tab with my finger.

"Tons! I knew what to focus on before the quiz. Oh, and hey!" He pulls his bag toward him and reaches in, exaggerating his motion as if he has to crawl inside to find something. I shake my head and roll my eyes, but really? It's cute when he acts like this.

"Ta da!" He pulls out another quiz, this one with an eighty percent circled on the top. "Definitely not failing."

"Logan!" I rip it from his hand. I'm truly proud. Two weeks ago I figured I'd do my best to survive a semester of frustrating review, but now? I think he's going to pass! And the only frustration I'm starting to feel is the nagging temptation to touch him.

Logan holds up a palm for me to high five, and I slap his hand. Before we part, though, he grabs hold, and his fingers suddenly weave between mine. He coaxes my hand down to rest on his thigh, and my gaze follows, my mouth hung open as he flips my palm over and runs his thumb along the vein in my wrist. I'm sure it's pulsing like the heart of a baby bird. He must feel it.

"Dude! No weights tomorrow morning, bitches!" Deep and bellowing voices fill the house, breaking the magic. Logan's on his feet in less than a second, his brow pinched and shoulders raised.

"What part of *I'm studying with Rachel so try to be chill* did you miss?" he scolds. Four guys pour into the kitchen, filling the space instantly with their presence and sucking up every last breathable molecule. Oh, wait, nope. That's just me hyperventilating.

"Oh, yeah. I know, and *hi, Rachel!*" The tallest of the bunch leans across the table, his bronzed arm like a sculpture, tendons flexing and forearms flexed. I feel like I'm living in a charity calendar.

I take his hand, and his palm is literally twice the size of mine. This must be Dante, the quarterback.

"Nice to meet you. I like your art," I say, nodding toward the misshaped can art attempting to spell TIFF.

His eyes light up. I guessed right.

"Thank you!" Dante stands up straight and rolls his shoulders before glancing to his equally enormous friend. Sizing this guy up, I'd say he's a corner. Maybe a wide receiver. He's mostly arms and legs.

"Rachel, you don't know what you have done," the second guy says, pushing Dante off balance and rolling his eyes. "He's going to make more of that ugly shit now. Can you tell he thinks he's an artist when he's drunk?"

He reaches for my hand and we shake as he introduces himself. "I'm Jax."

I've heard both of their names often from Logan. The roommates, but also good friends. There's an instant camaraderie in the room, and while it's loud and I feel as though I'm buried in a crowd, it's also nice. I envy this. It's what I thought I had with Dalton and Stella.

"I'm sorry. We can go to the library if you want. Or maybe push this to the morning since I don't have weights?" Logan says in a hushed tone as he leans on the table to give us feigned intimacy.

I shake my head, a little overwhelmed with the barrage of

bodies and also still racking my brain over the fact we held hands a minute ago. Like, *really held hands!*

"It's fine. Whatever you think you need, *Mister I got a B.*" His lips curl up at my compliment, and I dare say his cheeks seem red. I think he's embarrassed but also proud. I get that juxtaposition. It's where I thrive, which unfortunately means I'm always in a state of knowing my worth yet not feeling like I fit in.

The other two teammates introduce themselves and I do my best to tuck their names into my memory bank—Bradley and Liam. Everyone is either sitting at the table with us or digging in the fridge to piece together some semblance of a meal when Dante shoots up his hand and pulls his head from staring into the freezer.

"Party! We have a party!" He's reading a text on his phone, his eyes scanning what I assume are the details while he reaches around the kitchen and somehow high fives everyone but Logan without even looking.

"It's at Meg's, which means her dad's pit BBQ, which means kegs and food. Dude, no weights in the morning. We have to." Dante drops his phone on the table in front of Logan, who glances at the message then to me, his mouth pulled into a tight line. I can see the tug-of-war happening behind his eyes.

"Go," I say, closing up his folder for him. I tuck it in his bag, but before I can zip it shut, his hand covers mine. My gaze flies to his then darts around the room to see if anyone else is witnessing this. Jax is. His lips pucker into a smirk and he turns his back to us.

"I don't need to go to a party," Logan says, but there's a slight lilt in his voice. He wants to go. I can tell.

"I know, but also, you deserve to go to a party. You've

worked hard. Reward time. Professor Rachel insists," I say, sliding my hand out from under his. I lean back in my chair and drop my hands to the hem of my dress, squeezing my knees together and tucking the cotton under my thighs.

"Come with us," Logan says.

My mouth waters with the vomit sensation.

"Oh, yeah . . . no," I say through nervous laughter. I get up from my chair and scoot it into the table, then turn directly into a giant chest.

"Yeah, come with us, Rach! You'll love Meg's barbecue. Her dad owns a meat shop. It's literally heaven over a fire pit," Dante says.

Rach. Like we're familiar. It's . . . nice.

"I don't know," I waver, turning back around and meeting Logan's eyes.

He's standing now, but keeping distance between us. An eyebrow ticks up and he mouths, "Please."

I swallow down the most vile taste and force myself to take a deep breath through my nose. I don't party. I don't really drink. I don't even know how to behave at something like this. *What if Logan leaves me alone? Who will I talk to?*

"Don't think. Just come," he says.

I exhale while holding his gaze, and there's something about the way he's looking at me that settles the butterflies in my chest.

"Okay."

There are actual cheers when I agree, and before I know it, I'm back in the passenger seat of Logan's truck and heading to the outskirts of town for fire-pit meat and cheap beer.

We pull onto a dirt road that leads to a huge white house with a sprawling porch. There's a firepit blazing in the middle of the yard, and at least forty people are clustered around the fire for warmth. The smoky scent knocks me back a step when I exit the truck, but the sweet touch of cherry wood draws me back in.

"Okay, now I'm glad I'm here," I joke, breathing in the gift being puffed out of a huge smoker.

"My company wasn't enough, huh?" Logan says, slinging an arm around my shoulder and pulling me close. My palm lands on his chest as my feet stumble and I end up grabbing hold of his flannel shirt. It's strange how well we fit—like his height was made for mine. Everything seems to have a place.

Logan guides me toward the group, not letting his arm leave my shoulder until he introduces me to a few girls sitting on a log bench near the fire. I don't catch any of their names because I'm too stupefied by this entire scenario. Plus, it's hard to hear over the music being blasted from the back of someone else's truck. The girls seem nice, though. One of them hands me a beer and compliments my shoes, either that or she's letting me know I stepped in farm gifts, a term my dad uses for horse shit. I thank her for the beer, then let Logan lead me to the next group of his friends. I feel a bit like I'm on tour, so I clutch my beer and take long sips until my nerves subside.

We make a full circle around the fire, stopping to grab more drinks from a huge metal bin filled with ice before sitting at a picnic table with plates full of food. Jax and Dante join us, but Liam and Bradley disappeared near the first set of girls I met.

Within seconds, the three guys are shoveling food into their mouths. My plate is crumbs in comparison. I manage to fashion together a sandwich with the scoops of pork and coleslaw I got from the tables near the porch. I lean forward so I don't wind up dropping half the meat down my dress and take a bite.

"Right?" Dante says from across the table.

"Err my gawd," I mumble through a full mouth, a piece of the bun flaking off. Logan catches it in his hand, then brushes what I'm guessing is a splotch of sauce from my chin. I can literally feel my eyes get dopey as I look up at him through my lashes.

"I'm guessing you like it?" His thumb brushes my chin one more time, but I know there's nothing there to wipe away this time. This touch is extra—a bonus touch.

I nod slowly and lick the flavor from my lips, Logan's focus dropping to my mouth. His smile spreads a hint, and his lips part to show his tongue caught in his front teeth. Maybe I drank that first beer a little too quickly, or maybe I'm feeling just right. Whatever the reason, I think Logan Ford actually wants to kiss me. And not just for show.

"Rach, you have to try the tots. I mean, everything is good deep-fried, but these—here, just try." And our moment is once again foiled by one of Logan's roommates as Jax slides across the bench until his thigh is touching mine and he's pinching a tater tot in front of me, begging me to try.

"Oh, sure. Yeah," I stutter, taking it from him and popping it in my mouth. It's piping hot, and I have to spit it in my palm almost immediately.

"And this is why Jax will never have a girlfriend," Logan scoffs, taking the tater from my palm then promptly cleaning my hand with his napkin. I dive into my second beer, drinking nearly a third of it down to quell both my nerves and the blisters I fear are coming.

"Sorry, Rach," Jax says, hiking his shoulders up and flashing an apologetic expression to Logan.

"It's okay. I was not expecting it, is all," I say. Not wanting to sour the mood, I reach across the table to his plate and take another tot, this time blowing it cool for several seconds before taking a bite. It's an average tater tot, but there's something sweet about Jax and the way he's hanging on the edge waiting for my response.

"Amazing!" I proclaim, finishing the rest and turning my focus back to Logan, who leans in and rests his forehead on mine.

"You're way too nice to him. Careful, you'll get yourself a stray," he says through a soft laugh.

"I haven't already?" I say, blinking up.

He leans back enough to look me in the eyes, quiet for a few seconds, then he pushes our plates closer to the middle of the table and grabs my hand.

"Come with me," he says, swinging his legs around and holding out his other hand to help me to my feet. I hold on and am careful not to flash my underwear to his roommates as I clear the picnic bench.

Country music blasts through the speakers, and Logan slide steps next to me, bumping my hip and sending me a few steps to the side. Our hands still tethered, he quickly pulls me back into him with a little spin then dips me. His breath tickles my throat, and I'm all too aware of how close his mouth is to the edge of my dress and curve of my breasts. Laughter spills out of me so hard it's silent. It's mostly from shock, but also, I'm truly happy.

I'm also definitely feeling the two and a half beers. Those went down quick.

Logan helps me back upright, the earth tipping a little in my mind, which translates to loose feet.

"Whoa, Shortcake," he says, steadying me with a hand on

my shoulder. I meet his gaze again as I hold my right arm out like I'm on a balance beam.

"I think I'm good," I say. My words sound like a giggle.

"Let's get you a water," he says, leading me up the porch and into the grand house.

The inside is even more breathtaking than the outside, the walls all painted a dark gray-blue, honey-colored wood accents and trim, and cream-colored oversized sofas by a roaring fire. At least five separate couples are making out by the fire, and my eyes linger on them as we zip through the space on our way to the kitchen. What they're doing looks fun. Dalton wasn't much into PDA. Of course, I've never really been into being out with the public, which I suppose is step one.

"Here we go," Logan says, pulling a cold water bottle from the fridge. He twists the cap off and hands it to me, and I guzzle down nearly all of it in one breath. I know how this chemistry works. I drank that water because I'm thirsty. It won't do a damn thing for my blood alcohol content. Time is the only factor that matters.

"Can we play a drinking game?" I hand Logan the now-empty bottle and he stares at me with an amused expression.

"We can play a *game*. I don't know that you need to add more drinking. I think you might be a lightweight."

I swing my dress at my side, the fabric swooshing against my knees.

"Oh, I am *definitely* a lightweight. But I always wanted to try one of those games. What's the one with the cups?" He doesn't know it, but I'm duping him right now. I might not drink much but you don't grow up in my family, the sister of a football stud and daughter of a Bears fan, and not know how to ace a ping pong ball in a Solo cup.

"Fine, but we're sticking with water." Logan reaches back into the fridge and grabs two more bottles, gripping them in one hand while he holds mine with his other. I'm enjoying his unrelenting hold. It's protective. And sweet. And his hands are warm, and a little rough.

I lick my lips, dashing the thoughts of his hands other places. Logan snakes us through the back yard filled with people, the crowd double what it was before. There are a few people playing cornhole near the driveway, and two of the picnic tables are already set up for beer pong. Logan scans the cups, finding the ball and handing it to me. He straightens the cups then guides me to the end of the table, where he proceeds to mansplain the rules. I let him, because I'm buzzed and because I'm caged between his arms and his chin is at my shoulder as he stands behind me.

"Now, the loser usually has to drink. And I do think you could use more water, but—"

I don't have the heart to tell him the water is pointless.

"How about the loser buys breakfast tomorrow? Since I don't have weights, and I have a feeling you're going to want some good hangover food?"

"Deal," I agree. He's likely right. I don't hold my liquor well, and I drink a couple times a year at best. I won't throw up because, sadly, I know it takes me four beers and a shot of tequila for *that* to happen. But I'm counting on a stinger of a headache to greet me when the sun comes up. Unless I drink more water. *Hmmm.* I grab the bottle from him and gulp down half, which seems to make him happy.

"I'll go first," I proclaim, squinting at the cups and lining up my shot. I'm not a bounce-it-in player. I'm far better if I treat it like basketball. With a flick of my wrist, I toss the small white ball across the table, sinking it in the center cup.

"Hey!" I celebrate and Logan joins me, high fiving me for what he will soon learn is the first of many. He'll be lucky to get a turn.

He sweeps the cup away and hands me the ball again. I wait for him to stand behind me and offer his advice on where I should aim next. It's cute. I go for the opposite side, though, and sink the next cup as easily as the first.

Logan clears his throat and wanders toward the cup on the edge, clearing it and tossing the ball to me with a bounce. I snag it mid-air and his eyes haze with a slight tilt of his head.

"Are you hustling me, Shortcake?"

I hold the tip of my tongue over my top lip and consider for a full three seconds.

"Maybe," I finally admit, returning my attention to the table and sending the ball into another cup.

"Well, fuck," he laughs out, scooping up the cup and tossing the ball at my chest. It pings off my arm as I turn to deflect it, and I realize our little game has garnered a bit of a crowd.

"Do you want to keep playing?" I ask, turning my attention back to Logan. He shakes his head, his lips tight but hinting at a smile.

My reaction time is slowed enough that I don't realize how close he's getting until his fingertips are under my chin. He licks his bottom lip then bites it, pinning his grin.

"No, Shortcake. I don't want to play beer pong anymore," he hums, leaning in, his gaze dropping to my mouth a fraction of a second before his lips cover mine.

As if it's automatic, my head tilts back and my mouth opens to deepen our kiss. His hands cradle my face, thumbs brushing along my cheek bones as his hands push into my hair. My hands grip the open ends of his flannel shirt, fisting the material as I lift up on my toes to keep this kiss going.

I have been the jealous one watching another girl get kissed by Logan Ford. This time, those jealous stares are fixed on me . . . and I like it.

10 /
logan

I BLAME THE KISS. Which was one-hundred-percent on me. So, I guess I blame myself. Rachel wanted to play beer pong for real, and I let her. She said please, and her bottom lip jutted out, which made me want to bite it. So I did. And we kissed more. And I may have let my hands flirt with the sides of her breasts a little. And that might have played into my weakness too. Along with the massive boner I sported for half the night.

Fine, it was my fault. I let her get shit-faced drunk.

The wallflower might have been a ringer when she was still hovering somewhere around sober, but after her fourth chugged beer thanks to one of our linebackers, she was toast. By her last game, she couldn't even hit the table with the ball.

She threw up in my truck.

Breakfast was definitely not going to happen. In fact, when I walked her to her dorm room and helped her into bed with the help of her roommate, I believe her last words were, "No more eggs." I'm not sure what that could have meant other than breakfast was off the table. I'm also pretty sure her roommate grabbed my ass on my way out.

"Ford! Office! Now!" I stop running the towel over my head and toss it into the laundry bin on my way to Coach's office. I exchange a quick glance with Jax, who makes the same face he always does when I get summoned to the office with those words. Like his lips are sealed and he's going to pretend he doesn't know me.

Shit. I should have stayed in the shower longer.

I shuffle my way into his office and plop down in one of the chairs opposite his desk. He holds up a finger and finishes typing something on his laptop, pecking his way through whatever it is two fingers at a time.

"There," he says, punching the final key with his index finger then turning his laptop around so I can see the screen.

"You wanna tell me what that is, Logan?"

I run my palm over my face, my skin still hot from the steamy shower. I know it can't be chemistry I'm failing, but I seriously thought I had my other shit handled. I lean in and scan my grade report—B, B, C, A.

"It's nothing!" I protest, snapping my gaze to Coach. He stays in character for about two more seconds before that broomstick mustache of his flies up with laughter and he leans back in his rolling chair.

"Exactly!" He slaps his desk, but not in the scary way I'm used to. I look at him sideways, skeptical and hesitant, but I go ahead and smile.

"Is this you . . . being proud?"

"Damn right it is," he says, slapping his computer screen shut then folding his hands over his protruding belly.

"What's going on in here?" Cam's been anxiously awaiting grade reports, ready to step in if I fuck up. He's mentioned it a few times, and I've held off popping him in the jaw.

"Just me killing my GPA," I say, glaring at him over my shoulder.

"Huh. What a surprise," Cam says, slinging his towel over his shoulder. He walks around with his shirt off a lot longer than he needs to. The man's a fucking peacock. So proud. Such an asshole.

I stand up, mostly so I can look him in the eyes while he's dissing me. Cam's not only from a major family, he's also pretty smart. He's an accounting major, a choice he made so he can *count all his money someday*, he said during media day. Gross.

"Whatever magic that tutor has is working," Coach says, affirming my request for Rachel at the start of the semester.

I knew she'd make a difference. Instinct told me. But I also wonder if there was a part of me that wanted a reason to talk to her. We've never had the occasion. She doesn't show up to parties—which now that I see how she handles them, I don't blame her. But it's not like I was in any of her classes, and I get the sense she wasn't all that keen on me before, which is probably why she helped other students in my class and stayed far away from me.

Things are different now, though. Hell, maybe I'm different. Logan in his post-Amy era.

"Rachel's a genius," I say as I leave Coach's office, Cam still lingering by the door.

"What does she see in you, then?" Cam lobs at me. I flutter my eyes at him and purse my lips. If I were twelve, I'd twist his nipple right now so hard it bled. I'm twenty-two and still considering it.

"Guess she has a thing for starting running backs," I

respond, slapping his bare shoulder with an open palm that leaves my handprint behind.

Coach doesn't say a word.

I'm not sure Rachel made it to her labs today. Knowing her as I'm starting to, I'm guessing she would drag herself in with one eye open and a vomit bag at her hip if she had to. I have a feeling she's still not operating at one-hundred percent, though, so I grab my bag from my cubby and slap hands with Jax and Dante on my way out.

"Got a hot date with the tutor?" Jax teases.

"Something like that," I say through a stupid boyish grin.

Fuck. I'm stuck on her.

Once I get to my truck, I shoot her a text to see how she's feeling. Her response is quick.

SHORTCAKE: *Did I really lose at beer pong?*

I laugh out loud, nodding for nobody to see.

ME: *Yes. You lost big time.*

She responds with the facepalm emoji so I leave it at that and head to the grocery store where I get a gallon of Ben & Jerry's Tonight Dough ice cream and the only bouquet that looks like it wasn't spray painted to appear alive.

"Lucky girl," the cashier says, giving me a wink.

"Oh, the flowers are for me," I joke. The woman chuckles but shakes her head.

"Honey, you can keep those. All we want is the damn ice cream."

I nod and grin.

"Well, all right then. Noted," I say, wishing her a good night then hopping back into my truck to zip straight to Rachel's dorm.

I didn't get a great look around the place the first couple times, and it was dark last night. But with the sun still up this afternoon, I'm able to scope out what these honors facilities are all about. The buildings aren't anything special, but when I walk by the cafeteria, I understand completely why Rachel never veers far from her quarters.

"Damn, they get real food," I mutter to myself. I scan the tables as I pass by the windows, and I'm pretty sure I see fresh veggies and whole chickens on plates. I'm pissed.

I charm the same resident assistant I met the first time I snuck into Rachel's dorm. I pull out one of the flowers and hand it to her, and she doesn't seem to mind that it's slightly wilted. "I'll put it in water," she says, waving me toward the stairs.

I take them two at a time until I get to Rachel's floor. When I make it to her door, it's cracked open, so I rap on it lightly.

"Hello?" I push it open tentatively and inch my way into the room, catching a glimpse of her roommate, Claire, sitting on her bed with massive headphones over her ears. I'm too far in not to scare her, so I wave a hand. The second she sees me she screams and throws her headphones at me. I clutch them against my chest, along with the flowers and ice cream.

"Shit. Sorry," I say, handing them back to her. She grabs them with a scowl.

"You seem to say that a lot when you randomly show up here," Rachel's voice answers from behind.

I spin around to find her clutching a laundry basket filled with clothes.

"I do, don't I. Probably because I'm a massive fuckup who needs to apologize a lot." I lean toward self-effacing with her. I'm not quite sure the reason, but it always seems to disarm her.

"You're not *that* much of a fuckup," she says, pushing past me and dropping her basket on the floor at the end of her bed.

"Is that because you mean it? Or because you saw the ice cream?" I hold out my gifts and her eyes bounce between the bouquet and the Ben & Jerry's.

"Who says it wasn't the flowers that got me all . . ." She flattens her hands over her heart and makes a swoony face.

I hold up the bouquet and four petals drift to the floor. We both follow their path and stare at them on her blue carpet. The bright pink isn't even a color made in nature. Finally, we both laugh.

"Yeah, those are weeds. And I think they might be dead," she says, taking the bundle from me anyhow and marching it over to a large cup sitting on her desk. "It's not water. It's an energy drink. From yesterday morning. So, science experiment?"

"I'm in!" her roommate pipes in, slipping off her bed and joining Rachel by the desk, both of them looking into the cup with an odd intensity.

"Oh, you weren't kidding about the science thing?" I move toward Rachel's bed, perhaps presumptively, but she lets me take a seat without questioning it.

"We don't joke about science," Claire fires back.

"That's fair," I say, now myself a little curious about the outcome of this experiment.

Rachel leaves the flowers on her desk, her lamp turned down so it's lighting stems. I hold out the ice cream and she grabs it quickly, pulling off the lid and rummaging through her desk drawer for a spoon.

"Not sharing?" I pout.

"Wait your turn," she scolds, taking a seat right next to me, our legs touching.

She's wearing dark gray sweats that match my lighter ones minus the fact hers are skin-tight and bunched at her calves. Her shirt says Southern Iowa State Football, and I keep glancing at it as she continues to take slow, languid bites of the ice cream.

"My brother," she says, twisting toward me more and holding the shirt out as if I couldn't read it before. "He graduated our freshman year. Tight end. He was good."

She builds another scoop and holds it in her mouth, letting it melt away slowly as she smiles around the spoon.

"Ah, the football thing. That's why," I say, pointing a finger.

She pulls the spoon from her lips with a sucking sound, and yeah . . . my dick twitches.

"Mystery. Solved."

Her lips are full, painted with a hint of chocolate ice cream, and my mind goes right to the visual of her taking my dick down her throat and grinning up at me like a good girl. I shift, scooting back against the wall to mask the massive hard-on growing in my pants.

"So, what are we doing, kids?" Claire asks, hopping on her bed and folding her legs up.

"Oh, uh . . . I don't know." I was kind of hoping Claire would give us some privacy, but I guess that's a fairly selfish assumption on my part. It's likely dark out by now, and this is a building filled with people who take school nights pretty seriously.

"You wanna watch *The Office* with us?" Rachel digs her spoon into the ice cream and holds it out for me. An offering.

"Would you cringe if I told you I've never seen it?" I take the spoon in the nick of time because apparently, yes, they would cringe. They are cringing. And gesticulating. Meanwhile, that's damn good ice cream.

I reach over to take another scoop but Rachel pulls the carton back and points a finger at me.

"I tried the party thing, and I think we can both agree I went all in." Rachel's chin lowers and she hits me with a hard stare, her eyes still tired-looking from what I'm sure was a long night and a rough morning.

"Yes, you went full-tilt on the party thing," I admit.

"I second that," Claire adds.

"*The Office* is a work of genius. Not everyone gets it. And those who don't are sorely missing out."

"Here, here!" Claire adds in.

I cough out a laugh at how seriously they're taking this.

"I understand," I say, reaching once again with the spoon. Rachel pushes it away.

"Do you?" She leans in, and I swear if we were alone right now, I would toss the ice cream on the floor and kiss her.

I meet her stare.

"I do," I say.

Her lips part with a tiny breath, and it feels as if long seconds pass with the two of us locked in this protected bubble. Even Claire has disappeared.

"You may have the ice cream," Rachel relents, shifting the tub between us and unveiling a second spoon. I narrow my eyes on it and tap the metal edge.

"You dog!" I chastise, earning me a smug grin.

"Are you guys going to do this all night? Because it's totally going to kill the satire," Claire groans.

I dig out a massive scoop and put the spoonful in my mouth, but my eyes stay glued on Rachel's. Neither of us seem to have an answer for Claire. But not because we don't know what she means. We do. And yes, we are going to do this all night.

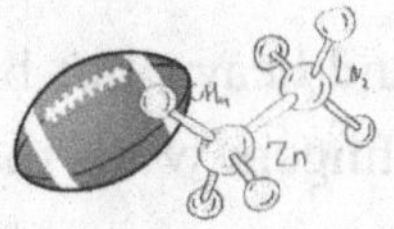

IT TOOK EXACTLY six minutes for this to become my favorite show. By the middle of episode two, I was hooked.

"You like Pam, don't you," Rachel says, pushing a finger against my bicep.

"I do. I really do," I say, almost in a trance from the seven episodes we binged and the gallon of ice cream we consumed. I ate most of it. I'm going to drag ass at practice in the morning.

"When did we lose her?" I roll my head to the side and glance to the pile of pillows and blankets burying her roommate. She's snoring lightly, the only proof that she's really sleeping and alive.

"I think episode four," Rachel says.

She recrosses her ankles, something she's done every ten minutes or so for the entirety of the night. I've memorized the pattern on her fuzzy socks, and have a permanent soft spot on my thigh where our legs have kissed for most of the night. We've remained very disciplined. At least, I have. I sense in her twitchiness, though, that Rachel is also very much feeling the heat between us.

My gaze travels up the length of her body until I'm looking her in the eyes. We're close enough that I can see the faint line of her contacts in her eyes. Her hair is twisted into a wild pile on top of her head, and her eyelids look heavy. She must be exhausted. Midnight came and went a while ago.

"I should go," I say, my eyes dipping to her mouth then back up.

"Stay," she croaks.

I breathe in, slow and heavy, but before I can convince us both I should go, her fingers work their way between mine. There's no Dalton around to see this. Our only witness is well into the stages of dreamland, so there's no way for this to become a story that's told and retold with the hope that an ex will be jealous. This moment is just for us. No Amy. No Dalton. Us.

"Okay," I say, sliding down so I'm lying flat in her bed.

She nuzzles up against me and I brush a few wild hairs from her face as she props her chin on my chest to look me in the eyes. I run my thumb over her bottom lip, so plump and soft. There's hesitation in her eyes, and maybe I'm reading into her measured breathing, but it feels as if she's holding something in.

"What's going on in here?" I tap gently at her temple and she leans into my touch, so I cup her face.

She bites at her lip.

"I really didn't want to tutor you," she says.

I laugh, but her weight on my chest holds it in.

"I know," I admit.

The quiet comes back, and I take the opportunity to truly study what makes her face so unique. The dusting of freckles that crest into a celestial map on her tiny nose. The golden touches on her eyelashes. Her sapphire eyes.

"I'm glad I did," she says, bringing me to her mouth.

I'm locked in now. Unable to move anywhere else until I taste her lips. Maybe it's the fact she's being vulnerable. Or perhaps I'm tired and her leg is pressing into my cock. Probably a little of everything. Whatever the cause, I need her mouth.

"Come here," I say, cradling her head and coaxing her mouth to mine. I take her fat bottom lip into mine and suck lightly, grazing my teeth against her skin then soothing it with a pass of my tongue. Her body shifts, her hands snaking up my chest and shoulders, fingers diving into my hair. She kisses back as her knees draw in, positioning her right above my dick. She rocks against me twice and I let my hands move of their own volition, trailing down her sides and grabbing at her hips, holding her down on me.

She pulls back, her lips redder than before, breath a little ragged as she glances to her right where her roommate is still sawing imaginary logs. Her cheeks flush, and I know she's both hungry and shy.

"How about we kiss a little while, until I'm ready to kiss you good night," I say, tucking more of her hair behind her ear.

She leans into my palm, attempting to hide her face, but I don't let her. What good are all those sit ups if I can't hold myself up enough to kiss her nerves away? The second our lips meet again, she melts into me, and I step right up to the line for the next thirty minutes, until I kiss her good night.

11 /
rachel

WHAT AM I DOING?

I did not want Logan to leave last night. I also did not want to stop where things were very clearly going. But Claire was there. And while I'm not ready to take on a bestie, I do like her. I might even call her a good friend, though that label still gives me pause. Friends can turn. So can guys.

But Logan is nothing like Dalton. He's silly and considerate and *my God, his hands!* I'm not naïve enough to believe I'm the only girl he's seduced with his good looks and puppy-dog charm, yet when I'm with him, he has this way. Logan Ford is nothing I expected. And he's making me feel things I didn't know existed. He makes me feel special—singled out in a good way rather than the overwhelmed way attention usually makes me feel.

Is what we're doing real, though? Making Dalton jealous was his idea. Honestly, that thought never entered my mind, and while I suppose it's a nice byproduct, I really don't care how Dalton feels about seeing Logan and me together. What I care about is figuring out why Logan and I are together and if it's really a thing, or something to pass his time.

It sure feels like more to me.

So much more that I changed six times between my lab and coming to the library. And I still got here an hour early. I've second-guessed my final outfit selection the entire time I've sat at this table, too. I never wear skirts, but the way Logan reacted to my dress—the way his hands felt under it— I wanted the possibility to exist. Now I'm all too aware of how short this plaid skirt is and how tight the white turtleneck is I chose to pair it with. To top it off, fall is making an ugly appearance in Iowa, and my legs are basically icicles, from the hem of my skirt to the ankles of my ballet flats.

Because fate likes to fuck with science, now I'm forced to have yet one more conversation with the last man I want to see. If I knew Dalton was in the library, I would have texted Logan and changed our meeting place. When we set up our schedule, I purposely planned around the days and times I knew Dalton was usually here. Seems he's changed his habits, though, because this marks twice that he's strayed from routine—three times if I count the whole cheating bit.

I brace myself, tucking my hands under my thighs and leaning into the table as Dalton closes in.

"Hi." His hair does that stupid thing where the longer front flops over and flirts with the rims of his glasses. I used to find that so adorable. Now, I want to cut that hair.

"Hi." I force a pleasant smile on my face. I have a feeling it looks more like I'm about to be sick.

Dalton grabs the back of the chair across from me and I dig my nails into the back of my legs. Dear lord, please don't let him pull that seat out and make himself comfortable. My chest releases when he simply fidgets with the wooden finials.

"How have you been?" He tilts his head as his features

melt into a sympathetic expression. What the hell? Is he actually feeling sorry for me?

I clear my throat and sit up straight.

"Great." I mock his head tilt with one that matches, but my expression is far from considerate. No, I'm well aware of my features right now—tight-lipped smile, lifted brows, gnashing molars. I'm wearing the annoyed mask.

"That's . . . good. That's good," he repeats himself. His brow pinches, and I think he's surprised I'm not more torn up.

I'm surprised I'm not more torn up.

I breathe out a short laugh at my thought, and Dalton's eyes narrow a tad.

"*Hmm?*" he questions.

I shake my head.

"Oh, nothing. Literally—" I draw a line in the air with my index finger. "Nothing."

"O—kay?" He's playing naive but he's smart. I bet he gets it on some level. And I hope it burns that I'm so over him.

"How's Stella?" I probably should have stopped while I was ahead, because now I'm venturing into spiteful territory. Truly, though? I have been curious. Not about how she's doing, but about how *they're* doing.

"She's well," he says with a tight-lipped smile and slight nod.

"Great." Oooh, that came out passive aggressive. I'm not portraying the *I-got-my-shit-together* persona I was a second or two ago.

"I mean it, Dalton," I add, relaxing my shoulders and flattening my palms on the tabletop. I slide a few inches in his direction as a gesture of caring. "I'm glad. And I hope you're doing well too."

My mouth waters with that statement, and I swallow slowly in an attempt to hide it. I don't think he notices because his body seems to relax as well. There I go, making it easy for him.

"Sorry I'm late." Logan's voice drifts from behind me. His bag plunks down on the table a second before I feel his arm swoop around my neck and his lips land on my head. My heart picks up immediately.

I glance up and Logan's hand cups my chin, tilting my face just enough for him to plant an upside down kiss on my lips. Dalton clears his throat, and while the jealousy bit wasn't really ever my plan, the grin on my face is worth it.

"I'll let you get to it. Rachel?"

I drop my chin to find Dalton's pinched face colored with unmistakable jealousy. *Yeah, you don't get to keep me in a cage, buddy.*

"Yeah, nice to see you. Take care," I say, lifting a palm in goodbye.

Dalton does the same before cinching his backpack straps tighter on his shoulders and pivoting to leave the library.

Logan gives the back of my neck a gentle squeeze then pulls the chair next to me closer and takes a seat.

"You all right?" His hand finds its way back to my neck, and the soft kneading is delightful. My eyes blink slowly, much the way they do when I'm drunk.

"I'm honestly amazing," I say, taking him in.

I reach my hand over to his thigh, his muscles filling out his black Tiff U joggers. He's dressed in his practice gear, a black long-sleeved compression shirt under a dark blue and gold football shirt. He looks incredible in black and blue, the dark colors making his auburn hair and green eyes stand out.

His hair is always so neat, combed into waves that I'm dying to mess up.

"You're looking at me like you want to jump my bones," he says.

I spit out a laugh and my face heats up. I reach for his bag and pull his folders out while nervous tittering quakes my lips.

"No. That's not the case," I correct. *I lie.*

"Good, because, I mean . . . we're in a library." His mouth is suddenly close to my ear. My shoulder hikes up as shivers run down my spine. *Sweet Jesus.*

"Who even says that? Jumping bones," I laugh out. *"Pfft."*

His hand cups my bare knee and I freeze.

"You sure you weren't thinking about it? Just a little?"

He nips my earlobe and my shoulder hikes up again. My mouth falls open, but before words find their way to my tongue, his fingertips begin to walk up my inner thigh. I draw in a quick breath and hold it, opening my legs as he travels to the hem of my skirt, his fingers flirting with the fabric.

"Good girl," he says, his nose grazing my ear.

My fingernails scrape against the table as I ball my hands into fists. Logan reaches forward with his other hand and flips open his folder, pulling out a few random papers and spreading them out as if either of us are reading them at all. My eyes dart to the librarian, our favorite one, as in *the one who hates us.* Her back is to us as she sorts through a cart of reference books. Other than her and a few people in the study rooms, we're alone.

Alone, but not alone. And that is . . .

"Spread."

We're not looking at each other, our gazes lost in the

scene Logan created on the table. I do as he asks, sinking down a little more in my chair and parting my knees. My mind is racing to calculate the dimensions of this table. Is it long enough to shield me from anyone walking in? Can the librarian see me if she turns around? What would people at my sides see? Behind us?

Logan's hand bunches up my skirt and his finger slides down the center of my panties, and I quit caring about numbers and voyeurs.

"Someone is very wet," he says.

I gasp.

"*Shh*," he says, his mouth back to my ear.

"You just keep your eyes on my study guide. Right here." His left hand pats the papers, which aren't study guides at all. I stare at my own handwriting. I stare so hard that my eyes haze and the words blend into fuzzy pictures.

Logan's finger slides down my center again, and my legs part even more.

"There you go," he says, his voice a low hum, not quite a whisper but low enough it's just for me.

I exhale a ragged breath. Nobody has ever touched me like this. Everything before this moment was so clinical. Textbook. We are way off script. And I like it.

His finger circles my swollen middle and I squirm in my seat, wanting more relief. He teases me this way for almost a minute before his fingers slip under the cotton strip covering my pussy, pulling it aside as his knuckles graze against my tender, wet skin.

"Ah," I eke out at the feel of him against me.

He flicks my clit, and I slide down lower in my seat. My legs are spread under the table and my skirt is bunched up around my hips, but my eyes are still glued to the pages on the table.

"Next time, we go to the stacks so I can drop down there and taste you," he says, his voice a little louder this time. My body rushes with adrenaline and my gaze flashes to the librarian. She's still sorting texts, completely unaware.

"She can't hear me," he says. "But she might hear you."

His finger sinks in and his thumb presses against my clit, circling it slowly. I bite my lip, which isn't going to be enough, so I bring my fist to my mouth and bite that as he pushes his finger in and out.

Logan's free hand pulls my fist away, then he nudges my chin so I'm facing him. I'm in a trance, my eyes unable to blink, my lips parted just enough to breathe. My inhales and exhales are controlled by him, matching him stroke for stroke as he pushes two fingers in and works my center.

"You want to come in the library, Shortcake?"

I nod and breathe out, "Uh huh."

His eyes dip to my breasts, and I suddenly regret wearing a turtleneck. Logan glances to his left then back to me, a devious smirk pulling up as his eyes dim. His left hand jerks my sweater up enough for his hand to slip underneath, leaving me still covered but clearly being groped.

"Logan—" I utter.

"*Shh,*" he coaxes, glancing again at the librarian then scanning the library space before sliding his hand over my breast and tugging the lace cup of my bra to the side. I don't care if it's torn at this point.

He takes my nipple between his thumb and index finger and rolls the hard peak with sweet pressure. His other fingers push in deep and I drop lower against them, wanting more. I writhe, unable to keep myself from bucking my hips under the table as he tugs my hard nipple, pinching then flicking while he palms my pussy and sinks his fingers in and out.

My mouth falls open as my climax builds and I flash a glance to the reference desk when I hear the librarian sneeze. My wide eyes are pained with pleasure and panic, and it's the hottest fucking thing I've ever felt. Just as I'm about to fall over the edge, Logan's mouth covers mine, and he sucks in my bottom lip, sliding his tongue against my skin as he rubs his thumb around my soaking wet pussy, drawing out the longest orgasm of my life.

I want to pant, but his mouth covers me. My moan is muffled as wave after wave drives my hips toward his pressure until it finally eases, and he squeezes out every last drop before pulling his hand away then sucking on his two fingers.

"Library tryst," he says with a smug grin.

I guffaw, my body limp. I don't even have the strength to straighten my skirt.

"What was that you said about the stacks?" I murmur.

He chuckles, then says, "You'll see."

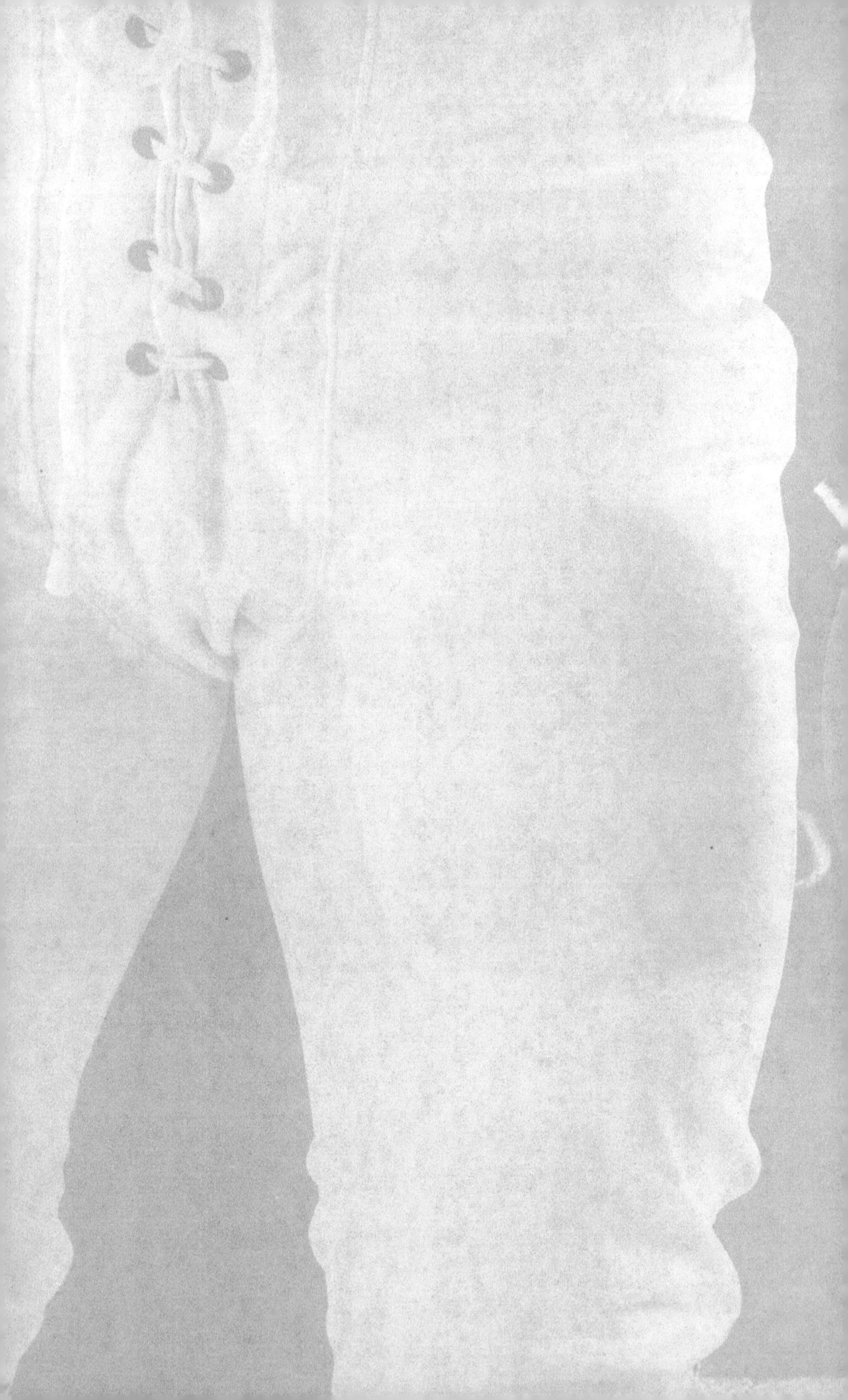

"COME TO MY GAME."

I've never asked a girl to show up to my game in my life. They were always just there. And maybe that's what I've been doing wrong. I've been following the lines drawn for me, playing the parts people expect.

Dumb jock.

Bubble player.

Life of the party.

A good time but not a serious boyfriend.

Unambitious. That's the word Amy used when she said it wasn't working out. I took way more offense to that than her not wanting to be with me anymore. I have aspirations. I'm not sure why people don't see them.

"I don't know. It's not like I have anyone to sit with. And aren't you going to lose anyway?" Rachel wrinkles her nose, and I stumble back a step as I slip my sock on. She came to the house early so we could review for my test Monday before I have to leave for pregame.

I clutch at my chest and drop my jaw.

"You have that little faith in me?" I know she's kidding

about the losing part. She might not be about coming to my game, though.

"Eh?" She squints. "I've never seen you play, so I don't want to believe the hype."

I toss my sock to the side and lunge at her, pinning her under me as I poke at her ticklish sides. Her giggle echoes out my bedroom door and Jax makes sure to groan and yell, "Get a room!"

"We're *in* my room!" I shout over my shoulder, still needling her.

"Fine. *Fine!*" She laughs out the words so I let up, dropping to my elbows and resting my forehead on hers. I love the way her eyelashes flutter when she looks up from this angle.

"Is that a yes? You'll come?"

My chest is tight with hope. It's weird.

She sucks in her lips but a faint smile curves them as she nods. I drop down and kiss her, and she places her hands on my cheeks.

We've been doing this a lot. Kissing. I can't seem to quit, and it doesn't matter if we're alone or in the middle of campus. Everyone on the team assumes we're dating. I guess we are dating. Aren't we?

She pushes up on my chest and I climb off the bed, back to my abandoned sock.

"You're going to be late," she warns.

I check my watch, and I've got time. I'm cutting it close, for sure. And I might have to sprint into the team room. But I'll make it.

I finish slipping on my compression sleeves then stuff my aftergame clothes into my gym bag using the roll method so things don't get wrinkled. Coach likes us to look like "grown-ass men" when we leave the locker room. I'll probably be spending some time in the media room, too. Hopefully talking about our amazing start to the season.

My bag zipped, I sling it over my shoulder and turn to take Rachel's hand. She's biting her thumbnail, her gaze lost somewhere out my door. I bend forward to scope out her view, but nobody is out there. I look back to her and her eyes flit to mine.

Shit. She meant that part about not having anyone to sit with.

"Hang on," I say, setting my bag on my bed and darting down the hall to Jax's room.

"I was just kidding, man. Relax. I like seeing you happy," he says the moment he sees my face.

"No, that's not it. I mean, thanks, though." I pause for a second and embrace his words. Happy. Damn, I *am* happy. "It's the game. Is Trisha going? Or Meg?"

Both girls are sort of on- and off-again girlfriends for Jax. At one point, I think he was dating both, and I think they were okay with it. Hey, good for them. Whatever makes people happy.

"Meg will be there. You want her to save Rachel a seat?" he offers, picking up his phone and already firing off a text.

"Oh, man. Yes, please. That would be great!" I slap his hand and head back into my room. Right as I step in, Jax shouts, "Section one-eleven, row thirteen!"

"Got it!" I holler over my shoulder.

"What's that?" Rachel asks. I rush to my backpack and rip a page from one of my notebooks, jotting down the seat location before I forget. I hand it to her.

"Meg's saving you a seat."

Her eyes flash to mine and her lips part slightly with what looks like grateful surprise. At least, I hope it is. She glances back at the paper, her fingers fidgeting with the edges.

"Thank you," she croaks.

"Of course," I say, wrapping my arms around her neck and pulling her head into my stomach. I lean down and kiss the top as she snakes her hands around my waist. It feels nice holding her this way. She feels precious.

I glance at my watch and see I've definitely pushed my limits.

"I've gotta go. But I'll see you after. And during! Row thirteen!" I tap on the side of my head as I snag my bag and rush down the hall to Jax's room, where he's still dragging ass. I pound on his door and he flips around, startled again.

"Dude!" he scolds at first, but I point at my watch and he kicks it into gear.

We're out of the house seconds later and speeding to the stadium in my truck. Dante has been there for an hour already. Quarterbacks have to get their heads on right. At least, that's what he says.

Despite leaving late, Jax and I manage to squeeze into the team room before Coach starts to ask questions. We're dressed, taped, and ready to go by the time he tells us to get our asses on the field.

I love pre-game. The hype fills my chest, always has. Being a senior has its perks, too, as does being a team captain. Jax, Dante, and I got to build this year's pre-game playlist, as long as it was language appropriate, according to the athletic director. It might be borderline, but our tunes are fucking epic.

Drill after drill, my muscles get more pumped. Guys bump chests and we nail down plays, our timing on for everything. I feel faster today, and I definitely feel ready to take a hit. That's the most important part. And the reason my mom hates tuning in, and showing up for parents' weekends. My dad comes to half the home games, but mom can't handle watching me get hung up by an O-line or tackled out in the open.

As the pre-game clock winds down and we gather to head back into the locker room, I scan the crowd in search of section one-eleven. It's the student section closest to the end zone, where I plan on spending a lot of time today. The stadium is barely a quarter full right now, but that's because people still have thirty minutes before kick-off and this is the Midwest. They're all getting beer. I search the rows closest to the field, counting up to thirteen, and then I spot her. Dark blue beanie, braids, and I swear she painted my number on her cheek.

I give a subtle wave and she raises her hand in response.

"Hi, Rachel!" Jax shouts, pushing up over my shoulder.

"You're an asshole," I huff, glaring at him before looking back to Rachel, who is now shading her face with her palm. A few students sitting nearby are straining their necks to look at her.

She lifts her palm and I mouth, "I'm sorry," but I don't think she can tell what I'm saying from this far. I throw an elbow behind me and catch Jax in the ribs, right where the pads end. *Good.*

We break our huddle and jog into the locker room, everyone taking a knee and setting our helmets on the floor. Coach calls up our defense coach, Allen, and he leads us all in prayer. Even our Amens are said with a different tone this season. We sound like winners.

For the most part, I'm in my head for the next ten minutes. Coach runs through scenarios I have imprinted in my mind. I've never been more ready for a game in my life, and I swear it's because Rachel has somehow changed my brain. I study differently. Information sticks. My eyes are fixed on the board, and I'm taking in the motions, but internally I'm playing my own mixtape.

You're going to be faster than them.

Nobody can catch you.

Ball first. Protect the ball.

Ball. Ball. Ball.

My head snaps up when Coach starts to clap, and we all get to our feet and pool into the center of the room. Fists raised, we wait for our center, Artemis, to fire us up for the field.

"Do I have your attention?" he shouts.

"Yes, sir!"

"Do I have your attention?"

"Yes, sir!"

"Let's get it, then. Three, two, one . . ."

We all bellow, "Knights!"

The rush back out to the field through the tunnel is special. Only a handful of these left for me here, maybe ever. Unless I change my narrative. No more bubble. I'm putting people on notice. Right now.

We break through a cloud of smoke. Flanked by stacked cheerleaders on either side, we sprint onto the field, helmets raised as we chase the two guys running ahead with the T and U flags. We form a half circle and line up for one final stretch.

This part? It isn't for us. This is for the fans. Somehow we still sell out. Hockey does but that's because they're nationally ranked. Our fans are just loyal. Or maybe it's the beer.

Whatever it is, they deserve this show. And they deserve the win as much as we do.

"Hey," Jax says over his shoulder as he holds an arm across his chest.

I nod.

"Kill it today."

I chew at my mouthpiece and nod again, a little vigor in my confidence. I don't let go of it through the national anthem, and I let it power me through the coin flip, which we win for the first time in maybe fourteen flips. A good sign.

We opt to kick first, saving that second half momentum in case we need it. But it means I have to sit on my boiling energy while our defense goes out and gets it done.

Every time I look over my shoulder, I find her. The stands are definitely full now, students packed shoulder-to-shoulder. Frat boys have their shirts off with blue and gold letters painted on their chests. It's a sea of twenty-something-year-olds' bodies. Yet through it all, I find her. My eyes go right to her. Always.

It's actually her lighting up I see first before I realize our defense just forced a turnover. Pushing my helmet down as I jerk around, I charge onto the field, slapping defenders' backs for a job well done before huddling up, my legs buzzing with the need to run.

"Seven draw thirty-four," Dante barks.

That means Jax is going out for a fake pass and I get the ball. I'm so fired up I growl my response.

"Hell, yeah. Let's go!" I rush to the line and follow the count, breaking right on the edge and juking the defense, making them think I'm there to block. I pivot and rush behind Dante for the quick handoff and my legs take over.

Five yards.

Ten.

Fifteen.

I get brought down by the last guy on St. Mary's team who could catch me, and I roll the ball off my fingertips to the ref when I get up. I pound my chest and jump into Jax, shoulder to shoulder.

It's a hurry-up play next, catching St. Mary's off-guard. We jump to the line and Dante gets the ball out before they know we're coming, this time a short dump pass to Jax.

Thirty seconds have gone by and we're already in the red zone. My gaze finds her, above the helmets in the huddle. The blue hat and strawberry hair. Dante looks over to Coach for the call, pulling us in tight and repeating our first play. Putting it on my shoulders. I can carry it.

We break and I make my way to the line, my teeth biting into my mouth guard with so much force I swear I'm going to bust through the plastic. My focus zeroes in on the hard count and I fake like I'm going to rush the line then reverse, sweeping behind Dante, the ball heavy in my gut. I cradle it. This time, St. Mary's is expecting me, so I dart through bodies and hurdle thanks to a block. I'm mid-air, and if I break this I'm free. I'm in. I can see it.

The pull on my leg is swift. I'm not sure what part of my body hits the ground first, but my upper leg goes one way while the calf goes the other, and the pain is fucking excruciating. I roll on the ground and instantly push my helmet off, teeth gritting as I growl so I don't cry.

"Don't move, man. Don't move!" Jax is over me first, our trainer, Terry, not far behind. The hush in the stadium feels surreal, and I'm not sure whether people are freaked out or if I'm in shock. Perhaps both.

"Logan, I need you to tell me what you feel here," Terry directs, making a slight adjustment to my leg.

"Everything hurts," I shout, but quickly breathe out and follow up with, "Okay, okay."

I let him maneuver my leg, doing my best to pay attention to the nuances of pain. Some positions and pressure points hurt like the normal kind of game-play pain. But there's one spot, in the inside of my knee—that spot's trouble.

"Yeah!" I sit up when he twists it. He relaxes his hold and exhales through his nose. Terry has zero poker face.

"It's probably a sprain. Let's hope for a sprain, all right? But we gotta look. You gotta come out." His eyes hit mine and I take it in stride for exactly half a second.

"Fuck!" There's zero chance half the stadium didn't hear that.

"No cart," I demand, glancing to my side where I can see them getting it ready. "Fucking don't let them bring that thing on the field, Terry. I swear to God, I'll get up and sprint out of here and tear the shit out of my knee if they bring that cart on the field."

Terry shakes his head but waves the cart off.

"Good to see you're thinking with a clear head," he grumbles.

"Fuck off." I'm being a dick. I'll apologize later. Or now.

"Sorry," I mutter.

His hand lands heavy on my back.

"I know, Logan. It's all right. Keep thinking sprain."

Sprain. Sprain. Sprain.

WE ENDED up winning twenty-one to three. Jax made it to the end zone twice, but goddamn Cam Ledger scored on the last drive. And all I could do was watch from the sideline, balanced on these fucking crutches with ice and this goddamn bionic brace fastened around my entire leg.

"Yeah, Mom. It's just a sprain. I promise. And yes, they took real scans. It's a real doctor. I will heal. Two weeks."

I fall back in my bed, head heavy in my pillow as I let my forearm flop over my eyes. I called Dad to fill him in because I know he was watching. My conversation with him lasted fourteen seconds. And then he handed the phone to Mom. That was thirty-eight minutes ago. I pull my phone from my ear to check the screen. Scratch that. Thirty-nine.

"Hey, Mom. They gave me some pretty strong anti-inflammatories, and it's making me a little sleepy, so I'm—"

"Were they muscle relaxers? Those can be addictive, you know. Your Uncle Johnny had issues with pain pills." She whispers that last part as if someone is tapping our phone line and listening for those key words.

"They're not. I'm just tired. I promise. I'll call you tomorrow." I roll my head to the side and find Rachel leaning against my door jamb, a paper bag in one hand and a bottle of orange juice in the other. She's wearing her gray sweatpants and her brother's football shirt, but my number—34— is still smudged on her cheek. I smile at her, my knee suddenly not so bad.

"I love you, too," I say to my Mom. Rachel's eyes flicker.

I end the call and toss my phone to the foot of my bed, skootching myself as far to the left as I can to make room for Rachel next to me. She hands me the orange juice and sets the bag on the bed between us.

"You didn't have to come," I say, really glad she did.

"I'm missing *The Office* for you, too," she teases.

I laugh out then wince, pretending it hurts. She bends toward me but stops herself, placing her hand on my chest.

"You ass. Your knee is hurt!"

I smirk then pull her into me, moving the mystery bag to my other side. I kiss her without even thinking, her comfort so natural. Her presence natural.

"I heard that last part. It's a sprain?" She grimaces, likely because she knows even a sprain is going to have me out longer than I want. I told my parents two weeks, but that's probably optimistic.

"Yeah. At least the next two games are really shitty teams." Of course, that means easy numbers. TDs Cam will get instead of me.

"Yeah, that's when they put the bench players in anyhow," she says, winking so I know she knows. They don't do that in college. She's trying to make me feel better.

"What's in the bag?" I bring it back to my chest and Rachel sits up, folding her legs in but staying close, her thigh tucked against my side.

"Only the best donuts in the state of Iowa," she says, unrolling the bag and pulling out a golden ring glazed with bright pink frosting and party sprinkles.

"Go Nuts Donuts?" I lift a brow, hopeful.

"Like I said, only the best." She holds the donut out for me and I sit up on my elbows, letting her feed me a bite.

"Oh, my God, that's good. I needed that." My gaze hits hers as I chew. She reaches forward and touches her fingertip to the corner of my mouth, picking away a sprinkle that she promptly sucks off her finger.

"I'm jealous of that sprinkle," I say, which makes her eyes flare again.

"You are the patient tonight. No dirty talk."

The blush on her cheeks only increases my urge, but she's right. I actually feel pretty awful. And I don't want my bad mood to come anywhere near the things I want to do to her. With her. For her. On her.

"Eat your donut. And give me your laptop. I'll put on *The Office*." She hands me a napkin and I follow her orders, but while she's setting up my laptop at the foot of the bed, I do come back to the sprinkles for just a moment.

Her. Sprinkles. Everywhere. And my tongue.

"Your mom is calling back," she says, handing me my phone and pouring cold water over my erotic imagery of me and Rachel. And Sprinkles.

rachel

I KNEW it the second he hit the ground. My brother has been through it all when it comes to football injuries. Two concussions, that we know of. One broken rib. A tooth situation that required my mom to hunt down a carton of milk to drop his canine into until we could get to the emergency dentist. And then my brother's knee. His was supposed to be a sprain, too. It was his senior year. It ended up being his last high school game ever, and he missed playoffs because of a tear. He probably missed out on some bigger scholarship offers too. He was never quite as dynamic because of it.

But for my brother, football was always extra. It wasn't life. And he wasn't nearly as amazing on that field as Logan is. I hope this sprain holds true. I hope it heals fast. And I hope he keeps the fire lit because watching him out there was breathtaking. I've never loved football more.

Despite what I know has been a crushing blow, Logan's kept the proverbial sunshine out. I admire it. Maybe even aspire to it. It's also made me glad I never entered the pool. I'll find another way to earn money. Another scholarship.

Maybe even at tonight's Dean's Dinner. I can be charming when I have to. Or I'll go to Germany another time.

That's probably not going to happen.

I'm less crushed over the whole thing now, though. Three weeks with a guy I didn't think knew my real name before we started studying together and my perspective is shifting. Now, if I can just find the courage to ask how phony this fake dating scheme really is. Because it feels pretty real. As in, *I'd really love for him to meet my brother, then maybe my parents* kind of real.

I roll up my lab coat and tuck it in my satchel, along with my leather-bound notebook containing my latest experiment notes and a few copies of my embossed resume. Leaning close to the mirror, I touch up my pale pink lipstick and push the few stray hairs back into place, hoping the loose bun I pinned at the base of my neck holds up for the next three hours.

Logan isn't going to recognize me in a black pant suit and heels. I smirk at the thought, and a part of me wonders if he's going to like this grown-up business woman look. It's why I didn't want to cancel our study session. I figured I could go right from the library to the dean's house across the street with plenty of time to spare. Plus, this way Logan would get to see this side of me. I watched his game, and he gets a glimpse of mine, rubbing shoulders with a room full of academics. The end goal is simple—secure a chemistry apprenticeship after graduation.

With my bag tucked to my side, I make my way out of the chemistry building, my heels clicking against the terrazzo floors. The clacking sound turns a few heads at the front desk, and I spot one of the first-years push his glasses up his nose as he stands to catch a view of me. It's rare, this feeling, but I think I like this attention. I feel beautiful and smart.

It's breezy out, so I cup my hand over my bun as I rush toward the library, pausing at the glass door to check my reflection for more stray hairs. It seems to have held up, so I head inside and stop in my tracks when I'm greeted by Logan Ford, wearing a suit and holding a rose.

"What is this?" My mouth hangs open as I drink him in. Dressed head to toe in dusty blue, his jacket hugs his muscles and his pants are snug around his hips and thighs. The crisp white dress shirt must be new because I know the man doesn't own an iron, and his tie is pink. I step forward, taking the rose in one hand and his tie in the other as my eyes scan up and down one last time.

"You said most people have dates, and I thought—" He licks his lips, then takes a step back, palm rubbing his chin as his eyes drop down my length.

"I'm sorry, but you're sexy as fuck," he says through a kind but surprised laugh.

I turn slowly to show off every last bit of my Ann Taylor clearance find. These miracle black pants are sheer in places and drape my curves. I almost didn't try them on but the manager at the store begged me to. I'm glad she did.

"Yeah?" I hum, meeting his gaze again.

He reaches up and nudges my chin, urging me closer.

"If you kiss me you'll smudge my lipstick," I warn.

His gaze drops a hint and he smirks.

"I don't care," he says, giving me a soft peck.

I don't care either.

"You don't have to do this. I am fine handling it solo, truly. And you're going to have to stand all night, on your leg." I gesture down to his right limb.

He lifts his pant leg up several inches, revealing what looks like an intense compression sock.

"If I could pull this up any higher you'd see the impressive wrap job and weird mechanical contraption Terry put on my knee. It's practically not even sore anymore," he says, faking some type of tap dance. *I think that was tap?*

I laugh, then reach for his tie again, and he cuffs my wrist in his hand and lifts it to his mouth, pressing his lips on the soft tender spot. I don't want to look away, but I also heard someone gasp to my right, so I venture a quick look and see a younger version of me sitting in one of the leather chairs, headphones on but hand over her heart. Her eyes scream of swoon. I'm pretty sure mine do too.

"If you don't mind a slight limp," he says, reaching for my leather satchel and pulling it from my shoulder.

"I love a good limp," I respond, causing him to spit out a laugh, shaking his head and shutting his eyes.

"Yeah, that sounded way lamer out loud," I admit.

He nods, then tucks my arm around his.

"It did. But you're hot as fuck, remember? You can say anything you want."

I let that sink in. Normally, I would be a nervous wreck for this dinner. Last year, I accompanied Dalton as I wasn't officially invited. Watching him work the room was educational. It's no wonder he's going into law because he won over every law school rep in the room the way he'd sell a jury on a verdict. Since I can't concoct some sort of potion to put people in a trance—*or can I?*—I need to muster similar charm. Maybe some of Logan's will rub off on me tonight.

Rather than sticking around the library for tutoring, I let Logan walk me through the school's modern art gallery to kill the forty minutes until the dinner begins. The long building stretches nearly the entire block on the east end of campus. It's steps away from the library yet I've never been inside.

"I come here all the time," he says, waving to an older woman dressed as a security guard.

"Good evening, you two," she says in a teasing tone.

"That's Nora," he mutters by my ear, his voice hushed. "She has a thing for me, but she must like you. She wouldn't make that face if she disapproved."

I hug his bicep, but give him a sideways look.

"You bring a lot of girls here, Mr. Ford?"

He holds my gaze through a few slow steps then shakes his head.

"Not a one."

Oh.

Logan leads me to a room in the far end of the gallery. It's a quiet space and the light inside is dimmer than most of the other rooms. There's a sense of calm the moment we step inside, and my skin feels cool. It's mental, I'm sure. Every painting hung in this room is blue. It's as if water and sky collided and left works of art behind.

We stroll through the space slowly, Logan pointing out his favorite pieces, including one of a hill covered in trees.

"Sometimes when I'm in here, this one feels like night. Other times, I see a storm. It's a chameleon."

A short breath leaves my nose, an amused laugh that Logan doesn't miss.

"What? Too nerdy for you?" He touches the tip of my nose with his finger.

I shake my head.

"I was just thinking how fitting it was. You're kind of like a chameleon too."

His head falls to the side as he looks at the painting again, a serene expression settling over his eyes and mouth. It proves my point without him saying a word. This man is a monster on the football field, and yet now, in this room, he's the embodiment of peace.

We leave the gallery a few minutes before six-thirty and make our way to the dean's house, a Craftsman-style bungalow with a massive front room already buzzing with suits, dresses, and young people with resumes. I pause at the steps, feeling my throat close up for the first time today.

"Are you all right?"

I exhale and widen my eyes as I look to Logan.

"I didn't think I was going to be nervous until right now. I kind of wish I wore my glasses tonight. They're like a shield."

His lip quirks up.

"I'll be your shield. Come on. You got this."

He leads me up the stairs and opens the screen door as I step inside. Professor Combs spots me first, and is quick to rush to my other side and point out the most important people in the room.

"Mr. Ford. How nice to see you here," he says, taking a step back and eying Logan with what feels like suspicion.

"Nice to see you, too," Logan responds, jutting out his palm. There's a slight tic in his jaw as he waits for my professor to shake his hand, and the moment they're done, Logan drops both of his hands into his pockets.

"Right, well. I'm not sure if they have seating placements. You may want to check, Rachel," Professor Combs says, his eyes lingering on mine for a beat. There's a warning to them, and my chest grows heavy. Logan is an outsider here. That's what he's saying with that look. I feel it. And I think Logan feels it, too.

"Okay, thank you," I answer, glancing over my shoulder to Logan and nodding toward the hallway that leads to several more rooms packed with so many other academics.

Logan's mouth stretches into a tight-lipped smile, but I can tell his teeth are pressed together underneath. I recognize the small dent above his brow, too. He gets it when he's struggling with one of the chemistry subjects. He wears his frustration. I wear my panic, and it looks very similar.

Despite how uncomfortable I can tell he is, Logan follows me to the next room, and he remains at my side while I introduce myself to a science dean from Stanford and another one from Northwestern. A few Tiff professors recognize him and ask questions about the season, only one realizing he was injured. His shoulders stiffen and his jaw starts to work more as he gets cornered. I catch his gaze across the room and lift my brows, offering a rescue, but he shakes me off, waving his hand to encourage me to go on.

I finally find the rep from Iowa State and reintroduce myself, having met Dr. Rebecca Callahan once last year at a symposium. She says she remembers me, but I think she's being polite. Regardless, when she asks questions about my studies this year and is piqued by my latest research on hormones, my jitters subside.

"Do you have your resume with you tonight? Or a card?" My pulse jacks up at her request.

"I do! Yes, I mean. Yes, ma'am. I do." I twist and lift up on my toes, my height already nearly maxed thanks to the two-inch heels. I catch Logan's attention above the heads in the crowded library room and Logan excuses himself from the conversation he's been trapped in for at least ten minutes.

"Thank you," he exhales, turning his attention to Dr. Callahan.

"Hi. I'm Logan," he says, holding out his hand just as he has all night. Dr. Callahan's gaze drops to his hand as she quakes with a short, and rather judgmental, titter. She's a fairly formal individual, and I think Logan's casual greeting has thrown her.

"Logan's one of our most talented football players. He's projected to go high in the draft," I brag, leaving the whole *bubble* out of the picture. I give Logan a quick glance and when our eyes meet, his mouth twitches for a brief crooked smile.

"Well, how nice for you, Logan," Dr. Callahan says, finally taking his hand. She meets his firm shake with her own, and it feels a little like a pissing match. Maybe that's how I'm reading it, though.

"Can I get something out of my bag?" I tug on the strap, which he's carried on his shoulder for the last forty minutes.

"Oh, yeah," he says, enthusiasm coloring his words. He winks at me as he holds my bag open for me to reach inside, and his genuine thrill on my behalf tempers my worries.

I pull out my resume and one of the business cards I made last semester, when I applied for the scholarship I didn't get. I hand them to Dr. Callahan and she pulls a pair of reading glasses from her clutch purse and gives my credentials a quick scan.

"Very impressive. Let's set up a meeting. Call my office on Monday," she says, pulling a card from her clutch as she puts her glasses away. I take it in my hand and stop myself from staring at it in awe, instead pocketing it and doing my best to play it cool.

A bell rings, calling us all to the dining room in the very back of the house. It's an awkward stampede of well-dressed students and professors through the narrow opening, but once inside, the room is large enough to breathe in. Long tables form a square, white linens draping them, and golden chairs pushed close to mark each place setting.

I'd forgotten about the place cards, and as I scan the names and find mine on a corner near the fireplace, I realize I don't have a plus-one next to me. I twist and flash my eyes to Logan's, but he brushes my chin with the back of his thumb and smiles.

"I'll be fine. I'm sure there's a place somewhere. Go. Do your thing."

I swallow hard, taking his hand and squeezing it. His palm is sweaty, and mine is cold.

The mess of bodies scurrying around the room in search of their assignments eventually sweeps me toward my chair, so I settle in and wait to see who I'm seated near. I introduce myself to a chemical engineering professor from Berkeley to my right and another rep from Northwestern to my right. When everyone finally seems to have found a place, I scan the room until I spot Logan, tucked in the center of the table opposite me. I hold up a hand.

He gives me a thumbs up and promptly pulls apart the folded napkin to lay it on his lap. Dinner and conversation take over for the next thirty minutes, and while I'm keeping up with the talk of research papers and who was recently published, my attention never fully strays from the man twice the size of everyone else. His tie now loosened and his jacket on the back of his chair, he's staring at his half-eaten plate of chicken piccata, pushing around the garnish with his fork.

The second Dean Fisher, our host, finishes his toast, I excuse myself from my place and make my way back to Logan. Cocktails are flowing, and more mingling is in the works, but I don't feel any desire to stay. I can tell Logan wants to bust out of this place, too, so when I find him and offer to leave, his grin is instant. He slips his jacket on in one smooth movement.

We're on our way out of the dining room when Dr. Callahan stops us at the door, her hand on Logan's arm, a man who looks to be about fifty behind her. Her husband, I'm guessing.

"I'm sorry. I forgot your name, but I wanted to introduce you to my husband. He's a big football fan," she says.

Logan's brow rises, his expression skeptical.

"Sure. It's Logan Ford. I play for Tiff," he says, squaring his shoulders and holding out his hand.

"Henry Callahan," the other man says, chuckling through their handshake. "Wow. Some grip!"

Henry flexes his hand when they part, and I'm not sure how much of that was him kidding. Logan's hands are back in his pockets, so I loop my arm through his elbow and hold on to the fabric of his jacket.

"Tell me, Logan. You make it to many of these kinds of dinners?" Henry asks.

My brow pinches at the smugness of his question, and Logan's arm tightens around mine.

"Like this? Not really. They feed us braised beef and corn-bread muffins on Fridays in the stadium dining hall. Those are pretty special, and the food, well . . . it's better than that piccata stuff." Logan's turning up the stereotype, and I'm not sure why . . . until—

"You were talking to my colleagues before dinner, in the library. What was it you said? Something about—*Huck Finn*? Or was it *Treasure Island*?"

Logan's mouth has dropped into a hard line, and he blinks slowly before lifting his chin a tick.

"It was *Tom Sawyer*. And I said it was my favorite book."

Henry's laugh is instant. And it's mocking.

"Oh, man, you football guys. You're always so simple," he says, daring to put his palm on Logan's shoulder.

"We should get going actually," I cut in, spotting the slight shirk Logan gives Henry. I want to punch the man in the face. I can't imagine Logan doesn't.

"Dr. Callahan, it was nice to meet you. I will call your office Monday," I say, no longer sure I want to.

"Pleasure," Logan grits as I lead him out of the room and through the haughty crowd. Drinks started flowing with dinner, and much like the party Logan took me to, it has raised the volume and emboldened the attendees. Apparently, though, in this crowd liquor brings out the assholes.

We walk in silence down the steps, and I bite my tongue until we get to the sidewalk, sheltered by the deep shadows of the oak trees that still haven't lost their leaves.

"Logan, I'm so sorry for that."

"It's fine," he grumbles, continuing his stride from the dean's house. I jerk his arm and force him to twist into me. My hands grab the lapels of his jacket and I shake them against his chest.

"It's not fine. Let me apologize!"

Logan's nostrils flare.

"Fine. You're forgiven. Even though you didn't do anything wrong. Can we go now?" He looks back toward the house, his neck flexing. His mind clearly still rearing with negative energy.

"We can go. But Logan, hear me. I'm sorry."

His eyes drift back to mine, and there's a tinge of redness to the whites.

"Like I said. You didn't do anything wrong. It's just . . ." He exhales and looks out toward the street, chewing at the inside of his cheek. His gaze comes back to me, and I finally see it. His shame.

"You know they had to come up with an entire plan to deal with me failing chemistry last year? Like, there were meetings and shit about how to sweep my grade under the rug and just usher me through, the way they did with those basketball guys who got caught up in the scandal. I actually had to fight for them to let me take this class again. But they told me not to worry about it. 'Just worry about football, Logan. We'll get you a passing grade.'"

His eyes dim, his face somehow sadder.

"Do you know how stupid I feel sometimes? Even with you, and I know you don't mean to make me feel that way, but you're just so smart. Every class is easy for you. I bragged about a few A's in literature, but you know what? Those classes were remedial. And the materials were dumbed down for people like me to understand. It doesn't mean I didn't like it. And I did read the real texts because I wanted to learn. *I want to learn!*

"But people like Henry . . . they want me to play football. Earn the school big money. Take a few hits. *Fuck your knee up. We'll give you an A.* But then what? Huh? What happens if I fall on the other side of that bubble, Rachel? Who am I? A dumb jock who isn't even fucking good at working on cars?"

"Oh, Logan," I say, stepping into him, my hands cupping his cheeks. His stubble scratches against my palms, and as he tries to shake my hands away, I press against his jaw even harder.

"No, you look at me. Logan, you are . . . you are that chameleon. You are *so* smart. And you can fit in anywhere, thrive in any room, on any field. I showed you how to study and look at what you've done?"

"What, get a C?" he scoffs.

My fingers curl against his skin and I shake my head.

"No, Logan. You tried. You're relentless. Maybe a little stubborn. And so brilliant. You walked into that gallery on your own, because you had to know what was inside. You found the blue room, and you understood it as if you were the artist yourself. Henry can't do that. He sees a room where the lights don't work. He sees blue, but not what's underneath. Not the cold. Not love. Not the stillness."

I'm barely into my barrage of all the things I admire about Logan when his mouth covers mine, his hand at my back as he lifts me into him. I arch my back with the roughness of his kiss, and my hands cling to the sides of his face as he drops my satchel and runs his other hand up my spine and into my hair, unfurling my pinned hair until it spills down my back and weaves through his fingers.

Someone whistles in the distance, and I'm not sure whether it was from the house or a passerby on the street. I don't care. All I want to do is stand here under this tree, away from the glow of the streetlights and the brightness of the moon. I want to live in the blue. To swim in it, and all things Logan Ford.

[illegible]

[illegible] [illegible] it [illegible] [illegible] [illegible] [illegible] the [illegible]
[illegible] the [illegible] and you [illegible] it [illegible]
[illegible] all [illegible] I [illegible] [illegible] [illegible] [illegible] the [illegible] [illegible]

[illegible] the [illegible] I [illegible] [illegible] [illegible] [illegible] [illegible]
[illegible] [illegible] [illegible] [illegible] [illegible] [illegible] [illegible] [illegible]
[illegible] [illegible] States.

[illegible] [illegible] In the [illegible] [illegible] [illegible] and [illegible]
[illegible] [illegible] more [illegible] [illegible] [illegible] [illegible]
[illegible] all [illegible] to [illegible] [illegible] [illegible] [illegible]
[illegible] [illegible] [illegible] [illegible] [illegible] [illegible] [illegible]
[illegible] [illegible] [illegible] [illegible] [illegible] [illegible] [illegible]
[illegible]

AFTER ALL THAT, she came home with me. I'm not sure what to say after the word vomit I dropped at her feet outside the dean's house. When she pushed it all to the side and still saw me as someone special, I didn't know how to handle it.

So I kissed her.

My lips were saying thank you. They were begging her to play along. To stick with me. To let me show her how real this arrangement can be.

We didn't talk in the truck, other than me asking her if she wanted to stay at my place tonight and her saying yes.

Yes.

Now, here I am in the driveway, truck in park but still idling. My teammates inside and asleep early because they have a game tomorrow. One in which I won't play. One I'll watch from the sideline. Where I'll be expected to help Cam be at his best.

I run my palm over my face and laugh against the heel before resting my wrists on the steering wheel. My head swivels and my gaze hits Rachel's, her soft smile and hazed eyes toying with seduction. How can I want to do dirty things to someone so sweet? So kind?

"I don't remember whether I told you this or not, but did you know I asked for you to be my tutor?" My cheek pushes up to the right, a guilty smile forcing me to squint my right eye.

Her mouth puckers, like she's holding in a laugh, and she shakes her head.

"No. I didn't know that. My professor told me the administration chose me for the job." Her voice is raspy.

I nod slowly and drop my half smile.

"Job, huh?" I drop my chin to my chest. That word lands heavy.

"Oh, you've been a job all right," she teases. I glance sideways and quirk a brow. "Real work, Logan Ford. What with your swagger and your perfect hair."

She unclasps her seat belt and leans across the console, flicking a lock of my hair with her index finger. It flops over my forehead and I quickly push it back in place.

She purses her lips but they hint at a smile as she shakes her head. "Everything is always in its place with you, isn't it?"

I blink a few times, flitting my gaze down her chest then back up to her eyes. She twisted her hair into two loose braids while we drove, and I want to point out how she likes things in their place too.

"Not always," I say instead. "I was a bit of a mess tonight. My whole self was kind of out of place."

She shifts in her seat, leaning in close, and runs her hand along my chest, slipping it inside my shirt, between the buttons.

"I'm always out of place. It's why I thrive on the edge,

just out of the picture. It was nice to have you there with me. And for the record, *Tom Sawyer* is my favorite book, too."

I wrap my hand around her wrist and hold it still, dropping my chin a bit and holding her stare.

"No, it's not," I say.

She blinks a few times, then glances down with a smirk.

"Okay, fine. It's not. But that's only because I'm a girl. And Mark Twain wasn't really about the romance. He was more about the skipping rocks and sword fighting and—"

I chuckle.

"I don't think that was really the point of *Tom Sawyer*," I say.

"Oh, yeah?"

I shake my head.

"Uh uh." I lick my lips and take a long, slow inhale of air. "It's more about the pull to be an adult, but this inherent desire not to follow the paths our parents laid out for us. To make our own mark. And to slow down and just be a kid sometimes."

She studies me for a few seconds, and I'm not sure whether her inner voice is echoing the opinions of those people at dinner tonight, or something else. Something better . . . or worse.

"Hey, Logan?" she finally utters.

I lift a brow.

"When you talk like that? You're sexy as fuck."

And there it is, that flicker in her eyes. I've only seen it a handful of times, and each time it makes me want to pick her up in my arms and consume her.

"You said the real F word," I tease.

"I did."

"I'm going to need to take you inside now," I continue, unlatching my seat belt.

"You are," she agrees.

I'm out of the truck in half a second and to her side in the other half. I help her swing the door wide open and then pick her up from her seat and hoist her over my shoulder. Her hands slap at my ass as I kick the truck door shut and swing her around, carrying her up the driveway and through the front door.

Her giggling is muffled the moment we're inside, but I can still feel her laughing as I take her up the stairs and into my room.

I close the door and set her down against it, pinning her hands above her head with one hand while cradling her jaw with my other. She titters for another second or two, biting her bottom lip, which slips free when our eyes meet. Her chin lifts and she breathes in through her nose, pushing her chest up, almost in defiance. My mouth drops to her throat, my tongue dragging up her neck and along her jawline until my mouth covers hers and my teeth find the soft plumpness of her bottom lip. I bite her gently, pulling as I let out a soft growl.

My head rests against hers as I let her hands go and drop both of mine to the braids on either side of her head. Her hair is long enough that I can wrap it around each palm, and she hisses when I lightly tug.

"You know why I call you Shortcake? Because I bet you taste sweet. And those strawberry braids are begging me to grab hold and give you a lick."

It's her whimper that pushes me over the edge.

I toss away my jacket and drop to my knees, unbuttoning her pants and sliding them down her hips, the fabric pooling around her feet. She kicks them to the side and reaches for one of her shoes—strappy black heels that crisscross her ankles and wrap around her legs. I stop her.

"These stay," I say.

Her foot lowers to the floor. My hands begin just where the leather straps end, about halfway up her calves. I glide my palms up to her knees, pausing there to coax her legs apart. She obeys, and her willing submission makes my dick swell.

I lean in, first pressing a soft kiss to the inside of her knee. Her breath falters, and I smile against her, tilting my head to gaze up at her. She's biting her fist, eyes locked on me.

"It's the anticipation that does it, huh?" I kiss her inner thigh and look up again.

"Uh huh," she whispers with a tiny nod.

Turning my focus back to her black lace panties, I slide both of my hands up until they meet the thin band on her hips. I toy with it, hooking my fingers around it and pulling them down an inch before stopping to kiss her inner thigh again, this time inches from where I really want to taste.

I look up at her again.

"Are you wet for me, Rachel?"

Her eyes are pained with need. It's so fucking sexy. And when she moans, "Uh huh," it takes all my restraint not to tear through her panties and suck her pussy. But it's the anticipation for me, too. I want to take my time. To enjoy this. For *her* to enjoy this. Besides, I don't have to be well-rested tomorrow. I'm on the bench.

I kiss her right in the center this time, letting my lips linger on the thin satin strip that barely covers her. I can smell how much she wants this, her scent so fucking sweet.

"I bet you taste so good," I say, kissing her center again. This time, I press my tongue against the strip of fabric, dragging it along the length, feeling how swollen she is underneath. Her head falls back against my door and she lets out a soft cry.

"Oh, you want to be fucked, don't you?"

She cries out again, softly.

"Uh huh."

My right palm flattens against her abdomen, my other hand still hooked in the lace band at her hip. My thumb slides between her legs and I rub her swollen pussy, pressing into her and circling where she's most sensitive. Her hips buck, pushing out from the wall, and I push her back, holding her still while my thumb hooks into the soaking wet center of her panties and tugs it to the side.

"One taste," I hum, my lips brushing against her pussy as I talk dirty to her. She's so fucking sexy, innocent and wild at the same time. I give in and drag my tongue from her center all the way to the beginning of the small trail of copper hair. Needing more, I kiss her pink skin, sucking in her clit and flicking my tongue against it. She gasps and I let go, smiling.

"Let me see you," I say, pulling her panties down her hips and thighs until she lifts one foot at a time to step free of them.

I rub my thumb over her glistening skin, slow circles that seem to force her eyelids to flutter shut. Her hands weave into my hair, urging me toward her, begging. Fucking hell, she wants me to lick her more.

My turn to obey, so I do as she asks, clawing up the backs of her legs until my hands grab her ass cheeks and my tongue dives into her pussy. Her gasp is loud this time, propelling me to be rougher, to take more. Groaning, I hook her leg over my shoulder for better access and dip my tongue inside.

"You're so fucking warm. So sweet." I flick her clit with my tongue, then sink it inside her again, my hands rough on her ass, hers grabbing my hair. I tease her clit with my tongue and run my finger through her wet folds, finally diving inside and working her with my hand.

"*Ooooo*, Logan." My name vibrates from her lips, driving me harder, and I push two fingers in, fucking her like this until her center clenches around me and her pussy grows wetter as it shudders against my tongue.

Her hands fall from my hair, and her body is instantly limp. I swoop her into my arms and spin around to drop her on my bed, pulling her ankles off the edge. I stand at the foot of the bed, my cock hard as fuck as I stare at her pussy. So perfect. I unzip my pants and kick them off along with my boxer briefs, then tear through the buttons on my shirt, my impatience getting the best of me. Stroking my cock, I stare at her as her back arches, the top several buttons of her white blouse open. She took her jacket off in the truck.

"Touch yourself." It's a request but I say it more like a command. The quirk in her lip seems to show she likes it. She moves her hand inside her blouse, slipping inside the lace of her bra, gliding over her nipples.

"Lose the shirt. I want to see."

A coy smirk paints her mouth as she draws her knees up, resting her heels on the bed while her hands undo the buttons on her shirt. I drop my cock and step toward her, unwrapping the leather straps from her legs while she slips out of her white dress shirt. I drop her shoes to the floor just as she unclasps the center snap on her bra, the lace relaxing but clinging to the hard rosy peaks of her tits.

I nudge her legs apart with my knee and crawl on the bed, lowering myself enough to grab the edge of her bra in my teeth. I shift the lace over the curve of her breast with my mouth, revealing her hard nipple, and I swipe at it with my tongue.

Rachel's hands fly to the back of my head as she arches her back and holds me near her breast, pushing her tit into my mouth. I bite it, clasping the hard tip between my teeth and flicking the skin with my tongue as she writhes beneath me.

"I want this," she murmurs, her hands sliding around my sides and lowering to my cock. She takes me in both hands, stroking me, her thumbs rubbing away the pre-cum dripping from my tip.

"You can have it," I say, my voice almost a growl.

I get up from the bed and move to my nightstand, grabbing a condom out of the drawer. I tear the packet open and slip the condom over my cock, returning to the foot of the bed where she is splayed out and ready for me.

"You sure you want this?" I put a knee between her legs and push her thighs farther apart. She nods then bites her knuckle, her lips quivering with her stuttering breath.

I hold myself over her, guiding my cock to her entrance, and I push in the tip then pull out, dragging my length through her wetness. She whimpers as I dip into her again, a little deeper, holding my position a little longer.

"You're so fucking tight, Shortcake. Your pussy is like heaven." I slip back out and run my cock over her pink skin again.

She arches her hips in anticipation and I guide myself into her one last time, sinking in deep and shifting to hold myself above her. I rock my hips slowly at first, and she welcomes each push with a soft moan. Her arms stretch above her head as her hands grab at my blanket, fisting it as I pump into her harder, faster. Our gazes lock and her lips part, the sweetest, hungriest cry escaping her lips each time I push in. Her tits shake with my force and I drop my mouth to her nipple, sucking in one then the other as she meets each pummel by raising her hips and pushing into me.

"Fuck, Rachel. I'm going to come," I warn her, and as if it's a challenge, her legs wrap around my waist just as her arms swing around my neck.

I sit up on my knees, my cock inside her, and maneuver so I'm sitting on the edge of the bed and she's in my lap. My hands grip her ass and I pump my hips as she bounces on my cock, her moans now a constant hum, only broken by my dick pushing deep inside.

"I'm coming," she says, her raspy voice ragged with sex, hot against my ear.

I'm unable to form human words, simply groaning as she grinds against me and I push up into her a few final times, releasing and pulsing until her body is damp with sweat. I fall back on the bed, holding her to me, her braids now a wild mess, her bra hooked on one arm, and my dick still hard inside her.

"You can thank *Tom Sawyer* and the sword-fighting scene for that," I pant.

Her body quakes with silent laughter. Our skin is slick and stuck together. It's perfect.

"I knew it was the sword-fighting," she says.

I laugh in response, lifting my head enough to kiss the top of her head.

This girl. I think I'm in love with her.

"LET ME WALK YOU UP." Logan is already parked illegally in the loading zone for my dorm. He insisted on bringing me home this morning on his way to the stadium. Apparently, I look "properly fucked."

My response was, "As long as it's proper."

But really? I'm glad he saved me an awkward walk of shame. I have my own car, but I rarely pull it from the garage. It goes to my parents' house and back because I rarely leave the half-square-mile radius around my dorm. And so far, Logan's driven everywhere we've gone.

"I think I can manage," I say, leaning over the console and tugging the center of his jersey toward me. He leans in and kisses me softly, lips holding on to mine for extra seconds.

"You look good in my clothes," he says when our kiss breaks. His gaze dips down to his hoodie that I paired with my dress pants from last night. It's a solid fashion choice for sure.

"I'll see you at your game," I say, slipping out of the passenger seat and shutting the door before he can question me. He insisted I not come since he won't be playing. He knows I have lab hours to make up, so he encouraged me to go there instead. I think he's afraid I'll somehow be wowed by his replacement. To be frank, Cam Ledger sounds like a real ass.

I'm almost to my building's door when he calls my name out his window, having turned his truck around. I spin on my heels but keep walking backward, cupping my ear as if I can't hear him shouting at the top of his lungs.

"I'm not even playing!" His palm is out the window as he shout-reasons with me.

"I don't care!" I give him two open palms then shrug and spin around, ducking inside before he can yell anything back.

The front desk girl's name is Kira, I found out. Logan officially introduced us since he and she have become friends thanks to his drop-by visits. She's hugging an enormous vat of iced coffee as I approach the desk, her mouth fixed to the straw, on constant suck. I wonder what party she went to last night.

"Hi Rach—*oh* . . ." Her mouth snaps shut, and I look around me quickly, wondering what her reaction was for. I brush a few stray hairs from my face, tucking them behind my ear, and then my hand gets caught in what feels like a tumbleweed. I smash the mess of hair against my ear and it hits me.

Properly fucked.

"Oh." The same word she used.

Leaning toward her tumbler, she shows me a smug, knowing smile for about half a second before taking her straw and drawing in a big swig of coffee. My face is hot. Which works out since my hair probably looks like flames.

I skirt around the desk and head to the elevator, but before I'm out of her earshot Kira says, "Atta girl."

Palm over face.

Thankfully, I'm on my own in the elevator, and it's early enough in the morning for the halls to be clear still. Even the nerds are still asleep. At least one nerd is awake, however. And she's sitting on her bed, legs crossed while *The Office* streams on her laptop.

"Well, *hello—oh!*" Claire makes the same face Kira did, and the blush that ended at my cheeks before now crawls all the way to the top of my head.

"That bad, huh?" I wince and open our closet door to check the mirror.

"Oh, fuck!" I smash both sides of my hair to my ears.

"Yeah, you did," Claire jokes.

"Oh, my God!" My gaze hits hers in the reflection, and she falls back in her bed with uncontrollable laughter.

My frustration and embarrassment boil over, so I grab hold of my towel and shower caddy, clutching them to my chest while I rush to the shower to erase the scarlet letter I'm embodying. When my hair finally resembles normal again and the burning mortification has stopped climbing up my neck, I wrap my body in my towel and carry my things, wrapped in Logan's sweatshirt, back to my room. I set everything on the bed before looking Claire in the eyes, but eventually turn and take a seat on the edge, ready for my judgement day. Surprisingly, she doesn't seem to be on pins and needles waiting for gossip. She's back to her laptop, some murder mystery playing that I don't recognize.

"You feel better?" She doesn't look up from her screen when she asks.

"Yes," I say, but then quickly reverse. "No."

She exhales with enough force to drop her shoulders a few inches then shuts her laptop screen and pushes it to the side. Scooting to the edge of her bed, she folds her hands in her lap before blowing up at her grown-out bangs that skirt her eyes.

"You like him," she says.

I shrug.

"I don't know." I'm lying, protecting what I'm afraid of, holding things close.

Claire scoots off her bed and climbs up on mine. She unfurls his sweatshirt, moving my hair care bottles and day-old clothes to the side so she can hold it up and read the back.

FORD – 34

"Rachel, this might as well be a letterman jacket," she says, tossing it to my lap. I catch it against my body and stave off the temptation to bring it up to my nose and breathe in Logan's scent.

"You can talk to me, you know. I'm not Stella. I am not going to drive a wedge between you and Logan or steal him away from you. Really? I just want to be your friend. Your *real* friend."

My face tingles with an anxious rush to my bloodstream and I do my best to smile.

"I'd like that," I say, and I mean it. Tears prick at the corners of my eyes, so I give in to holding his hoodie close, burying my face in it for a few seconds so I can choke back my emotions. I miss Stella, yet I *don't* miss Stella. I guess I never mourned the end of our friendship, and I've been in denial over the hole it left behind.

"You like him," Claire says, pulling me out from hiding. I peek around his sweatshirt and find her encouraging expression, so I drop the hoodie back to my lap and bite my lip.

"I *really* like him," I admit.

A giddy grin spreads from cheek to cheek on Claire's face, and my body rushes with tingles. It's as if a weight cleared my shoulders simply by saying it out loud, and also, a parade kicked off inside my chest.

"And the sex must be good," Claire adds, which pops my eyes wide. Instead of being embarrassed though, I give in and embrace having a girlfriend again.

"Sooooo good," I add, moving the hoodie back to my face to muffle my delighted scream. Claire grabs my heart pillow from the corner of my bed and muffles her own reaction, I think mostly to make me feel at ease.

I tell her the rated PG parts, about him showing up dressed in a suit, and how he *looked* in the suit. I mention the gallery, and how special it felt, how he read into the works of art and showed this emotional side I never knew he had. And then, without divulging Logan's insecurities, I walked her through what happened at the dinner, and how snobby everyone was. It's Logan's story to talk about how he felt. I would never put words in his mouth or speak on his behalf unless he wanted me to. But I sense from Claire's heavy expression that she has some idea of how the evening may have made Logan feel out of place.

When I get to him carrying me up the stairs, I stop at the door closing, insinuating just enough for her cheeks to turn cherry red. The rest, I save for me.

"So, are we going to his game, then?" she asks.

I slip into a pair of leggings and a sports bra, my body sore from our long and very active night. I can still feel his touch when I close my eyes. And the ache between my legs is a sweet reminder of what it was like to feel so close to him, to be connected.

"I was planning on going. He won't play today, but I

thought the support would still be nice. Plus, I miss football." I slip his hoodie back on, hugging myself with the oversized sleeves. I towel my hair dry a little more, then braid it to one side.

"Can I come?"

I twist around mid-braid, surprised she would be interested. Then again, why wouldn't she? Claire isn't me. She's far more social. I'm not one-hundred-percent certain, but I think she even sits on a committee for live-action reenactment play. I've seen her cardboard sword in our closet.

"That would be awesome," I say, finishing up my braid.

Claire slips on a dark blue Tiff Science Department sweatshirt that reads BIO BITCH across the front, and we both put beanies on since the clouds are out today in full force. I offer to drive, but Claire insists we make the seven-block walk to the stadium as a tradeoff for beer and a bratwurst. It sounds like a good idea until we're about four blocks in and the wind picks up. I wish Logan would drive by and see me, but even though he's not playing, I'm sure he's already on the field.

We make it to the basketball arena, the gathering spot for students and fans to make the march to the stadium. I wait on the concourse while Claire stands in line to buy us two water bottles, the marching band kicking off the tailgate walk into the stadium from the arena floor. The cheerleaders all kicking their legs to their foreheads, poms shimmering as alumni and season ticket holders clap along with the fight song. Huge cardboard letters spell out TIFF TUFF.

"You thinking about joining the squad?" Claire nudges my elbow with the water bottle. I take it from her and chuckle.

"Do you think they have a position for someone who trips on stairs and whose splits make it clear to a forty-five-degree angle?" We both stare at the arena floor where six girls are all perfectly straight in their splits, arms over their heads as if it's nothing.

"There's always the mascot," Claire jokes. As if on cue, the second she makes the suggestion, the giant-headed cartoonish Knight mascot slides into perfect splits.

"That's a hard pass." I laugh.

We walk around the concourse to the other side, saving ourselves some distance by exiting to the west, and as we reach the door, the band and cheer squad climb the steps to make the walk to the stadium with us.

"Great," I mumble.

"Oh, where's your spirit," Claire chimes in, elbowing me then tucking her water bottle under her arm so she can clap along with the band.

I roll my eyes but give in, clapping along as well. For the next block we make up our own lyrics for the fight song, substituting elemental symbols for words—like AU for gold. I'm genuinely having a good time, which of course means something has to balance out. My spoiler comes in the form of a leggy blonde cheerleader who rushes around me just to block our path.

I spotted Amy in the arena, and I recognized the blonde curls of her ponytail as she passed. She skips in place a few times, clapping her poms and turning slowly until her gaze stops on me. She planned this, and it's obvious. Even the way her face lights up with fake surprise when she sees me makes my stomach churn.

"Oh, my God, Rory!" *She knows my name.*

"It's Rachel," I correct, stuffing my water bottle into the front pocket of Logan's hoodie and balling the ends of the sleeves into my fists.

"Right. Rachel. Sorry, I'm bad with names," she laughs off. Her eyes shift to Claire, her face shimmering with a sheen of glitter, her eyelashes about twice as long as humanly possible.

"Hi, I'm Amy. I'm a friend of Logan's . . . and I guess now Rachel," she says. Her lie comes out smoothly.

"Nice to meet you. You can call me Rory," Claire says, and I spit out a laugh that I quickly bury with a fist over my mouth.

My friend's response puts a dent in Amy's fake bravado, but she shores up her mask quickly, simply playing along. "Nice to meet you, Rory," she says, returning her gaze to me with what I'm sure is no intention of ever looking Claire in the eyes again.

"So, how are things going . . . with Logan?"

We've started walking again, with Amy matching our strides as she shimmers her poms in the air next to me.

"Things are fine," I say, not offering more. When she approached me in the parking lot at his truck a couple of weeks ago, I offered little information as well. I could tell it infuriated her, but I have a feeling she's done her homework since then. My gut says she knows most of the details about my arrangement with Logan, from starting as tutor and student and morphing into . . . whatever we are now.

"He's a really great guy," she says, sidestepping for a few steps so she can look at me.

"He is. He's working hard." I decided from the first time we met that I would offer zero details about anything remotely personal.

"*Mmm*, I'm sure. Did you mean with the injury? Or are you talking about teaching him? It's so nice of you to volunteer your time." She does a poor job of masking her conde-scension this time.

"He's working hard at both," I answer, snapping my mouth shut into a tight smile that I hope gives her the idea to fuck right off.

We get a reprieve from her barrage of questions thanks to the drumline, but the minute they're done, she's right back at it. There's still a block left to walk, and a few times I've thought about breaking into a sprint. I'm not very fast, though, and with my luck, she'd keep pace with me.

"So, did he take you to the gallery yet?"

I feel her question burn down my esophagus and diffuse into a toxic gas within my chest. My breath falters and I feel my lips twitch as they work to keep my smile in place.

"Not sure what you mean," I mutter, not wanting to answer either way.

Claire's elbow brushes against my air as we walk, and I give her a sideways look. She blinks at me slowly, as if trying to message me in code, possibly checking whether I'm all right. I'm sure my voice gave me away. I heard myself. Amy's words threw me, and I know I sounded upset.

"That's his place. Has he shown you the blue room? He must have by now. That's his big move, and you look like you have that glow about you." She lifts a knowing brow, but I maintain a straight face despite her insinuation landing spot on.

"Did he show you the painting of the trees? I love that one. We saw it differently, of course. We saw a lot of things differently." Her specifics cut deep, but I'm somehow strong enough to hold it together and not let my eyes well up.

"Oh, I don't know. Sounds nice," I say, with very little inflection to my words.

"Shouldn't you be somewhere? Else, I mean. Shouldn't you be somewhere else?" Claire's leaning in front of me as we walk, her words darting at Amy. I'm no longer sure whether I'm trudging through my own tension-filled air or the mix Claire just created. I doubt it matters. It's all thick. All uncomfortable.

"I have time. But thank you," Amy bites back.

"*Hmm,* all right. Well, we do have somewhere to be. So if you don't mind—" My roommate links her arm through mine and she tugs me to the left. Before she's able to steal me away completely, though, Amy tugs on my other side and I spin around.

I'm not a rope!

My protest only happens in my head.

"I just wanted to tell you that his hoodie looks nice on you," she says, her bright red lips forming a haughty but tempered grin. Everything about this woman is calculated.

"Thank you," I croak out, kicking myself for speaking at all.

"Yeah, it fits you so much better than it ever fit me." Her smile pushes into her cheeks to punctuate her dig at me, and with a flutter of her fingers, she tucks her pompoms behind her back and prances away.

"She needs my sweatshirt without the BIO part," Claire says, and all I manage for a response is a faint, "Yeah."

CLAIRE SAID she wanted a real friendship. Well, she's getting one with me now, and has been for the last hour. I haven't stopped overanalyzing and venting over the things

Amy said since we got to our seats. I've lumped Logan together with Dalton and all other men and then come up with a million excuses for everything Amy said.

"She's jealous, Rachel. And she may be dating someone else now, but that doesn't mean she wants Logan seeing someone else. She wants him pining after her. It's what we do—all of us. We wish to be the one who got away in every single ex's mind forever across time. That girl is just a little more . . . aggressive." Rachel lifts her half-drunk beer and holds it up, waiting for me to tap my plastic cup into hers.

"Are we toasting?"

"We are," she says. "To benefits of the doubt. And to having hard conversations."

I hold her glare for a beat but knock my cup into hers eventually, knowing she's right. I need to ask Logan about the things Amy said. And I need to ask him again, while looking into his eyes, about how many girls he's taken to the gallery. Depending on that answer, I may need to burn this sweatshirt.

16 /
logan

I'VE STARED at my message left unread by Rachel for at least twenty minutes. I sent it the second I got to the locker room, asking her if she wanted a ride home or to go out with me and the guys. So far, nothing.

I know she stayed for the end. I saw her sitting next to Claire with a minute to go, and there's no way she bailed before seeing that last-second hail Mary pass from Dante to Jax for the win. I was almost willing to root for a touchdown by Cam to come away with a win today. *Almost.*

My roommates are in the mood to celebrate, and I want to be there for them. But also, it's not the same watching the game and having no real input on the outcome. I can't stand being injured. I'm not gracious enough to take a bench role.

I scratch my head and lean back against the wall while I wait on the bench outside the locker room. Cam is one of the first to walk out, and he spends a few minutes with one of the reporters for the student paper. He's beaming while he spits out one-liners about stepping up and filling a role and how the team misses what I bring, but he's doing his best to fill my shoes.

Dude doesn't deserve to *clean* my shoes. I smirk to myself at that thought, and try to focus on it as he heads my direction.

"How's rehab?" He swings his duffle into my knee. It doesn't exactly land soft.

"Running program starts this week. With the bye week, I might be back for game three. Hey, but thanks for keeping my spot warm for me." My self-satisfied grin is joined by a thumbs up.

"Guess that's what I was doing with your girlfriend, too, huh?" His expression is now on the bitter side, his jaw flexing with the slight lift of his chin.

"I have no idea how warm you keep Amy, Cam. Nor do I care." My phone buzzes in my palm, so I drop my gaze to my lap and shield my screen with my palms.

RACHEL: *I'm catching up on my labs tonight. I probably shouldn't have come today.*

My stomach sinks with guilt. I know Cam just said something else likely meant to needle me, but all I can focus on is the tone, or lack thereof, in Rachel's message.

"What, is that her texting you now?" he says, and I snap my gaze up to his. His brow is all bunched up, mouth in an irritable tight line.

"My girlfriend? Yeah, she's texting me. What the fuck do you care?" Seriously, I'm done with this guy.

"*Pfft*, whatever. I was done with her anyway. You can keep her this time." He walks away and I stare at his back, trying to piece together the puzzle pieces he just dropped at my feet.

And then I see Amy.

Shit.

I can't say for sure, but I have a feeling the timing of Amy dropping Cam has something to do with Rachel suddenly regretting spending her day watching me sit on a bench. Granted, I think she has every right to regret watching me sulk, but not because I didn't want her there. And not because someone I dated before I knew what I really wanted made her feel like she should.

Amy's left side is loaded down with her travel bag, stuffed with all her cheer shit. Her joggers are sitting especially low on her hips, rolled down to expose her belly button stud, which I used to find so fucking appealing. I was so basic before I met Rachel. Superficial, just like the girl heading my way with the knowing smirk.

She bunches her hand up at her side to wave hello, and I have a choice. I can wave back and wait for her to reach me. There's no way in hell I'm giving her a ride anywhere, though, and I'm especially not bringing her home with me. I could ask her what the hell happened with her and Cam, the guy who supposedly had it all figured out. His family is still rich as fuck, so I'm not sure why that no longer appeals to her.

Or, I can get up right now and leave.

It takes me about three seconds to play each scenario out in my head, and I'm on my feet before Amy's within earshot. I don't head to my truck, though. Instead, I march to the science building, where the side door is propped open and the stairwell is dimly lit.

I'm surprised how many people are using lab rooms on a Saturday afternoon, but I'm not surprised to hear the classical music spilling out of the open door at the end of the corridor. I step through the door to find her back to me as she holds up a glass tube with yellow liquid and begins to swirl it.

"Please don't drop that," I say in a soft voice. There isn't really a good way to walk in on someone in this situation, and I'm not about to sit here and wait for her to turn around and drop it. Again.

Her shoulders drop, and it takes her a few seconds to speak.

"You have a thing for acid, don't you?" She puts the tube in a rack, then glances at me over her shoulder.

"I think maybe *you* have a thing for acid. I'm simply the guy showing up." I give her a half smile and raise my shoulder. Her laugh is soft—short. Courteous, but not truly amused. She's upset about something.

"I'm sorry I made you fall so far behind." I step fully into the lab, stopping at the first table and running my palm along the immaculately clean surface.

"You didn't make me do anything. I wanted to spend time with you. But now I have to make up for that." Her mouth draws in on one side, and while she's trying to project a smile, all I see is disappointment.

It's the words she chose. *Make up for that.*

"What's going on?" I move around the table as she turns back to her workspace. She's avoiding me. It's obvious. I've always had solid instincts for other people's emotions. I can read a room, read a face. Just like I can read her silence and lack of eye contact.

She flicks the tube with her finger and leans down, studying the light behind the liquid. Her eyes flit to my face now that I'm beside her, and she exhales before straightening her spine.

"What is this?" She glances to her side for a beat then her eyes come back to me. "Are we a fling? Or, is this all part of the plan to make exes jealous, or—"

"Wait a second. Hold up." I stop her with my words and an open palm in the air. She said *exes*. "What did Amy say to you?"

It's the only logical reason for this sudden cold turn in her emotions. She overrode my offer for her to stay home, to choose chemistry over football, with zeal this morning. And now she's sunk with regret. Only Amy has that power.

"She asked me if I'd seen your place yet. Your *favorite* place. She said it was your move." Her mouth slips into a slight frown, her shoulders ticking up with defeat. Her eyes sunken in.

All I can do is fall into her eyes and search for an answer, a reason. *Why would Amy say that?*

"Rachel, I have no idea why—"

Shit.

My face falls.

I do know why. And how. I pinch my brow as I mentally fall back in time, this month last year, in fact. It was a party her sorority threw. We weren't even officially a couple yet, and I was trying to impress her by winning some stupid game of hide-and-seek. I knew the gallery was open late.

"It didn't mean anything." That's all I can say because she doesn't want or need the reasons that led me there. I was trying to score with a cheerleader. She doesn't need to hear that.

"She said the painting of the trees was your favorite." She blinks slowly, her lashes mimicking a door shutting in my face. At least, that's how I feel it.

"Rach—"

Her head falls to the side, eyes welling up.

"It's fine; I'll get over it. It's not like I thought I was anything special. You took another girl there before me. So what? It's your move. And it's a really good one. It just hurt hearing it from her, that's all." Her slight shrug cracks open my chest and I step into her, palm on the side of her face so my thumb can erase the tear that slipped out.

"That's the thing, though, Rachel. You *are* special. And that's not my move. I brought Amy there for a game. I brought you there to share a part of me. You know I called you my girlfriend today? Ironically, I said it to Cam, who I guess is now Amy's ex. Which is probably why she's playing games with you. But I'm not interested in games, or in Amy, or in what Cam thinks. I'm interested in how you feel, right now. It hurts me when you hurt."

She sucks in her bottom lip, but I think I see a smile trying to break through the storm. I cradle her face in both palms and stare deep into her eyes.

"You called me *girlfriend?*"

I let out a faint laugh and rest my head on hers, closing my eyes. My thumbs caress her face.

"I did. To my mortal enemy. I hope that's all right."

Her hands wrap around my wrists.

"It's all right," she says, and I pull my head back enough to meet her gaze. I glance to our right, to the acid tube and chart on her work station.

"Do you *need* to finish this right now?"

She shakes her head and slips on a wry, crooked smirk.

"I'm not really behind. I mean, you know me. I'm way ahead."

I chuckle and step in to press a chaste kiss on her lips, smiling against them.

"Of course you are," I say. "Clean up. There's something I'd like to show you."

I FEEL Rachel's hard stare as we walk toward the gallery.

"Please trust me," I say before she can dig her heels in and protest.

"I'm trying," she says, a hint of skepticism coloring her words.

We step inside and find a few patrons in the space. It's not quite evening, and it's a weekend. It's usually when the gallery is busiest.

"Seeing a lot of you lately, Mr. Ford," Nora teases. "As well as your miss."

"She likes you," I whisper in Rachel's ear.

"He likes you," Nora blurts almost in unison.

Rachel giggles.

"I like him, too," she responds to Nora.

I weave my hand into hers and squeeze her palm.

"You do?"

She nods, and I want to tell her I'm falling in love with her right now, but I should probably win her back completely first. Instead, I settle for her confirmation of liking me.

When we get to the blue room, I lead her directly to the tree painting. When I pull it from the wall, she gasps.

"I don't think you're allowed—"

Her words stop fast. She sees it.

With the painting propped against my stomach, I run my finger lightly over the signature in the bottom right corner: Annabelle Ford.

"Is that your mom?" It's a good assumption, and close.

I shake my head.

"Grandma," I say, and I can feel my face beaming. I hold the piece, careful to keep my hands on the frame. I shouldn't have touched her signature, but I haven't pulled it from the wall in a long time.

"You were close?"

"Incredibly," I say, a slideshow of my amazing childhood speeding through my mind.

I hang the painting back in its space and take a few steps back, Rachel's hand snaking around my bicep.

"She was an artist. Not famous, but she made a living. She taught art, and she let me play with her paints. I was . . . no, I *am* terrible." I close my eyes, shaking my head with a short laugh at the memory of the dogs I attempted to paint when I was in junior high.

"She passed away the summer before I came here. She painted this for me when I was a kid. I felt like it deserved a wall better than the one in my bedroom back home."

Rachel's hand coaxes my gaze to her, and her hand runs along my jaw and cheek as we stare into one another.

"I'm guessing Amy doesn't know about that," she says.

I shake my head but keep our gaze locked.

"I wouldn't dream of sharing that with her," I say, and I mean it. To my core.

Rachel steps up on her toes and presses her lips to mine. I leave my eyes open, taken in by the way her lashes flutter when she kisses me. Like a butterfly, or a bird. She sinks back on her feet and returns her focus to the sea of blue trees, my favorite color, just like her eyes.

"It's beautiful," she says.

I want to tell her I love her.

"So are you."

rachel

WHILE I TRUST my gut most of the time, my brother Casey has never steered me wrong. When I didn't think I could handle the pressure of majoring in the sciences as a woman, he called bullshit and told me I would thrive. And when I almost drove straight home after my first night in a dorm at Tiff, he stayed on the phone with me and promised me I'd find my lane. He also pegged Dalton as a cheater after only meeting him once.

In terms of my life, my brother is batting a thousand.

Which makes what should simply be a nice lunch date with my brother and Logan about a million times more important. And stressful. And I'm going to vomit, I'm so nervous.

"So, this guy's a football player you said?" Casey reiterates. When I told him I was seeing someone on the team, he basically did a cartwheel through the phone.

"He's good. Running back," I add.

My brother nods with a slight air of arrogance, picking up his beer and sipping it slowly as his eyes study me. I figured lunch at Patty's would be casual enough, and since it's a bye week for Tiff, there'd be plenty of seating. It's a little more crowded than I bargained for, though. I didn't consider that the guys would all probably spend their off weekend at the bar watching their competition.

"Hey, Rachel! Good to see you," Dante says, stopping by the high top I'm perched at with my brother and an empty chair—Logan's chair. He gives me a sideways hug then folds his arm over his chest and nods toward my brother with a suspicious glower on his face. Casey is a good looking guy, but also . . . gross. Because, duh.

"Hi, Dante. This is my brother, Casey. He played at Southern."

Dante lights up, probably more with delight that my brother played Division I than the fact I'm not stepping out on Logan.

"Oh, nice! My cousin was there a few years back. Left tackle. Kaholo Riven?"

My brother's on his feet now, as excited as Dante, apparently knowing Kaholo well. They fall into easy conversation that skips from funny stories about Dante's cousin to my brother's favorite games and how they think Tiff will do this season. I take the opportunity to check my breath, and my phone.

LOGAN: *On my way.*

I relax, but it's only temporary. I'm not sure I'm ready for my brother's crystal ball to descend on my relationship.

ME: *Dante and Casey are talking football. Take your time.*

Logan had a scan this morning, and some more physical therapy. He's been going doubly hard, which can sometimes backfire. He's determined to get back on the field next weekend, so I hope he got good news today.

LOGAN: *Now I'm running. Your brother is going to like Dante more.*

I laugh silently to myself then look up through my lashes in time to see them laughing and clapping over some game they both saw three years ago. Logan's right. My brother might.

"He's on his way," I say, breaking up their bro-fest. Dante's eyes catch mine and I try to convey my nerves with a quick flare. He winks at me.

"Ah, great. Man, you're gonna love my boy, Logan. He's such a good guy. This one here makes him better, though. Like, *way* better." Dante gives me another sideways hug and while I appreciate the compliment, the fact he showered me with it has my brother moving him up the ranks for sure. I can see it in his familiar grin.

"Nice to meet you, Dante. Hey, good luck next week!" Casey says, holding out a fist. The two of them bump, then Dante heads toward the back of Patty's to join a few other guys from the team.

"That's a cool dude right there," Casey mumbles over the rim of his mug.

"I knew you'd like him. But I'm not dating him, Case. Give Logan a fair shake."

My brother's gaze hits mine as he takes another sip, and he nods as he puts his mug on the table.

"I will, I will. Promise," he says.

Thank God, Logan walks through Patty's doors a second later, his T-shirt a bit soaked with sweat, and his black joggers pushed up on his calves. He's delicious when he looks like this, post workout, sporty, and a dash tired. He pauses when our eyes meet and he rolls his shoulders back as he draws in a visible breath. My brother catches my fawning expression and follows my gaze to the door, spotting him.

"Oh, you're in trouble," Casey says, chuckling as he turns back to the table to take another drink of beer. His eyes flit to me, his mouth this amused slight curve.

"What does that mean?" My voice is panicked as I lean into him, but all he does is chuckle and get up from his seat, meeting Logan the second he steps up to us.

"Hi. I'm Logan. I'm so sorry I'm late. I'm rehabbing a knee, and apparently I don't get to control the healing process." Logan shrugs as they shake hands, and my two favorite men quake with this strange, quiet, similar laugh.

"How bad do you hate those bands?" my brother asks.

Logan huffs out a laugh then covers his face with his palm.

"Dude, the worst! You know what I did today?"

My brother leans in a touch, interested, but also testing Logan. Everything for the next hour will be a test.

"I was doing this one," Logan begins, bending a knee then drawing in the air with his hand to show how the band was around both his feet.

"Let me guess. You shot that fucker off like a bow and arrow?" My brother's relaxed with him, all part of his test. Making Logan feel at ease, and seeing how he handles bro-speak and swear words.

"Worse! I shot that fucker in my face!" Logan says, pushing his hair back to reveal a still very present welt across his forehead.

"Dude!" My brother actually touches it lightly. Even from here I can see the raised skin.

"I asked our trainer if that was all part of the process," Logan says as my brother drops his hand. He pulls out the third chair and takes a seat, holding up a finger when the waitress walks by. He taps on the side of Casey's mug and leans back as she gets close.

"Make it three for the table," he says. "This round's on me," he adds, slipping our waitress his card and nodding yes when she asks if she should open a tab.

My brother's gaze passes mine behind Logan's back throughout the exchange, and it's hard to tell for certain, but I think that might have just been an impressed simper he's sporting on his lips.

The three of us ease into conversation quickly, Logan and Casey comparing knee injuries for a while, then moving into strategies that might help Logan clear through some of the defenses in our conference. My brother has always aspired to coach one day, and I think he's flexing those muscles with Logan right now. But also, I think there's a genuine bond forming. And respect. Or I'm blinded by love and hoping for a miracle. That could very likely be the case.

We dive into our burgers but the conversation never stops flowing. After a while, Logan calls Dante over to join us, and the three of them sink into a natural comfort that, to anyone new, might seem as if they grew up together and have known each other for years.

Dante excuses himself first, noting that he's off to hang with Meg. I'm guessing they are on again. And while Logan's in the bathroom, I pin my brother down for a report card.

"So, am I still in trouble?" I ask, his warning weighing on my chest from the moment he said it.

My brother drains the dregs of his beer then rotates the glass on the table, his mouth pinched as he falls into his thoughts for a second. His gaze lifts to mine, and there's a look to him that I don't think I've ever quite recognized. I see his adoration for me, the soft smile that stretches the width of his face. But his eyes are heavy, and I swear he seems about to cry.

"You're in worse trouble than I thought," he says, sliding from his seat and pulling my head into his chest, kissing the top.

"What does that mean?" I mumble against his chest, pushing back to look him in the eyes. His expression hasn't changed much, but his smile has grown a tick.

"You'll figure it out," Casey says, pulling his wallet from his back pocket and fishing out forty bucks. He drops it on the table.

"Let Logan know we should do this again sometime," he says, leaving me with that lingering stare before he takes off through Patty's doors.

What the hell?

I push my brother's money toward the center of the table and replay his words. I can tell he liked Logan. I'm sure of it. And if he had any reservations, he would have said something. Casey isn't usually vague.

A warm palm covers my back, and soon Logan's lips are on my cheek.

"Your brother take off?" He sounds edgy, probably bummed he didn't get to say goodbye.

"He had to run," I say, making up an excuse. He didn't have anywhere to go. He simply *ran*.

"Oh. Shit. I hope I did all right. He's a great guy. I see why you two are so close. Your parents are lucky." Casey flips open the bill on the table and sees my brother left cash behind. "Damn, I wanted to buy."

"He's like that. He remembers living on college money. I'm sure he appreciated your offer, though. That was a good move." I study Logan's profile as he gnaws at the inside of his cheek as if he's still worried he blew it despite my reassurance. He fills out the tab, putting the entire bill on his card and leaving my brother's cash for a tip, and I think how Casey would like this move, too. Logan is full of a million kind gestures that nobody ever sees. He's constantly finding ways to shift fortune to others, to share, and to give.

And then it hits me.

I'm in trouble. We're in love.

I'm so much in love with him it almost suffocates me right here in this seat. And I can't hold it in any longer.

"I love you," I blurt out.

Logan's hand freezes mid-air, his eyes blinking slowly as he stares at the bill he just finished signing and the pen he dropped on the table. His mouth tugs up on the side nearest me as his head shifts to look at me sideways. It's the elated smile and twinkling eyes of a kid on his face, and he drops his gaze with a faint chuckle before stepping into me, cupping my face and kissing me before I have a chance to breathe.

Our kiss breaks but he holds me close, his gaze roaming my face. When we connect again, I see the sudden peace deep in his eyes. Like his favorite place, and his favorite painting. Still. Quiet. Settled.

"I love you, too, Shortcake."

18 /
logan

APPARENTLY, the first month of Intro to Chemistry is review. What it's reviewing, since it's a fucking intro, beats me. But review equals easy. Or easier, at least. But now? Now, this shit is hard.

Rachel's been drilling me for my test tomorrow morning, but all I want to do is sleep or rip her clothes off. There's no in-between for me.

I'm exhausted, having gotten up at six this morning to put in tons of rehab and soak in the ice for a while. I'm cleared for the running program. I got the call late last night, so I made a commitment to myself to be cleared for play by Saturday. That means every spare second needs to be spent in preparation. The right food. The right cardio. The right stretching and cool downs. All the ice. The wraps.

And rest.

"Just a short nap. I promise we can set an alarm and I'll wake up," I say, my fingertips crawling along her back. She's lying next to me, propped on her elbows as she grades my latest practice test.

"You can sleep after we go through this one more time,"

199

she says, her serious tone hitting my chest with dread. I failed the practice test again. I can tell.

"Am I getting better?" I roll to my side and rest my head on my palm.

"You're not getting worse," she says, holding up the edge of the paper where she's written a sixty-four. I scored the same the last two times we practiced.

"You seem to be missing the same types of questions, so let me find something we can use to practice that."

I groan, shoving my face into my mattress. Rachel ruffles my hair, and I roll my head to the side so I don't accidentally fall asleep.

"Okay, so no nap. Sex?" I quirk a brow.

Rachel picks up the pillow above her head and throws it in my face. I roll with it but grab her to take her with me, lining her body up on top of mine. My cock is hard from all the dirty thoughts I've had over the last two hours we've been studying.

"I thought you said you were tired?"

I push my hips up, pressing my cock against the center of her legs. She bites her lip, which gives me hope. Her gaze sparkles, her focus shifting from my right eye to my left, so I lift my chin and nip at her bottom lip.

"What's going on in there?" I tap on her temple.

"Well, how about this." She shifts, pushing herself up so she's straddling me. My hands drop to her hips and hold her down as I push up again. We're both wearing cotton shorts, which is basically nothing with how hard I am.

"I'm going to ask you some questions and when you get one right, I'll give you a prize." She rolls her hips, grinding into me, and I let my eyes flutter shut.

"Fuuuuuck. Are they going to be hard questions?"

She drops her palms on either side of my head and touches her lips to mine.

"Yes, Logan," she whispers against me. "They are going to be . . . very . . . hard."

I flip her to her back, pinning her under me and pressing my forehead against hers. I shift lower, grab the center of her T-shirt with my teeth, and attempt to tug it up. She pulls it from my grip though and palms the top of my head.

"Uh uh uh. No cheating." She squirms out from under me as I grumble, like a whiney baby. I want her pussy so bad. And I hate chemistry so much.

"Fine. But give me a few seconds to focus. I need my blood back up to my brain," I joke, though I'm not entirely kidding.

Rachel flips through the new notebooks she started for me.

"Ah, okay. Here," she begins, stopping on one of the pages she flagged with a purple tab.

"Shoot," I say, fighting the urge to adjust myself under my shorts. There is no calming my dick down. I better get these questions right.

Rachel flips to a blank page and writes down a compound for me.

"Give me the empirical formula," she says.

My eyes narrow on her writing, and I search my mind for every single step we've practiced. I overthink these, and I know that's part of my problem.

"Okay, give me that pen," I say, holding my palm out as I shift to prop myself on my side.

If the substance contains 1.11 g of Se and 1. 6 grams of F, what is the formula? It takes me the entire expanse of the paper and two false starts, but after looking up the weights for fluorine and selenium and run them through the process, I come up with SeF_6. I push the paper toward her and hold my breath.

"Oh, no! I'm so sorry, Logan. But . . ."

I'm about to dive back into the mattress and scream when Rachel slips her T-shirt off and tosses it to the floor. I lunge for her, but she holds me back with a stiff arm, her grin crooked. Fucking she-devil.

"I'm sorry but you're going to have to do this next one while I sit here like this."

My gaze drops to her tits, her nipples barely covered by the lace bra. I want to bury my face between them.

"Give me the next one now," I growl.

She giggles, but flips another page and writes me another formula. I snag it and click my pen anxiously, my eyes scanning it. I finish this one faster and push the notepad back to Rachel. I adjust myself, leaving my hand in my shorts and wrapped around my cock. If we don't fuck soon I'm going to have to take care of things myself.

"Very good, Logan," Rachel praises, unclasping her bra with one hand and letting her tits spring free. I roll to my back, staring at her, as I stroke myself and bite my fist.

"You better have that next one ready," I say.

Rachel giggles again, and it's fucking torture to hear. "*Grrrr*, you're so cruel, all flirty and naked and shit," I mutter, taking the notepad before she's finished writing. I fill in the rest, working my way through the problem while she laughs at me and slips off my bed.

"Done," I announce, pushing it toward her. I shift so I'm sitting on the side of my bed, stroking myself while she stands topless in the middle of my room and reviews my work. She's careful not to give anything away until finally dropping the notepad on the floor and meeting my gaze with her hazed eyes.

"Very, very good, Logan," she hums, her thumbs hooking in the band of her shorts. She slides them down her hips and I realize only then that she's not wearing any panties. She's completely bare. Fuck me.

Fuck me now.

"Come here." I call her with a finger, my other hand wrapped around my cock, which I have now completely pulled out of my shorts.

Rachel takes long, languid steps toward me, and I run my fingers through her wet folds the second she's within reach. She steadies herself with her hands on my shoulders and I let go of myself to grab her ass and pull her close enough to take her nipple in my mouth. My fingers sink into her soft, warm pussy and she moans. Her head falls back at one point and her hands clutch my shoulders.

I brace myself when she steps back, leaning toward my night stand to grab a condom, but she grabs my wrists and shakes her head.

"Uh . . ." my brow hitches up.

"Trust me?" She throws that ask back at me, and while I do, I'm not quite sure I trust myself to pull out before we risk something.

I give a hesitant nod, and Rachel bends forward, her hands grabbing at my waistband. She tugs my shorts and boxers down to let my cock spring free. Before I have time to question anything else, she drops to her knees and takes me deep in her mouth.

"Oh fu-uck." My words stutter as my breath is knocked out of my chest from the feel of her lips wrapped round my cock. My hands sink into her hair as she sucks me, sliding her mouth up and down. I start to work my hips, careful not to push too deeply, and Rachel moans with her full mouth.

"Your mouth is almost as good as your pussy," I say a second before her lips let go with a popping sound. Her hand wraps around my shaft and she strokes me a few times, looking up with raw, swollen lips and a pleased grin on her face. She runs her thumb over my tip and I feel myself flex in her grip.

"I want you to come in my mouth," she says, and I swear with those words on her lips I'm in danger of doing it right now in her palm.

"Yes, please," I say, my voice vibrating with my racing pulse.

"Stand up," she commands, and I'm quick to obey.

Stepping out of my shorts and boxers, I pull my shirt over my head and toss it to my bed. Rachel aligns herself with me, one hand on my hip while she grabs my cock with her other. She strokes me a few more times before glancing up to stare at me with her big, blue eyes while my dick slides into her mouth.

"Goddamn, are you beautiful," I say, triggering a smile that forces her lips to tighten and move. I wrap her hair around my hand and hold her head in place, then rock my hips, fucking her mouth until she whimpers every time my tip hits the back of her throat. She pulls back for air a few times but always comes back, her tongue teasing my tip, drinking my pre-cum until I'm unable to hold back any longer.

My breathing grows more ragged, and Rachel braces both hands on my hips, pulling me in and out, guiding me so I'm not afraid to be rough. I push in as far as her mouth will take me, and my pumps become faster and harder until, finally, I fill her mouth with my semen. She's so full with me that she has to wipe her chin as she falls back on her heels, swallowing with a proud grin.

I fall back on the bed, my head suddenly light and my chest soaring with euphoria.

"Fuck, that was good," I say, my arms out to the sides and breath still panting.

I lift my chin as she stands, her naked curves teeming with the need to be touched.

"Come here. Let me please you," I say, holding up a hand but staying on my back.

She shimmies toward me, placing one knee on the bed then straddling me. I slide down as my hands grab her ass and move her so she's directly above my mouth, and without pause I drag my tongue along the length of her folds, stopping at her swollen click and sucking her tender skin in.

"Oh, my God, Logan!" Her hands flatten against the wall and her legs quake, so I grip her thighs and ass harder.

"Hold still, Shortcake," I say, retracing my path down and up again, each time flicking her clit with my tongue and causing tiny cries of pleasure to fall from her lips.

I push my tongue inside her, pumping her with it a few times before falling back into the pattern from before, and soon her hips begin to rock. She glides against my mouth, writhing above me as my tongue circles her center and dips inside.

"Loga—" She can't finish my name when the first wave comes. I hold her open and on me as I cover her pussy with my mouth and suck and lick through every pulse. She hums the word please over and over, her hands sliding down my wall and eventually grabbing hold of my hair, and I drink in her taste.

When the quakes finally stop, she shifts so her head is on my chest, her hair stuck to my skin. I tickle her arm softly for several minutes until she finally adjusts her head and peers into my eyes. I tuck my chin and smile at her.

"Too bad you can't bring me into your test like a study guide," she jokes.

I laugh hard and gaze up at the ceiling, remembering the look on her face as she took me in her mouth. So sexy and so trusting. I don't think I've ever wanted to be so completely owned by someone in my life.

"I don't think they'd allow you in the test room," I laugh out, again tucking my chin to meet her eyes.

"Cuz I'm naked?" she teases.

I chuckle but also give in and look at the rest of her. My cock flexes against her arm.

"Yeah, Rachel. Because you're naked."

LOGAN WOKE up early to study more before his test. Since I really do have some catching up to do in the lab now, I spent extra hours working on my hypothesis. It's morphed into something fairly unique, and I'm excited to tell Logan more about it. He was really the spark for my final idea.

I'm adding to research on pheromones. What started as a search for a real love potion has morphed into how pheromones are used to communicate, with the question being whether certain human scents carry messages. My work is really a cross-over study into psychology, so I've had to shore up a lot of my research on that end. I was able to conduct a video chat interview with a psychologist in London famous for this research. My morning has been so busy I don't realize it's nearly time for Logan's class to let out.

I clean up my station and pull my satchel together, and I'm tucking away my research when I notice Dr. Callahan's card. Leaning into my workspace, I turn it over in my hand a few times, not sure whether I want to throw it away or drop it back into my bag to deal with later. I was so put off by her insolence at the dinner party that I'm no longer in awe of her work. I've always had a hard time when people I respect behave badly. My opinion is easily swayed against people. It's so much harder to earn my favor.

My phone buzzes in my bag, so I drop the card in and trade it out to check my phone.

LOGAN: Library. STAT

Oh, no. I hope he did all right. I told him to request a re-test if he wasn't satisfied with the first score. It's not something many students take advantage of, but all Chem 101 courses offer one re-test. I know it's in the syllabus because I put it there.

I tug my bag up my arm and tell him I'm on my way. I make it to the hallway when I hear my name called from an office a few doors down.

"Yes?" I respond, backtracking a few steps and craning my neck to attempt to see who is in the adjunct office. Dr. Combs steps out and startles me.

"Sorry," he says, his serious face attempting to form what I think is a smile. And is that . . . is he laughing?

"Boo!" he adds on.

"Uh, yeah. You got me," I say, moving into the office where he and one of the biology fellows seem to have uncorked some pretty expensive-looking brandy.

"Oh, I see," I chuckle.

"*Shh*," my professor blubbers. He's toasty, and his very pretty companion isn't doing much better.

"I wouldn't say a word," I say, holding my finger to my mouth as a promise to keep his secret. It's actually nice to see this human side to him.

"I heard you in your lab, and I wanted to make sure you

got this while you still had time to respond." He moves to the leather sofa and slides his coat out of the way to unveil a light purple envelope. I get dizzy at the sight of it but manage to keep my feet under me.

"I didn't apply," I say, taking the envelope in my hand as I lean my weight against the wall of this suddenly small-feeling office.

"Well *someone* applied for you," he says, his words a bit loopy.

"Yeah, I guess," I say, holding the envelope up to the light.

"Oh, go on. Open it!" He moves to sit on the desk, uncapping the brandy to pour more into his tumbler. I feel like maybe he's had enough. But also, he is in his fifties and what the fuck do I know.

"Oh, the abroad program is wonderful!" his companion says, in a thick South African accent. I might be attracted to her at this point.

"That's where we met, silly," Dr. Combs says, holding his glass up to toast her. The two of them are quiet for a beat then burst into laughter.

Now that I'm the only person in the room to not have attended the abroad program, I thank him for giving me the letter and bow out of the office with my shrinking and frail ego. My heart is racing as I slide down the hallway, the weight of this letter like a solid gold knife heavy and cutting my hand. I clutch it, crinkling it as I pick up my pace and finally slip into the library doors where Logan is waiting for me at our usual study table.

"Well, I didn't fail," he says, stepping up and presenting a test with a seventy-two written on top.

"Oh, that's—" I slump into the closest chair and drop my

hands to the table, resting my forehead on my arm. "That's amazing, Logan."

"Rachel, are you okay? What's wrong!" He's at my side, kneeling, which is nice because if I lift my head right now the world will tilt. I'm hyperventilating. Panic attacks. I haven't had one since, well, since the last purple envelope showed up in my life.

I slide it toward him from under my hand and he stands, reading it.

"Hey, this is that program you wanted to go to. Is it happening again? Are you in?" His genuine excitement at what may or may not be possible squeezes my heart. He's so positive, and all I can think is how this must be a cruel joke. And how I don't want to leave him if what's in this envelope is another chance. I no longer want to go, and it's crazy to give up on something like that for a guy. But he's that guy for me. The kind you make adjustments for. The kind you stick around for.

The kind who finds something better when you're gone.

"You want me to open it?" he asks.

I glance sideways and up, still not quite convinced I'm ready to sit up tall.

"Sure." I shrug, but quickly recant. "Actually, no. Throw it away."

He laughs and moves back to his chair, turning it sideways so he's close enough to swoop in and catch me if I faint while I'm in this chair.

The crisp rip of the envelope is followed but the quieter sound of paper being unfolded. "Dear Miss Edwards," he begins.

"No, not out loud. I can't . . . not out loud." I draw my hands in to shield my face, holding my breath while Logan gets silent. The longer he takes to speak, the more anxious I become, until finally, I lift my head, feeling that so much time has passed he must be reading a lot of bad news. Or a sales pitch.

The library lights are brighter than normal for a few seconds, but eventually my focus adjusts on him, his lips moving as his eyes scan across the page. A slight smile plays at the side of his mouth.

Oh, my God.

"Rachel." I love the way he says my name.

His eyes flit up to my face, and that one-sided smile becomes two-sided.

"You've been invited for six months of study. It's not spring, but right after graduation. I mean, I don't know exactly what some of this stuff is that they're talking about, but it sounds pretty spectacular. You have to do this!" He flattens the pages on the table and I nervously drop my gaze and turn them to face me.

The German Institute for Chemical Biology and Future Sciences would like to invite you to be a part of our prestigious post-graduate studies program. Classes will commence on June 1, and complete at the end of the calendar year.

I speed read the rest, noting the credits I would accrue toward a master's degree and the guaranteed entrance to any program I want. The catch? I still need a whole lot of money that I don't have.

"Wow," I say, folding the pages, my focus lost somewhere between me and the table. I'm swimming through the problems, through all of the hurdles that stand between me being here and being there. And then I look up and find the biggest obstacle of all. Green eyes, soft smile, strong arms, and this ability to make me feel alive. More alive than I knew I could.

"So? You're going, right?"

I open my mouth, but without knowing what my real answer is, all I can do is exhale and plead with my eyes.

"Rach," he says, his tone full of expectations. He's not wrong, but also, I can't focus on this right now. It's too much.

"I know. And I'm taking this seriously. It's a lot for me, though. And it's also . . . well, a lot of money." I don't like talking about finances. My family has always been so private about that stuff, probably because my dad has gone through his fair share of economic ups and downs. There was a time he almost lost the store when I was in high school, and Casey probably wouldn't have gone to college at all if it weren't for football. That my dad and brother have been able to turn the family business into two stores is a big deal. But they had to take out some hefty business loans to get it done. And the thought of me taking one on too, just so I can study overseas, has never felt like a fair thing to ask. Even though the burden would be mine, the stress would fall on my parents. It's how the Edwards family is built. We share hardships and joys.

"Okay. That's fair," Logan says, scooting his chair closer and sliding his palm across the table to me. I cover his hand with mine and mouth, "Thanks."

A few people take over the tables next to us, sliding a pair together for a study group meeting. I reach for Logan's test, finally giving it the attention it deserves.

"I'm really proud of you, by the way," I say, scanning his answers and spotting the ones he missed. Out of habit, I wince with disappointment and Logan notices.

"I miss an easy one?" he asks.

I waggle my head.

"Not easy, but it's one you got right, well, last night." An impish smile touches my lips and I feel my face warm.

"I told you I needed to bring you in as a study aid," he teases.

Our hands have begun to intertwine on top of the table while I look over his test.

"Maybe you can get one of those exceptions next time," I say, forcing my eyes on his test instead of him. If I look at him, I know he's going to have heat in his eyes. And I'm feeling weak.

A few more people take over seats at the tables near us, and the discussion is louder than our favorite librarian usually allows.

"Do you want to try to take it again? Or save your retest in case you need it later," I suggest.

Logan twists his paper so the words are facing him as he chews at his lip.

"I'm not really eager to take this one again. And I did pass." His fingertips have started to roam along my wrist, his thumb grazing the inside of my arm. Every touch from him is electric. Distracting. Exactly what I need.

"You know," I begin, looking up through my lashes. I check to see how engaged our neighbors are in their discussion, then shift my focus back to Logan, his hair a bit messy, eyes tired from a long night, wearing his dark blue hoodie and black joggers. He takes up so much space sometimes, and yet moves with this grace that lets him slip in and out of places without notice. Not that women don't notice him everywhere he goes. He's classically handsome, and his body is like dangling a steak in front of a bulldog.

"Yes, Rachel," he says, jarring my attention out of my brief fantasy and back to my very possible present. His eyes have that streak to them, the slight squint that indicates he's willing to be bad as long as it involves me. His smirk says so, too.

My stomach tightens and my core clenches at the thought of what I'm about to say. How I've gone from a girl who rarely leaves her room to one who wants to sample the full menu of library sexcapades is beyond me. But I've changed. And more than I want to study in another country, I want to know what is so special about having sex in the stacks of the Tiff Library.

"It's a little loud in here. I was thinking maybe we could find another place to . . . study." I suggest, putting a very obvious inflection on the word.

Logan slides his paper toward him and reaches down to slip it into his backpack. He zips his bag up and stands, reaching for my hand. I barely have time to shove my grad program letter into my satchel before Logan's hand is woven through mine and he's leading me to the stairwell in the back of the library.

He flings the door open and leans over to check the steps leading down to the basement and the ones that climb up five stories. Satisfied it's quiet, he turns into me, chest to chest, walking me backward until my back is flat against the door.

"Do you want to study? Or do you want to know what it's like to be fucked in the stacks, Rachel?"

My knees quake. I lift my chin and meet his stare.

"I don't need to study. So I guess I want to get fucked." I meet his filthy mouth with my own. His eyes flicker and his mouth crashes into mine a second later, his kiss rough and deep.

He breaks away after a few seconds and winds our hands

together again, barking, "Come with me," as he leads me up to the very top floor. We slip in the door and wind through several rows of shelves, most of them filled with texts in other languages and old reference books with layers of dust. There's an entire section devoted to *The Times* and another for old reels of film. It's like a time machine, an entire floor that's the last vestige for some mediums. It's the part of the library that's rarely visited, but there are people on this floor. We passed at least four, all searching for some obscure text that can't be found online.

Logan leads me down an aisle lined with classical studies, older copies of books like *Crime and Punishment* and *The Iliad*, and without warning, he turns me around, tossing his bag and mine to the floor, before he smothers me against the books' spines. His mouth covers mine as he unfastens the snap and lowers the zipper on my jeans. His hand sinks into my panties and his finger is inside of me in a breath. I cry into his kiss, my center already pulsing from his touch. He must feel how close I am because he slows, slipping out of me and sliding his fingers along my wet skin.

"You've been thinking about this, haven't you," he says in a raspy, hushed tone, his lips brushing against my ear. His breath is hot and sends shivers along my neck.

"So much," I confess.

Logan continues to tease me with one hand while he pulls his wallet from his pocket with the other. He takes out a condom and drops his wallet to the floor, holding the packet with his teeth. He pushes his joggers down and pulls out his hard cock, then lifts his chin and grunts lightly, I think asking me to take the condom and open it. I pull it from his teeth and tear the packet open, slipping the condom out and rolling it over his length. His cock is hot to the touch, and I swear it's harder than it's ever been.

"Turn around," Logan commands, slipping his hand out from between my legs and guiding me to the right angle as I grip the shelf I'm now facing. He tugs my jeans and panties down, exposing my bare ass to the cold library air, and I gasp out loud. If anyone is remotely close to us, they'll hear me. And the thrill of that turns me on even more.

"Arch your back," he says at my ear, and I lower myself a little, giving him access. He plunges his fingers into me first, stretching me wide before grabbing his cock and guiding it to my entrance, sliding in slowly at first.

I cry out louder this time, but quickly cover my mouth with my hand as he sinks in, the angle so different—so incredible.

"You like this?" he asks.

"Uh uh," I whimper, his hips rocking into me again.

"Tell me," he says, and I flush with heat, my body beading with instant sweat and chills all at once.

"I like the way you fuck me," I say, giving him the dirty words I know he wants. His skin slaps against my ass as he picks up speed, pumping into me faster, one hand snaking up my sweater and under my bra, the other rubbing my clit in the front.

Logan rolls my nipple, pinching hard as he pumps deep inside me, and my voice wavers as I crane my neck to look over my shoulder. All I can see is the hard line of his jaw and his full lips. He kisses the side of my mouth as I beg for him to go faster.

"Yes," I plead, my orgasm building from every sensation. No part of me is left untouched. My breasts are tingling with ache, my clit is swollen, my pussy full with his width. His breath is ragged against my jaw, and I feel the need to come build even more between my legs.

"I'm so close, Logan. Please, I'm so close," I beg, knowing he's close too. His cock flexes inside me, and I arch my back in an attempt to take him deeper, to feel him hit my most sensitive spot inside, and as he grunts with his orgasm I feel my own peak. Logan lifts himself into me, clutching my body against his as he drives himself in, making sure I'm satisfied even after he's done.

He waits until I'm done breathing hard, his cock pulsing inside of me as his hand works out every last second of ecstasy. Finally, he slips out of me, pulling off and tying the used condom and pulling his pants back up, making sure he has his wallet. He stands guard as I adjust my jeans and straighten my bra and sweater, then picks up my bag and tucks it over his shoulder along with his own backpack.

Just as quickly as we entered the fifth floor we disappear back down the stairs, neither of us saying a word. But before we walk out the stairwell door, Logan circles my wrist and urges me to wait with him just inside the door. Gone is the rough and hungry running back, and present is the sweet man who wants to make sure I'm all right.

"That was incredible," I say, anticipating his need to hear that I wanted all of that. He brushes his thumb over my bottom lip then kisses me softly.

"I love you," he says, his eyes still closed as he breaks away.

And I know right now that if Logan and I can make this work, if we stay together, he will have to force me to leave the country, leave him. And even if he begs, I doubt I'll go.

logan

I MADE the mistake of telling my mom I met someone. I didn't want to freak Rachel out, but that's the real reason my parents are driving up to watch the game this weekend. My mom couldn't care less about watching me play football. It makes her a nervous wreck. But if there's a girl to meet, Olivia Ford will bust right through a halftime show to get her hands on the girl who caught her pumpkin's eye.

She'll be sure to call me that, too. At least once. Probably twice. *Pumpkin*. She knows I hate it. Fine, okay. There is a part of me that loves it, but that part is in private, like when I'm helping her pull the turkey out of the oven on Thanksgiving. That's when it's called for. Not when I'm introducing the only girl who's ever made me want to be a better version of myself.

I'm afraid she's going to drive Rachel absolutely nuts. But there's no way around it, because they have to meet. I love Rachel, and I can't keep her hidden from my mom forever.

She spent the week in my bed. I mean, not the entire time —we did go to class, and I went to PT while she worked late on labs. But every night, her body was next to mine. The warmth of having her here, being able to reach over when I woke up just to feel her, it was a comfort I've never understood. Things feel possible. Like I'm on top for once. Not on a bubble.

She's been watching me dress this morning. She woke up early and went to her place to get ready for the big meet and greet with the Edwards family before coming back to my place. Even my sister is coming, though I think she wanted a reason to ditch the husband and twins for a weekend. Lola's also nosy, though, and she likes to watch Mom embarrass me in front of girls.

"Are you sure you're okay on that knee?" Rachel asks, stopping short of poking it with her finger.

I give her a sideways glance and hold my gaze on her for a few quiet seconds, my open-mouthed smile caught.

"What? I'm worried about you. That's all."

I drop my compression sleeves into my gym bag and walk over to her, stepping between her legs and pulling her head into my stomach so I can hold her. I kiss her head.

"I was worried about my mom making you crazy today, but I'm starting to think you're going to get along swimmingly."

She links her hands behind my back and twists her head so her chin is against my stomach, her eyes blinking wide, blue and beautiful. She's wearing braids today, so I slide my hands down her hair and tug gently.

"You know how I love these," I say.

"*Mmm hmm,*" she hums, her chin pushing into my diaphragm as she nods. I slide my hand down her jawline and cup her chin, holding it in place before bending down to kiss her. I nip at her lip, a nonverbal promise of how I intend to celebrate a win today.

My phone buzzes on my nightstand, so I pull myself away from Rachel and check the message.

"My parents are early. Not a shock at all," I laugh out.

"Oh, man," Rachel says through an exhale. She stands and stretches her arms up as she shoots me a toothy, overexaggerated grin. She's adorable in overalls that roll at her ankles, blue sneakers, and a yellow long-sleeved shirt. She's wearing contacts today, though she's cute in her glasses too.

"They're going to love you," I reassure. She's putting up a good front but I can tell underneath she's pretty nervous.

"I wish I knew how to make a potion to guarantee that," she jokes.

I roll my eyes at her nerdy chem humor.

After zipping up my bag and shoving my feet into my slides, I link our hands and promise I won't let go until she has to shake my dad's hand.

"Mom will hug you," I warn as we walk out to my truck.

Rachel sits on her hands for the entire trip to the stadium. I don't mention it because I know it's her nerves. She does this move a lot when she's feeling out of place. It's her coping tool, and I respect it.

We pull into the player lot, and I spot my parents' SUV near the suites entrance. Tiff reserves one of the boxes for family and friends every season. When my dad comes alone, he likes to sit in the seats, as close to the fifty as possible. He indulges in the luxury when my mom tags along, and I'm sure Lola insisted they take the offer. My sister never passes up freebies.

"Wait here and I'll walk you up," I say, squeezing Rachel's shoulders and kissing her forehead before jogging to the team entrance. I let the training staff know I'll be right in for prep and remind Coach that I've been cleared as I pass his office. By the time I get back to Rachel, she's sitting on my tailgate, swinging her legs and staring at her phone. I pause for a second so I can remember her this way. Her head pops up just then, catching me, and she holds out her palms.

"Are you torturing me?" she shouts, kicking off from my truck and pushing the tailgate closed. She walks toward me, her hands shoved in her pockets as she scans left and right. It's early yet, so there's not much traffic. I think she's looking for somewhere to run.

"I was taking a mental picture," I say when she finally reaches me. Our hands link, just as I promised. I hold on tight and kiss her knuckles.

"Yeah? You want to remember what I look like shitting my pants?"

My laugh is swift and loud.

"I can't believe you said that," I say, shaking my head.

"Yeah, well, I can't believe I'm meeting your parents. And that I'm here, at a football game. Holding hands with the hottest football player at Tiff. And he actually wants me here."

I stop at her words, tugging her into me so I can take both of her hands in mine.

"Hey," I say, my gaze on her worried expression. I shake our hands lightly, as if jostling her will help whatever this is all about.

"Sorry," she says, her voice vibrating through the single word. "I'm just . . . it's hitting me, is all. I'm not this girl. I'm used to spending my Saturdays on extra-credit experiments, or not leaving my dorm room at all and binging—"

"*The Office*," I finish for her. "Yes, I know." She relaxes a touch, her arms looser as I swing our hands back and forth.

"I want to make something abundantly clear to you right

now." I let go with my right hand to graze her cheek with my thumb and tuck a stray hair behind her ear. I leave my palm against her cheek, and she leans into it. I love it when she does this.

"I am in love with you. I have *always* admired you. There's not a moment when I didn't think you were the cute girl with strawberry hair. And when I found out how smart you were I was so jealous. I didn't fail my chemistry class on purpose but if I knew that's how I'd finally have the chance to get to know you, I would have gone right up to the professor on day one and said give me an F and a tutor to try again. And it would have had to be you. "

Her lids are heavy as a tears form in the corners of her eyes. I lean forward and kiss them away, my lips soft against her skin.

"You, Rachel Edwards, are too good for me. And I'm not this guy. I'm used to pounding my chest for an hour and listening to heavy metal to get into the frame of mind that I want to crush someone. I spend my Saturdays with a bunch of dudes who all prep the same way. I risk concussions for a stupid game that I fucking love. But not as much as I fucking love you, so get those thoughts out of your head. You might not feel like you belong here, but it's only because you're better than all of us."

She breaks our clasped hands to swing her arms around my neck and leap into me, and I catch her, swinging her around a few times in a massively tight hug.

"Thank you," she mutters into the crook of my neck. "I love you too."

And that's all I need.

I carry her for a few steps, mostly to coax her to laugh and shake off those tense feelings that gripped her heart and mind. Her body softening in my embrace, I set her on her feet when we reach the walkway that leads to the suite entrance, and when I hold the door open for her with one hand and hold her tight with my other, she gives me a squeeze.

"Pumpkin!"

Now, it's my turn to have tightness in the chest.

"Hi, Mom," I say, keeping a hold on Rachel even as my mom sweeps her arms around me. I hug her with my free arm and wince when she kisses my cheek with her plum lipstick-covered mouth.

"She did that on purpose, huh?" I say to my sister. My mom loves going big. Since the first time she left a lip print on my cheek my freshman year of high school, she has made sure to always have that stuff freshly applied to her mouth in time to mark me as hers. It's a mother's stamp, and it serves as a warning to everyone that she's close by.

"Good to see you, son," my dad says, stepping in while my mom admires her handiwork on my cheek. I shake my father's hand while my mom tries with very little effort to smudge her mark away.

"Mom, Dad . . . Lola"—I pause and take a deep breath— "This is Rachel."

"Hi, it's nice to meet you," Rachel says, giving my hand one final squeeze before she lets go and steps out in front of me.

From this point on, she's in my mother's hands. The plum mark of approval lands on her cheek in a matter of seconds, and my dad is making jokes at my expense within the first minute. My sister promises to share all of the most embarrassing stories with her during the game by the time I have to leave them and head into the trainer's room.

I get a text as I walk across the stadium grounds.

RACHEL: *Your mother is worried about your knee. I love her.*

I don't bother typing back, and while my eyes roll over the fact I have managed to amass *two* overprotective women in my life, I also love it.

MY KNEE IS WRAPPED TIGHTER than those mummies we studied in my world history class. I told our trainer I couldn't feel it and he said, "Good." I suppose he's right. I haven't felt pain in days. My sprints were on track all week. And I feel as though I can take a hit and keep going. The fear didn't stick, which is always the worry with a sports injury. Getting hurt can change the psyche. And football is a game you can't play with caution.

I keep checking the box, not that I can see much from down here on the sidelines, but I can at least tell where my family is. *Where Rachel is.* They've taken the four seats in the very middle, near the front. I'm sure that was my father's choice. While Mom came to talk to Rachel all afternoon, my dad came for the off chance I get to see the field today.

"Stay ready, Ford," Coach says after halftime as the offense heads out on the field without me.

I nod, chewing at my mouthpiece. I *am* ready. I'm more ready than that asshat he's marching out there in my spot play after pathetic play. I keep that shit in, though. Coach doesn't appreciate second-guessing, especially when it's from a selfish place. Which mine is. I want the time. I want the ball.

I want the chance.

Our offense goes out again, and after Dante moves them upfield thirty yards with one hell of a pass to Jax, the next play results in a turnover because Cam Ledger doesn't know how to protect the fucking ball. It gets punched out at the fifty, giving King State excellent field position. We're tied, and a score here will put them up.

"I need you in there," Dante grumbles as he steps in next to me and pushes his helmet up on his forehead. He sprays water in his mouth and swishes, then spits. "I'm fucking eating grass because nobody can block. All Ledger wants to do is run the ball. He doesn't know how to throw offensive blocks. And his hands are literally jelly. I mean, what the fuck! How do you drop that?"

I shake my head and bite my tongue.

"I know, I know. You can't say nothin'. But I sure can," my friend says, slapping my back and dropping his helmet down before striding down the line.

He's right. It's not as if our backup quarterback can throw half as far as he can, and with a tie game against a team we were projected to slaughter, Coach might break his rule about players stepping on his toes mid-game.

I watch from my periphery as Dante's hands flail, his head moving with his words. My roommate doesn't mince words and he talks a lot of shit on the field. Coach has tuned him out most of the last two years because he knows he can't shut him up, but I hope this time his words sink in.

Coach finally turns his head, but his mouth doesn't open. And his expression does not look like that of a man glad to receive input.

Shit.

I turn my focus back to the field and jump a few times, pumping blood through my legs. It takes King State six minutes to score, running the third quarter down to two minutes left. I glance up at the box, my family and Rachel still in their seats. It's hard to tell for sure, but I think my dad is leaning on the railing, his hands clasped. I fill in the details from memory, how he chews at the side of his mouth and twitches anytime our team fucks up. My dad isn't a vocal sports parent, but he sure wears his disappointment when his son isn't used the right way.

"I said my piece," Dante says, finally making his way back to my side while the special teams unit rushes out to try to make up for lost time with a killer return.

"And how'd that go?" I ask.

"Well, he didn't tell me to get out of his face, so . . ."

I laugh hard, but honestly? That is encouraging.

Our return team gets a few extra yards, but Dante has his work cut out for him. He heads out to the field, Ledger still in my position, and within seconds the ball is loose again from another drop. This time, our team manages to recover Cam's fumble, and we somehow get six yards on it. But I guess that's the last straw for Coach.

I'm on the field in seconds, Cam throwing a baby fit that sends one of the coolers of Gatorade to the ground along with a table full of towels and cups. The team managers are all scrambling to clean it up, and Coach is barking at him for making a scene.

My grin is massive. So big it hurts my cheeks. Karma is queen.

"Alright, are we ready to put this away now?" Dante slaps my chest a few times in the huddle.

"Yessir!" I nod, taking friendly hits from the rest of the squad.

Dante calls my favorite play, where I fake right and run a

sweep to the left. The Kings defense doesn't seem to realize I've subbed in, or maybe they assume I'm not up to my best stuff because I don't have anyone seriously tailing me. The ball is snapped and my legs take over, tricking the tackles and knocking them off balance as I juke and take the ball. I make it fifteen yards before I'm knocked out of bounds. I bounce back up to show how little I'm hurt, and rush to the huddle again.

"How'd that feel?" Dante asks.

"Like we're playing against a bunch of toddlers. Give me the ball," I growl.

"Ayyy, yeah. That's our boy!" Dante calls another play for me, a short dump pass that I take for another fifteen, and I feel like my legs are fire.

We run it again, and I find the end zone with ease, spinning the ball in the grass and holding up my arms as Dante rushes at me. We bump chests and I run sideways, scanning the box for her. My dad's on his feet with his hands up, so I give him a fist that he mimics, but then to the right, I catch another one in my honor. Rachel is jumping. My mom is hugging her. And my life is definitely out of the bubble.

I LOVE Octobers in the Midwest.

Yes, it's cold. But the colors make up for everything. This is when I wish I did something that didn't involve a lab. In a perfect world, I'd work in a lab made of glass in the middle of a meadow. Probably not the most conducive setting for a controlled environment, what with the shift in sunlight and massive costs to maintain a glass house one temperature. But if I'm fantasizing about such things then I'd probably be stupid wealthy in this scenario, so I'm sure I can have it built to spec.

Halloween is coming up. It's another one of those life events that I've usually taken a pass on. Growing up, I relied on easy costumes and my brother to do most of the doorbell ringing and candy hunting. I don't have much of a sweet tooth, so as I got older, the motivation waned. I became the pre-teen who passed out chocolate and complimented kids for talking their parents into buying whatever Marvel character costume was hyped for the season.

Tonight, though? I'm going to a Halloween party. At a frat

house. With my football player boyfriend. Maybe this is my costume—no one would believe it's my reality.

"I'm sure you look great. Let me see," Logan says from the other side of my closet door.

"Don't be shy. He's going to love it," Claire promises. I invited her to the party with us, even with my history of having third wheels steal my boyfriends—*okay, so it happened once.* But she opted for her own party with her dragon-fire friends. Her name for them, not mine.

"All right, but don't laugh," I plead as I exit the closet in the pink babydoll dress and puffy baker's hat. Strawberry shortcake, in all her glory.

"Oh, my God. This is my fantasy come true," Logan says the second his eyes hit me.

I grimace, but before I can give in to the desire to cover up and shelter myself all night, Logan hooks his finger in the neckline of my outfit and tugs me into him.

"Don't you dare run and hide. You are adorable," he says, himself dressed as a sailor from the fifties. We both picked each other's costumes, and naturally this was his choice. I went through a few options but ultimately settled on the retro white uniform with wide pants legs and a broad collar hanging around the back.

He pulls his cute hat from his head, his hair all tussled underneath, and he kisses me. I dip back in his hold, his palm on the arch of my back. My Shortcake version is a little more grown up, the skirt much shorter than I've ever worn, and the lingerie look underneath along with the bodice-style top is definitely more hot cake than shortcake. I was feeling confident when I clicked BUY on my shopping cart. When I unboxed it after it arrived, though, I was much less so. And now? Now, I'm going to freeze my ass off in this thing—literally.

"We should probably get going," Logan says, his eyes constantly roaming over my body.

"You like this a little too much," I tease.

"No such thing as too much. Not possible."

I play shove him and he slides his hat back in place, holding out an arm to lead me out of my dorm and to Sigma something or another.

"You kids have fun," Claire says, shutting the door to go back to work on the wings she's constructing for her party. Truthfully? Her shindig sounds way more fun. They're going to have a sword-fighting lesson with a professional stage fighter, and then they're going to eat s'mores made on spears and roasted by dragon fire. I'm going to listen to a twenty-one-year-old who thinks he's a DJ mash up decent pop songs with unfamiliar rap music to make something utterly unlistenable. What I'm *not* going to do, however, is get drunk. And vomit. I'm good never doing that again.

The Sigma house is packed when we walk up, the lawn filled with people standing around holding Solo cups. I'm not sure how they bend the public drinking rules along such a major road, but they've been propping up a keg out here every Halloween for years.

Logan fills two cups, mine mysteriously only to half, and we walk into the house, which is already thumping with indiscernible music. Something about people being in costumes makes them bolder, it seems. There's a couple making out on the front sofa, and the guy's hand is blatantly up her shirt. Or should I say, her green Crayola costume.

"You getting ideas?" Logan says low in my ear.

"Uhh, not into being a window display for the drunk and disorderly."

He chuckles and puts his hand on my waist.

"Maybe not for them." His eyebrows lift a tick as he looks down at me, ushering me through the crowded hallway to the stairs.

"You're not subtle in the least," I scold, the insinuation of him touching me sends tingles between my legs.

"I have learned, with you, that direct is the best policy."

Our hands woven together, we pass a few couples sitting on the stairs, including two dudes smoking a blunt. The sweet smell hits me and I shake my head, not a big fan of the skunk smell.

"You get a contact high there, Shortcake?" Logan chuckles, knocking on the first door we come to.

"Occupied," a male voice hollers from the other side.

"I think I'm legally under the influence after that," I joke. I take a big sip of my beer to chase a real buzz, but Logan shakes his head at me. "I promise, no overdoing it."

He now knows how very little it takes to push me into sloppy territory.

He tries the next door we come to, and when nobody answers, we slip inside. He locks the door behind us and I move toward the bed while scoping out the space. It's a neat room, likely belonging to one of the older guys who has his shit together. Business books are stacked on the classic wooden desk, and the large bed is made military style.

"I almost hate to mess that up," I tease, setting my beer down before turning around and pulling Logan into me by his black sailor's tie.

Before I can sit on the mattress, his hand cups my ass and he pulls me into him.

"So let's not use the bed," he says, tossing his hat onto a nearby armchair. I notice his beer is on the table. He leans his head to the left, and I follow his indication to a set of French doors that lead out to a balcony.

"And what does that overlook?" I arch a brow.

"Let's just say we're above the sofa couple and somewhere near the front lawn." He lifts me so my toes rest on top of his shoes and spins, walking me toward the doorway.

"So *above* the fray," I confirm.

"*Mmm*, indeed," he says, stopping at the door. "Would you like to see the view for yourself?"

His hand squeezes my ass and I yelp quietly, the sound quickly covered by his mouth. His kiss is rough, his last shave a few days ago, which rather perfects the whole Sinatra fantasy of mine. I run my hands up his sandpaper jawline and lean into him, his back against the door. His hard-on presses against my stomach, the thin fabric of his pretend sailor suit not masking much below the waist.

"I could use some air," I say, trying to sound sultry. I must have gotten it right because he bites my lip gently again, tugging as he releases it with a soft growl.

I step from the tops of his feet and kick my red heels off before following him out to the balcony. There's a small metal table with one of those large outdoor candles in the center, the wax melted down the sides. Other than two accompanying chairs, the space is pretty sparse, but the view is incredible.

"You can see the spires on Tiff," I say, gesturing toward the skyline.

It's a clear night with a full moon, and the rooftops before us glint with the reflection. I step up to the balcony's railing and scan the horizon, looking for familiar landmarks. Logan steps in behind me, one palm flat against my stomach, and the other wasting zero time and sliding under the cup of my bodice.

I fall back into him, his hard-on pressed against my ass, and he pinches my nipple when I press my backside into him.

"Careful," he says through a ragged breath at my ear.

"No," I say, moving one hand behind me and cupping his cock through his pants. I grip him and stroke as he pulls on my hard peak even harder.

"*Oooooh*, Shortcake," he hums in my ear.

I chuckle, enjoying both my nickname and this sudden power it's given me.

Someone below us shouts, "Who wants a keg stand!" and Logan quickly tells me to *not even think about it*. My head falls back against his shoulder as I laugh, but my amused tittering quickly turns into a moan as he hikes my skirt up and palms my pussy over my panties. He rubs his hand over the satin a few times before tugging the strip to the side and sinking two fingers inside.

Above everyone and shielded by a wall, there isn't anything anyone can see, yet the fact I can see them is so titillating. Behind my back, I dip my hand inside Logan's pants, slipping under his boxer briefs to wrap my hand around his cock. I stroke slowly, gliding my thumb over the wet tip and reveling in the way it flexes under my touch.

Logan's hand presses against me, stilling when I stroke him as he lets out a deep moan. His other hand slips out of my top, trailing down my side and lifting the other side of my skirt. I take in a sudden breath as his thumbs hook the sides of my panties and tug them down my hips. He takes a step back and runs his palms over my bare ass, squeezing both cheeks then kneeling, sliding my panties completely down my legs.

"Oh," I pant.

Logan's deep laugh is devious, and so fucking sexy.

Standing again, he pulls my hips back then presses the center of my back so I'm leaning against the rail with folded arms, my cheek resting on the back of my folded hands. He fluffs the skirt of my costume up so I'm completely exposed to him from behind, and I hear the distinct, slow tear of a condom wrapper.

"You came prepared," I say.

"I have been thinking about this since the second you agreed to wear this costume," he confesses, his palm smacking my ass then running over the skin to soothe it. He leans against my back as he works the condom on his cock.

"Was that okay?"

I nod, surprised how much I like to be spanked by him.

"Good," he says, doing it to my other cheek. His palm runs over my curved skin again, soothing it before I feel his hard cock trace the same path.

"Oh—" I lean down as flat as I can against the railing, my back arched and legs spread as Logan slides his length along my wet center.

"Nobody can hear you up here," he suggests before sliding into my pussy, his stroke long and deep.

"*Ahhh,*" I let out, a little louder than I would have had he not said that.

"Good girl," he praises, holding my hips as he rocks back, leaving me completely. I whimper at the loss, but he's quickly back inside, driving deep and hitting the most sensitive parts of my insides.

I grip the railing and lower my head to look at my bare

feet, Logan's dress shoes, his pants swaying as he pumps into me. I let myself moan, the sound broken up every time he pushes into me. The intensity grows as he fucks me faster, and his hand reaches around and dives into my bodice again, pinching and pulling my nipple. I place my hand over the one he's gripping my hip with, holding him in place as he pummels me from behind.

My core clenches around him, the build happening fast. I try to say his name, but my voice is gone, my air is gone, as the orgasm sweeps over me and all I can do is ride each wave. A low hum leaves my throat as I push into him, wanting him deeper, wanting it never to stop. He continues to slide in and out, even after the pulsing slows. I keep pushing into him, wanting to take him over the edge with me, the sound of his hard breath behind me tempting me to come again.

Before he comes, though, he pulls out of me, leaving a palm on my back as he holds me in place.

"Can I?" he asks, nearly unable to get the words out as I hear the slick sound of him stroking himself.

I nod and pant, "Uh huh," and he pulls the condom off and finishes on my ass, the tip of his cock touching my skin as his warmth coats me. He spreads it against me with his dick and I touch myself, suddenly wanting to come again. Logan notices and continues to slide his wet cock against my ass as he reaches around and helps me find my second release.

Spent and only slightly embarrassed, I tiptoe into the bedroom and find the bathroom door so I can clean myself up. Logan follows with my panties in his hand. He makes a point to stuff them in his pocket in front of me before warning that I'm not getting them back.

Freshened up and sore from being, as Logan likes to say, "properly fucked," I lead him down the stairs and back into the thickness of the party. He spots a few teammates and we join them on the lawn, forming our own little circle as we sip our beers and talk about nothing important. Every now and then, Logan runs his hand over my ass, reminding me that I'm completely bare underneath and that if I bend down to pick anything up, everyone will know.

We practically close down the party, leaving with the last few sober and awake dregs. A few people are heading to a twenty-four hour breakfast joint, and Logan and I both get invited. My heart lifts at being seen as a couple. Despite Logan's amazing speech, there is still a part of me that doesn't feel as though I belong. That part is shrinking, though. That negative voice is getting smaller.

We decline the breakfast offer, and Logan walks me back to my dorm, where he plans to stay the night. I have to work on a major lab early in the morning, and since Claire will likely spend the night with some mystery guy we've been hearing about who knows his way around a sword, we figured we would take advantage of having my room to ourselves.

The front desk is empty, so I use my security card to enter and we slip by the note that says someone will be right back. Logan flirts with my bare ass in the elevator on the way up, and I try my hardest to tempt him into hitting the big red stop button so I can learn all about elevator sex too. I almost don't care that he doesn't have a condom. I'm so mesmerized by him and how he makes me feel that I'm willing to take risks.

We exit on my floor and turn right to head down the long hallway. I stop in my tracks, though, when I see a familiar face waiting near my door. Stella is sitting on the floor, her back against the end wall, her legs pulled up, and her familiar boho purse resting in her lap.

Logan stops with me, his eyes taking in my visitor before shifting and studying me.

"Stella," I explain before he has to ask. His hand squeezes mine, and I squeeze back with equal strength.

"Do you want me to give you some privacy?" His voice shakes, and it's strange to hear him so uneasy.

I shake my head.

"No." I glance at him and take a deep breath.

He nods, then leans his head toward our path. I return my focus to my former best friend who is now on her feet, her bag slung over her shoulder as she knits her hands together. She shouldn't even be in this country.

"Hi," she croaks when I'm close enough to hear.

I pull my lips into a tight line and lift my chin. I can't seem to get myself to utter hello in return. I thought I was over the betrayal, but seeing her here, for the first time since the day she broke my trust, hits my gut like a thousand pounds of lead.

"I'm sorry to show up like this. I've been waiting for a few hours. I thought you'd be home sooner." Her words are a little insulting, though I don't think she means them to be.

"We were at a party," I say, making a point to flex my hand in Logan's and adjust my fingers through his.

Stella's gaze drops to the movement and her lips part as she says, "Oh."

"Yeah. This is Logan," I say, as if he needs an introduction.

"Nice to meet you. I'm—"

"Stella," he completes for her. It's a subtle way to let her know *he* knows. She gets it, shutting her mouth and letting out a soft, "*Hmm.*"

She averts her gaze, her eyes pained and brow low as her hands fiddle even more in front of her.

"Why are you here?" Maybe I'm still riding the high from feeling like a goddess all night or maybe I'm finally done feeling sorry for myself. Perhaps I simply hate her and want to get this over with.

"I wanted you to hear it from me before the rumors take over," she says.

I steady myself, my chest filling with a burning sensation, like a toxic gas, and this is just from her warning.

"Go on," I say.

She takes in a long breath, her eyes flitting to mine in beats, and her inability to look me in the eyes confidently pushes me even more off-kilter. Logan adjusts our hands and I squeeze him again, reminding myself of what matters— what's real.

"Rachel, I'm pregnant."

And I throw up, only two beers in me. All over the dorm hallway floor.

22 /
logan

I GET that she doesn't want to talk about it.

I understand.

But *I* want to talk about it.

Stella tried to help me with Rachel after she puked, but Rachel had enough energy to throw up a middle finger and tell her former friend to go away. I helped her clean up, rinse her mouth, change, and then we both climbed into bed. I propped her computer up on a chair and put on her favorite episode of *The Office*.

And neither of us said a word.

I know it wasn't from drinking two beers over three hours —beers I never filled to the top. It was shock. Some bio-chemical reaction I'm sure Rachel could explain, if only she'd talk about it.

She was at her lab when I woke up this morning. She left me a text, having put my phone on silent so it didn't wake me. I wish I knew whether it was considerate or calculated. And not in a mean way, but in order to avoid conflict. Because I think she knows what my biggest ask is.

Do you wish you were the one pregnant with Dalton's baby?

It sounds ridiculous, even now in my head. Of course she doesn't want that. It was just a big shock. A final blow after having been betrayed by two people she counted on. That has to be it.

Coach made weights optional this morning. Of course, the way he said it didn't sound so optional. And the guys dragging their asses in hungover the day after Halloween look bitter about it.

"You done already?" Jax says, one of the rougher looking dudes hitting the weights as I'm wrapping up.

"Got up at six," I say with a grin and wink.

"Fuck you," he teases, punching my bicep while I wipe down my bench press bar. "Look at you acting like an adult. Maybe I should get a super smart girlfriend too."

I chuckle, but the forced laugh shuts off when I turn my back to him and head into the locker room.

My smart girlfriend.

The unease in my chest lingered throughout my entire workout. And not only because of the conversation Rachel seems keen on avoiding. That formal ball she asked me to go to with her is this Saturday. Our game is at home and early enough, but Coach asked me to stick around for a while after the game. Specifically, for dinner. My numbers after coming back from injury have been more than solid. I'm sitting at nine TDs over the last three games with an average over a hundred rushing yards for the month of October. Not bad, considering the game on October first I was only really in for the fourth quarter. Those numbers might just land me a deal with a certain hydration beverage company.

I'm not sure what do to or if Rachel even wants to go to this ball thing. It hasn't felt like this is about making Dalton jealous in a while. But now, she seems like the jealous one. And I feel like an insecure weakling.

We have to talk.

My mom brought my tux from my sister's wedding when they visited. I have yet to pick it up from the cleaners, so I decide to avoid the hard conversation a little longer and head to the shop on the corner where it's been for the last several weeks.

I'm digging through my glove box in search of the claim ticket when someone raps on my window. I hit my head on the lip of the dash as I jerk up, and it's like I get kicked in the gut when I see who it is.

Amy smiles, then motions for me to roll the window down. I don't smile at her. I'm still pretty pissed off that she made Rachel feel like shit. It's my fault, though, for forgetting I took her to the gallery once.

I sigh, then reach for the window button, lowering it.

"Hey," I grunt. My stomach muscles are shredded, and holding myself stretched across the console with one palm on the truck floor is giving me the shakes.

"Hey, yourself," she says, attempting to be cute.

"Look, I have to find my ticket, and I'm in a hurry, so—"

"Oh, yeah. You're picking up your tux?" She holds up a dark green gown covered with plastic. I view it with dimmed eyes. How the fuck does she know so much? Like, that I have a tux here?

"I . . . am." My eyes drift from her gown to her face. Her mouth is smug. *Why did we date?*

"I figured. I'm going to see you at the ball. I got asked by this guy, Nelson. He's head of the physics club or something."

I nod slowly.

"All right," I say. "And you are going with him . . . why?"

I'm sure she has an angle. She's not about to pretend she's into some guy majoring in physics. Unless that guy owns actual rockets. And looks like a former boy-bander gone solo.

"Uh, same reason *you* are! The money," she says, giving her body a little shake.

"What money?" I ask, regretting every extra second of this conversation.

She doesn't answer so quickly now, and the lift to her brow feels like genuine surprise. She also gets this amused-looking grin that tickles her upper lip. It feels like an *I told you so*.

"Oh, my God, you don't know?" She clearly knows I don't.

I clear my throat and push myself up in my seat. I stay in the cab, resting my left wrist on the steering wheel while I twist to the side to stare her straight on.

"Oh, boy." She breathes in. Her acting job is painful. I endure it. "I found out that every year at this nerd ball thing, they host a pool where they put in a ton of money. I mean like, thousands, Logan!"

Her eyes widen to accentuate that word—*thousands*. My mouth sours.

"Okay, so?"

"So . . . whoever shows up with the most prestigious date, and has confirmation of, well, you know . . ." She actually pokes her finger through the hole made by her other hand. She's twelve.

"Like the hookup bet the freshmen athletes make?" I'm pretty sure Amy was a target for one of those. Maybe two.

"Yeah! Except bigger! And the winner is picked by

popular opinion. And since the prize is up to seven grand this year, I thought"—she lifts her shoulders and glances up and to the right—"Why not!"

Now I'm the one who wants to throw up. From this conversation. From the realization that Rachel was using me for more than making someone jealous. And from my fear that this is somehow going to ruin us, or that what we were isn't really that much after all.

"Well, I wish you luck. We might not even be going, so—"

"Aww," Amy says with a click of her mouth, her head tilting in a not-so-sympathetic way.

"Bye." I leave it at that, drawing my window up and backing out of the cleaner's lot. I head straight to the parking lot near the science building, not fully *wanting* to walk through the fire.

I decide I'm tough enough to push myself through and head up to the chemistry labs floor.

Per the norm, Rachel's back is to me. And once again, she's swirling what looks like acid. I laugh and shake my head, and she spins around but doesn't drop the tube.

"Seriously!" she shouts. It's not an angry face this time, however. It's almost a pleasantly surprised expression. But as I walk into the room and close the door behind me, her high cheeks sink back to normal, and her slight smile straightens. The worry dent between her brow deepens as she puts her test tube away and moves to take a seat in one of the chairs at the workstation.

"We need to talk," I say, and even coming from my mouth it sounds full of doom.

Rachel's face washes of color, her skin suddenly pale.

"It's not because I'm jealous or anything to do with

Dalton. I swear," she says, shaking her head side-to-side, her wide eyes pleading with me.

I settle my mouth into a reassuring smile and drag one of the chairs near hers, turning it around to sit backward. I hold on to the wooden backrest and sift through everything weighing on my mind.

"Okay, let's start with that."

She's kneading her hands so I reach across and place my palm over them. Her fingers scurry to hold on to mine. I let her have my hand for strength as she swallows hard.

"She didn't even go," she says, blinking her way up to my gaze.

My brow puzzles for a second, then I realize.

"Stella . . . she didn't go abroad?" And now my chest hurts in sympathy. Not that it didn't before, but now it's pure sympathy. And I feel like a dick for even thinking any of this was about me. That she wanted to break up, or trade me in for Dalton.

"Nope. I checked. And while her name was on the welcome page for the website, she never registered. I called, and they said she withdrew a few days before the program's start. It was too late for them to offer the scholarship to a replacement, and I was second on the list."

"Oh, Rach," I say, reaching up to touch her cheek. She covers my palm with hers and holds me to her. Her eyes are red, and I can tell she's been crying.

"I'm so sorry," I say. "You feel like she stole your shot, and then wasted it."

She nods, then drops her gaze to her lap, her hands moving back to their comfort zone, just under her thighs.

"I'm so mad at her. Not over Dalton, but over a trip to Germany," she laughs out. Her gaze shifts up, and her crooked smile is a window back into my girl. She's working through this.

"If you had gone—"

"I know," she finishes my thought.

Neither of us speaks, but we stare into each other's eyes for several quiet seconds. We know what we both meant. If she had gone, we wouldn't have gotten to know one another. She wouldn't have been here to rescue me in chemistry. We might not have ever *truly* met. We wouldn't have fallen in love.

"Do you regret it?" I ask, sucking in my bottom lip and holding my breath.

She shakes her head with little pause, and my chest cracks open with relief. It's temporary, though, because I have a new question. One that I suspect has just as easy an answer, but I'll only know if I ask.

"When were you going to tell me about the pool to win money by bringing me to a ball?" It sounds convoluted saying it out loud, so much so that Rachel flutters her eyes closed with a laugh that borders on absurdity.

"I didn't plan on it . . . since I never entered." She covers her face with flexed fingers and peers at me through the space between the middle and index.

No longer needing a physical barrier, I stand and swivel my chair around, then take her hand as I sit again, pulling her onto my lap. I cradle her into me, kissing the top of her head and feeling like the luckiest asshat on the planet.

I hold her in silence for nearly a minute. Eventually, she begins to tell me about the various issues she's been running into on her project. I understand none of it, but I love listening to her talk about her work. She's passionate about chemistry, and when she talks about chemical communication—whatever the hell that is—her eyes literally twinkle. I'm not sure what reaction in her body makes that happen, but it's a phenomenon strictly unique to her.

After taking up nearly an hour of time she should probably be figuring out all of those issues she attempted to explain to me, I stand and kiss her goodbye . . . for now. I halt just inside the doorway, though, deciding to work out one last hiccup.

"Since there's not really a financial reason to go to the ball, and since Dalton isn't as big of a concern as I originally may have thought, how upset would you be if I . . . maybe . . . went to an endorsement dinner instead?" I smile through my teeth, my molars clenching while I silently hope I didn't overstep any assumptions.

Her sharp intake of air worries me.

"Or, I can go. It's fine."

She holds a hand up and stares just to my side for a moment.

"It's . . . it's nothing, honestly. That's fine. Please. Endorsements sound big. And I know you love dinner."

I narrow my gaze and shift to look at her sideways.

"I do love dinner, but . . ."

She exhales, her shoulders dropping.

"I'm getting an award for student of the year. It's not really *that* big of a deal. And I'll just get my award then come home. It's before the ball anyhow. And you know how little I like the idea of hobnobbing with hors d'oeuvres being bandied about."

I shake my head.

"No, student of the year is a big deal." I immediately consider ways I can squeeze in both obligations, but Rachel steps up and twists the string on my hoodie around her finger before flitting her gaze up to mine.

"It's a big deal that I will celebrate with you later. I promise."

I take her on her word. But I also think she's underselling herself. Rachel is bound for greatness. And missing her big night feels like I might just miss out on her beginning.

**23 /
rachel**

I USED to show up to things alone all the time. Granted, I wouldn't stay long. Usually long enough to grab the freebie or find out the gossip and then leave. But I could do it. I was comfortable walking in and out on my own, knowing I'd get some looks but in that knowing, being all right with it.

But walking into a ball alone is a whole new level. My dress is tight. I loved it when I picked it out, thinking how the black drapery would trace my curves and how the slit up the side would accentuate my height and show off my favorite part of my body, my legs. Now it just feels tight for the sake of tightness. Uncomfortable, and showing off all my flaws.

Plus, turns out when you walk into a ball alone, stepping through grand doors where people are on hand to take your photo, people stare. *Everyone* stares. They're still staring and I walked in a full minute ago.

"You look nice," says a girl I faintly recognize. I think she's in the physics core.

"Thank you," I say, my voice barely above a whisper. I catch her gaze scoping out the expanse of my dress, a slight twist to her lips, like she's some fashionista keeping notes for her blog.

My anxiety is narrating this story now.

"I like your dress," I say, wanting to pay her back. She smiles and does a slow turn, I'm guessing to show off the open back of the deep blue number that's cut to perfection. She's pretty. Petite and blonde. I could eat her in one bite, just like the hors d'oeuvres being passed around.

I turn to face the bar, seeking an easy out of our conversation. I order myself a cranberry with a splash of vodka, watching to make sure the splash is tiny. I'll nurse this for the next hour over mingling, dinner, and then the awards. If all goes according to my plan, I'll be out of here by seven-thirty and in my pajamas by eight.

"Fancy meeting you here," a familiar voice chimes in from my other side. I glance up to find Claire, the self-titled hater of all things formal balls. She's wearing a gothic black dress made of lace, with lace gloves that spiral up her arms and are cut into diamonds over the backs of her hands.

"You came!" I hug her. Neither of us are big on hugs with people who aren't the guys we're currently sleeping with. Hers very well may even be a dragon.

"I couldn't let you endure this alone," she says, glancing over my shoulder.

I follow her gaze in time to catch Stella and Dalton enter.

"Are you gonna throw up?" Claire asks, having heard what happened last time I saw Stella.

"I ate a bagel for lunch, and this is a weak drink. I think I'm okay," I say, zeroing in on Stella's left hand. The sparkle is modest. I guess it's nice he's making it official, or honest, or whatever they want to call things. I guess it's possible they're in love.

"Does it help that she's showing?" Claire's chin lands on my shoulder as I'm now facing the entrance head-on.

"It helps a little. Does that make me a bad person?"

"Not in the least." She wraps an arm around my neck, I think a little to hold me back.

"Let's get this over with," I say, downing my weak drink to get the most out of that splash then setting the empty glass on a nearby high top.

Claire trails behind me as we head toward Dalton and Stella. My ex spots me first, and pulls Stella closer to his side. His move gives her a jolt and she scans her surroundings, finally landing on me. The two of them practically sink roots into the swirling carpet floor.

"Hi, Rachel," Dalton says. His voice is weak, and that pleases me.

"Nice to see you. And I hear congratulations are in order," I say, flitting my gaze to Stella. Her eyes are welling up, and there's a small pang in my chest for my former best friend. I wish this was something I could celebrate with her. Any other circumstances and I might. Though I'm sure none of this was planned. Well, the cheating part was planned, but the baby . . . probably not.

"Thanks, Rachel. We appreciate that," Dalton says on their behalf.

My smile comes easier this time with him, but it falters when I shift my gaze back to Stella. It took me a while to really get to the center of my pain after what they did, and while the affair part stung, it was really the dream theft that stuck it to me. *And to know she didn't even go.*

"Hi, I'm Claire. We've met a few times," my new bestie says, reaching over my shoulder to shake Stella's hand. I suck in my bottom lip, remembering how acerbic she was with Amy. I'm not sure whether Stella deserves better or worse.

"Yes, I think we have," Stella says, clear recognition in her eyes. The two of them have never mixed.

"Dalton," Claire tosses out, pulling her hand from Stella and not offering it to my ex. They've met too. Dalton tried to dismantle her LARPing club because they were too noisy outside the law school study rooms. Claire has said she would like the earth to swallow Dalton whole. I kinda would too.

"I hear you're getting the student of the year award," Stella says, pulling my attention back to her. Her brow is pinched with this forced caring expression. Maybe she's truly in pain and filled with regret. I can't believe anything from her anymore.

"Well, it's not quite an abroad study scholarship, but I can put it on my shelf," I say.

"And your resume," Claire pipes in.

"Oh, yeah. And that!" I turn to face her and hold out a fist for her to pound. She utters a faint "Boom" after we do.

Expecting to see a guilt-ridden face, I turn back to face Stella. But her mask is secure. Her eyes possibly droop more, from all the remorse echoing in her head, I'm sure. But other than that, she holds the truth close to the vest. Unable to stand it, I drop my chin and close my eyes with a breathy laugh.

"You're so unbelievable," I finally let out.

The weight on my shoulders lifts a touch, and I lift my head, rolling my shoulders and straightening my spine. Dalton's feet shuffle as he works himself into a protective stance as if I'm going to take a swing at Stella.

"Really?" I glare at him.

"Don't make a scene," he says in a gritted whisper.

My eyes widen as I laugh again, this one punchy and loud. There wasn't much vodka in that drink, but whatever there was hits me right now.

"Always assuming this is about you," I say, suddenly feeling nothing but pity for my ex. "It was always studying for *your* LSATs. We talked about living near *your* law schools."

I flash my gaze over to Stella.

"I hope to God for your sake that you have a say in things with him. If not, fix that now. Because I let him walk all over me. Clearly." I draw a line in the air up and down the length of her body.

"Hey," Dalton says, stepping in. The knight and shining nothing.

I hold a palm up, boxing him out of my view. Out of my life.

"You didn't even go," I say to her, point blank.

She sucks in her bottom lip and blinks wildly.

"Did you?" I want her to confirm it, not because I need her to but because I want her to feel any residual good in her soul go up in flames.

She finally shakes her head.

"I found out I was pregnant about a week before," she says. That checks with my research.

"You knew how important this was to me," I say, no longer able to hold in the ire. "I talked about it for *three years*. You read my application. *Oh, my God! Did you copy it?*"

She steps into me now.

"Of course not!" she says through gritted teeth.

Yeah, there goes that mask.

I huff out an incredulous laugh to my side and stare at the floor. We've got a few of the eyes in the room on us, but for the most part, nobody cares about our drama. I doubt anyone other than the handful of chem students who are interested in the abroad program this year even know who went and who didn't.

I let the silence build, eventually the sounds of the ball-room taking over and filling in the blanks. I look back to her face, into her eyes, and shake my head in admonition.

"Shame on you," I say, turning to walk away with Claire at my side. Before I can go, though, Stella's hand wraps around my upper arm and I twist to look at her sideways.

"Rachel . . ." My name cracks coming out of her throat. She licks her dry lips. "I really am sorry."

I hold her face in my frame, taking a mental picture so I can decide what to do with it later. Maybe I'll forgive her, maybe I won't. For now, though, I'll leave her with the last word. Claire and I will get another drink.

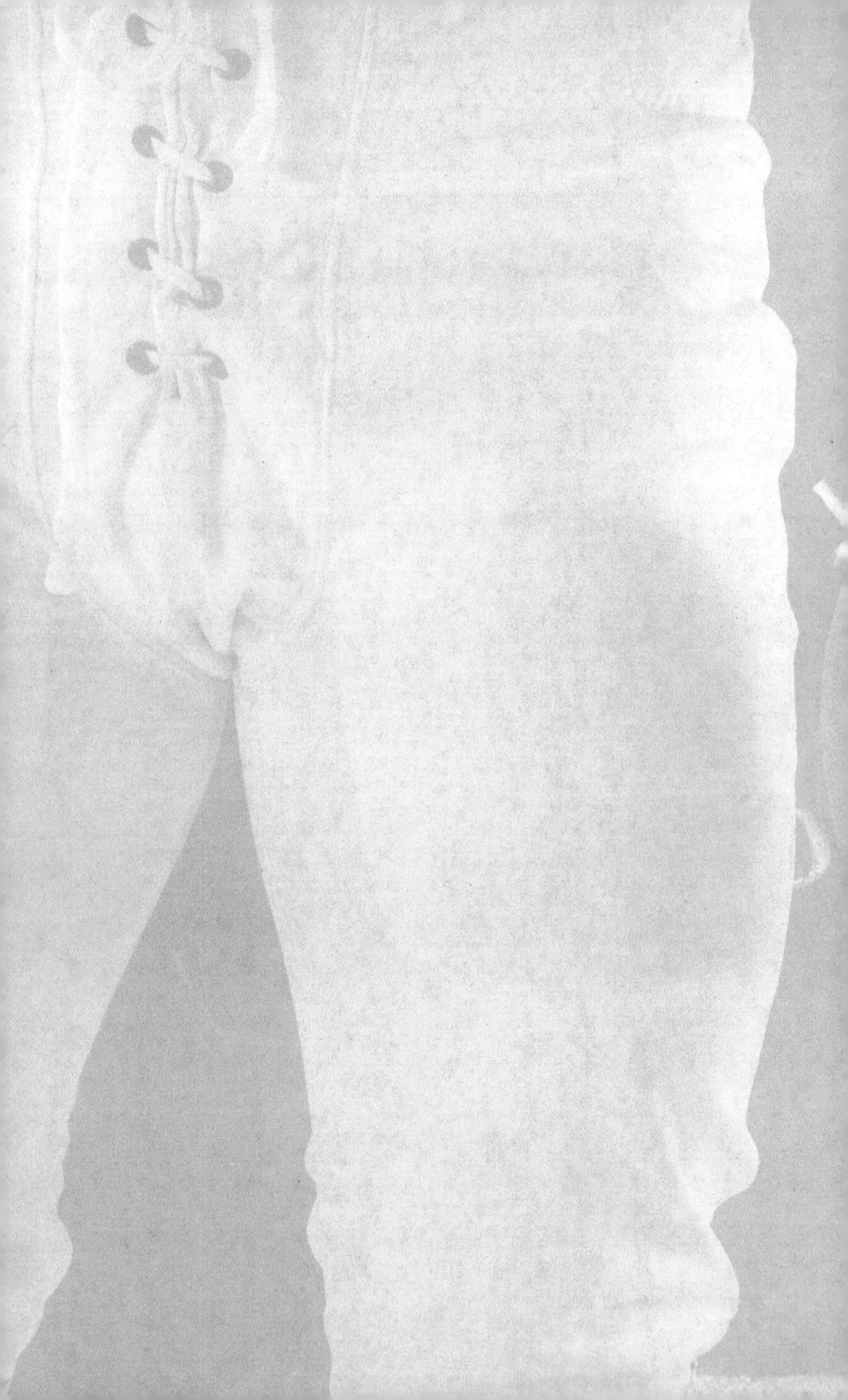

24 / logan

I'M GOING to have a billboard.

Sure, it's in a small town on the highway cutting between Missouri, Kansas and Iowa, but it's a billboard. And it's a busy highway. And it's my face.

My freaking face!

More importantly, I have seventeen minutes to get my ass in a tux and to the Ritz Carlton by the river for Rachel's award. We don't have to stay for the ball. But if I miss her getting praise for being amazing, I'll never forgive myself.

I make it to the cleaners five minutes before the place closes, but since I don't have a claim ticket, the manager asks me for a backup ID. She's a short, older woman with well-quaffed hair, the old-school kind that she likely gets done at a salon once a week. It's gray, mostly, but the tips are black. Stylish. Maybe she'll be reasonable.

"Your license has a different address than what's on file," she says, and I groan. *Reason out the window.*

"That's because I'm a student. That address is my parents' house. I live near campus for college."

She simply blinks, her mouth a hard line.

"Right," I huff, tucking my license back in my wallet and flipping through other options.

"Here, this is my credit card," I say, laying it on the counter.

She shakes her head, so I keep going.

"My library card for back home? Or maybe my student dining card," I flatten both of them next to the credit card, and she picks the dining one up, inspecting it.

"Hmm, there's no address here. It has your picture, though. It's a nice photo. Your mom must be proud. Very handsome boy." She gives me a polite grin, and all I can do is let my head sink.

"I need to get this tux. Please. It's mine, I swear." I shake my head before lifting it up and dumping out the remaining contents of my wallet, minus the condom I keep held in place with my thumb.

I hold her gaze, trying to evoke pity.

"It's for a girl. I have to show up!"

She pulls her mouth into a crooked twist and glances down at my offerings, spreading them around to give it all a good search. Her finger stops above the grocery store gift card, tapping on it a few times then sliding it away from the bunch.

"This one might do," she says, looking at me over the rim of her glasses.

I breathe out a short, amused laugh. I've had that card for a year. Hell, it might even be expired. My mom gave it to me when she was worried I wasn't eating enough. I weigh two hundred and five pounds. And that has not fluctuated for two years.

"Right, so the grocery card. Yeah, that works," I chuckle, sweeping up the remaining items and tucking them back into place while Mrs. Clean scoops up her evidence of extortion.

I'm at peace with it less than a minute later when she hooks my tux on the bar for me to inspect. I tear away the plastic and ball it up, pushing it into her trash bin, which makes her grumble.

"Hey, you made out pretty good here. I think the least you can do is take your plastic back," I say, returning my attention to the suit I haven't worn in three years.

It's going to be snug, but it was big on me three years ago. Before I really bulked. Once I'm sure the buttons are all intact and everything looks in order, I thank her for conning me and rush to my truck. That ticked off way too much time, so stopping by my house is no longer an option. Instead, I race the six miles to the hotel and find a spot shielded by hedges and away from the lights so I can change.

I keep the same dress shirt on, which helps, and manage to swap out my pants and change out my shoes, all in the cab of my truck. I step out, feeling the material stretched on my ass. There will not be any sitting. Or bending over. I can handle that.

After slipping on the vest and jacket, I reach across the seat for the small gift I bought for Rachel this morning. I planned to give it to her tonight, but since I made it here in time, I may as well come bearing gifts.

I fling the truck door shut and feel my jacket seams pull with the flex of my arm. It makes me chuckle, as does the blatant shortness of my pants. I look down, glad I went with the no-sock look when I realize how exposed my ankles truly are. Still, a tux is better than sweatpants. And my other suit isn't quite dressy enough for a ball. Not that I have a clue what is ball appropriate.

It takes me a few attempts to find the right ballroom, but when I do and pull open the set of doors, I find Rachel almost immediately. I close the door softly, someone on stage speaking and the rest of the room all seated for dinner. I didn't eat much during my meeting with Coach and the sponsor, so the smell of grilled chicken and fresh veggies is mighty tempting. Maybe Rachel will have some left. Or an extra plate.

"Can I help you?" A tall man I vaguely recognize leans into my shoulder. I think this is her professor.

"Uh, I think I'm good. I'm here for Rachel Edwards. I see her, but I'll wait for a break in the action," I say, gesturing to the stage.

"Well, good timing," he says. "This is her award."

My mouth forms an O and I take a few steps forward for a better view, now paying attention to the words being said. I'm not sure who the host is, but the man is reading comments from nearly every professor in the chemistry department, and they're all praising Rachel's intellect and drive.

"I am sure many of you have had the pleasure of this person correcting your presentation, politely after class, of course," the host says, garnering a round of laughter from the room.

I smile to myself, thinking how Rachel and I talked about this very idea weeks ago. Of course she corrects them discreetly. It's part of the built-in respect she automatically gives people. Only the first of many qualities I fell for.

"And how could we forget the great D'Amato Hall fire," he adds, this time the laughter lingering and loud.

Hall fire? I make a mental note to ask more about this one.

Another full minute passes filled with quotes about

Rachel's work, the headway she's made in her special lab studies, and her goals for finding solutions to help the business world make better use of science.

"Please join me in congratulating this year's student of the year, Rachel Edwards," he says. She rises, her hands on her cheeks to cover the pink color that always crawls up to her ears when she's under the spotlight.

Claire shifts her chair and stands to hug her, and I'm glad she's not alone. Though I wish I were a little earlier. I envy that hug.

Her tall, curvy frame navigates through the tables, the black dress swaying around her feet. She kicks part of it ahead of her with every step, and takes the presenter's hand as she climbs the few stairs that lead to the podium. She holds the award, a slender test tube set in gold and mounted on a wood base, then kisses it like they do in the tennis majors. This garners a good laugh from the crowd. She thinks she's a wallflower, but she can work a room.

Setting the award to the side, she adjusts the mic and leans forward, uttering, "Hello."

Hello.

I drop one hand in my jacket pocket and hold the small gift bag in the other, looking on as she delivers the speech she practiced with me all night. It's short, but it covers all the important pieces, thanking her mentor and the dean, as well as throwing a bone to the potential grad programs she would like to attend.

When she's done, she steps back from the mic, the spotlight clearing from her eyes just enough. I clap louder than anyone in the room, and her eyes find me.

"Hi," she mouths.

"Hi," I say aloud. Nobody is near me.

She shakes the cursory hands and makes her way back down the steps as I rush toward her table so I'm there to pull out her chair. Since hers was the last award of the night, it takes her a few minutes to maneuver her way back, and I ask Claire for the rundown of everything I missed.

"Well, there was the whole putting Stella and Dalton in their places thing. That was—"

"Oh, please don't say violent," I joke. But really? I don't put it past Rachel to go a little nuts. The more we talked about it, the more I understood just how much not getting the scholarship hurt.

"It went better than I hoped it would. I found out they were coming and that's why I showed up," she says.

I give her a one-armed hug, and she glares at me with dagger eyes.

"Sorry," I say, coughing and reminding myself to never broach her personal space again.

A bit of commotion stirs on the opposite end of the room, so I nod toward the growing group.

"Oh, yeah. About that," Claire begins, her mouth seesawing for a beat before she explains. "There's sort of this underground gambling thing going on, and well . . . you're the frontrunner."

I chuckle, shaking my head and utter, "What?"

"You know how you guys do that bet thing?"

My head falls back with instant understanding.

"Ah, yes. *The pool.*" My voice goes deep to show how ominous and important this tradition is. I guess it's no worse than what we do freshmen year. And it's way more lucrative. I'm about to dismiss it when the other part of Claire's explanation strikes something in my head.

"Wait, frontrunner?"

"Yeah," she sighs out. "And that's the other reason I showed up. Don't be mad at Rachel. She didn't enter. But I maybe sort of entered for her?"

Her mouth contorts into a quick and very guilty grin.

I hold her gaze for a few seconds, waiting for her to take it back with a *psych!* She doesn't.

"Wait a second. So you're saying Rachel is entered. And now I'm here, as her date. And word on the scientific street is I'm the frontrunner, which means by default *Rachel* is the frontrunner." I scan the room for my competition, spotting Amy in her green dress, sitting at a table near the cluster of people. Her date is, well, he's not tall. And he is definitely in over his head because even from across the room I can see the heart shapes in his eyes while he stares at his date.

"Pretty much," Claire confirms. "But I'm not sure she told you the whole deal."

"Yeah, yeah," I wave off. "You need to prove you did it. Whatever, that's . . . I mean, if I need to show people here I will. What's the pot up to?"

Claire checks her phone.

"You guys have an app for this?" *Wow!* Beats the group chat and napkin notes the football team uses for the freshmen.

"Uh, yeah," Claire says with that *duh* tone.

"Seven five," she says. And I know from what Amy mentioned that she means seven grand, not seventy-five.

"Hold my bag," I say, handing the gift to Claire and moving my way through the thinning crowd to Rachel. I step up behind her, my hand light under her elbow. She turns into me, her eyes flickering with that familiar joy I've come to recognize every time we're apart then come back together.

"Congratulations," I say, pressing a soft kiss to her cheek.

"You came!" She throws her arms around me, her strapless dress accentuating the curves of her shoulders and the crest of her breasts. I'm not the only man in this room who has spent time staring at her upper body, and that includes a few married dudes and so far at least six professors.

"I got done in time. It took . . ." I waggle my head and glance up, "a minor miracle to pull off, but yes. I made it. Your speech was great."

"Did you say it along with me?"

"Maybe in my head," I admit.

She picks the award up from the table at her side and hoists it in front of me.

"Watch this," she says, pressing a button on the side and lighting up the inside of the test tube. I smirk at the novelty.

"It's a lot cooler than the football plaques. That's for sure," I say. I'd still take a bowl ring over this, though. "Hey, mind coming with me for a second?" I take the award from her hands, cradling it to my chest. This sucker is heavy.

"Sure," she says, her brow raised on one side, her expression curious. I guide her to the far side of the room, and as we close in she realizes what we're walking into and stops.

"No, no. I told you. I didn't enter. And really, this thing is embarrassing, and—"

"You're going to win," I cut her off.

Her wide eyes click to mine.

"I'm going to win? How? I didn't—"

"Claire," I explain. She swivels her head and scans the room, spotting Claire, who holds up a thumb.

"She didn't," Rachel grumbles.

I tug her hand and draw her back to me.

"She did. But don't be mad. And did you hear me? You're going to win."

Her eyelids lift again, her blinking on hold. I stare into her pupils, watching as they stretch and shrink as if she's a computer calculating what all of this means.

"It's almost enough," I add.

She starts to shake her head, so I place my palm on her cheek to hold it still.

"It's almost enough. I want you to promise me you'll go."

She has to. Not getting to study in Germany was a blow to her passion. If my knee hadn't healed, I would have been in the exact same emotional, sinking boat. I can't imagine not getting the chance to try.

"But what if—"

"*When,*" I interrupt, "we have to figure it out, we will. We graduate in May. I have the draft. You'll head to Germany. Hell, maybe I'll visit. And then we'll see where I go. And if your grad school is close, I'll see you every night. If it's far, I'll see you in the off-season and whenever I can get there. And if none of this happens, I'll see you tomorrow and the next day and the next."

She steps up on her toes as I threaten to go on and on without taking a breath. Her lips stop me, her kiss soft and sweet, and landing on my mouth the minute I hear someone announce her name as the winner of this year's pool.

"Promise me you'll go," I say again, while we're still alone amongst the masses.

"I'll go," she says. It's still there. The flicker in her eyes.

And that's how I know we're going to make it.

"She's right here. And yes, she was amazing in bed," I shout, shutting down any threats to her legitimacy before they start. I'm willing to offer up anything they need, but kissing her hard in front of a room full of jealous geniuses seems to suffice.

THIS SHIRT HAS BECOME my lucky shirt. Logan gave it to me after the science awards ceremony, and while the pool prize money was a really nice surprise, I think I still like this shirt more.

JIM AND PAM = PERFECT CHEMISTRY

I'm not sure where he found it, but he managed to gift me a shirt that expressed my love for two of my three favorite things, *The Office* and chemistry. Thing number one, Logan, I wear every other day of the week.

Claire wasn't too upset when I decided to move in with him for the spring. And Dante and Jax have gotten a lot better about walking around naked, though I still have the occasional late-night surprise waiting for me under the glow of the refrigerator light. I always tell Logan I don't see much. But I look. And I see plenty.

"Lucky shirt?" Logan asks, tugging the sleeve. I nod then step up to kiss him. Tucking myself against his chest, I scan one side of the room, wondering how many relatives I have left to meet.

It's draft day, and Logan is pretty sure where he's going to land. All signs point to Buffalo, which is, well, very far away from Iowa. But, for the girl who never wanted to drift far from home, I'm finding the prospect of grad school in Manhattan to be very appealing. Less appealing is the six hours by car and eight hours by train standing between us, but it's more feasible than an entire country and a dozen state lines standing in the way.

"Your mom keeps trying to talk to me about how dangerous it is to travel overseas," I share after determining the coast is clear.

Logan kisses the top of my head.

"She's never left Iowa. She's not really one to talk."

I step back, surprised at his answer, but his quick nod and lifted brow assure me he's not joking.

"I suppose this means we won't get any visits in New York?" I question.

"Not from her," he says.

I actually quite like his mom, but she can be a bit much. Doses. She's good in doses. Her anxieties start to bleed into mine when we're together for too long, and I don't want to ever be afraid to leave the state of Iowa. Or this country. Especially two weeks before I'm set to pack up my life for six months and immerse myself in all things German.

"How's your vocabulary coming?" he asks.

"*Du bist sehr hübsch*," I manage.

"Wow, that sounded very legit. What did you say?"

"You are very handsome," I respond. "I think."

"I'm not sure you need to know how to say that," he says, leaning back enough to meet my eyes.

"You have nothing to worry about," I promise.

He shifts to give me a sideways look but quickly relents.

"I know. You love me," he says. I laugh, letting him swallow me up in his massive arms.

Our chatter is enough to draw his mom's attention, and she pulls both of us to the couch, standing back after we sit down so she can check the framing for the live stream. "Chuck, you have to move. Your head is too big," she says to her husband.

"Liv, my head is fine. You're just nervous. Sit down and let it happen," Chuck says, his patience for his wife's constant nettling hitting its limit. Having spent enough weekends with this family, I now know and appreciate the nuances.

"Maybe we should let Rachel's parents get in the shot," she continues, unfazed. Chuck rolls his eyes and recrosses his legs, doing his best to peer around his wife's pacing body so he can watch the few picks happening before we get to Logan.

"We're fine in the back," my mom says. It was really nice of Logan to invite my family. He wanted my brother to come, but didn't want my parents to feel left out. Like me, my parents would be happy to stay on the outskirts of this very packed room. And if I didn't express how important this was to me to have them there, for Logan, I'm pretty sure they would have been content to watch from home.

Of course, at this point, watching from home may have been the way to go.

"You really never wanted to experience all of this?" Logan asks my brother sarcastically.

"Tempting, but yeah. I'm sure I didn't want any of this," Casey says through a chuckle, his timing on point as Logan's mom steps up onto the coffee table to get a better view of the room.

"Mom, it's a small streaming camera. The news is going to cut to us for a few seconds. I'll have a real interview later when the news team arrives. You can sit down." Logan's mom seems to be looking at her son while he talks, but it's clear his words go in and out.

"Chuck, can you move that vase? The orange one, behind you," she directs.

Without blinking, Logan's dad reaches behind him and nudges the vase off the edge of the table. It falls onto the carpeted floor and survives, but really . . . I think we all wanted it to break.

I wrap my arm through Logan's and rest my head on his bicep while the chaos continues around us. His uncles debate over every pick that comes before him, and his aunts try to butt in and help his mom construct the perfect fifteen second live-stream clip. It's a cacophony of loud family, blaring television commentary, and one incredibly yappy dog. Through it all, on the surface, Logan seems perfectly calm.

But I know he's not. His hands reveal the truth as he's constantly clasping them together and squeezing. His knuckles are red from his kneading, and his palms are clammy when I slide my hand between them in an attempt to break up his fidgeting.

"That obvious?" he says, his words only for me.

"Not to anyone else."

He runs his palms on his jeans, his sweatshirt covering a Buffalo jersey, just in case. The hat is stuffed behind a pillow on the couch. Every prop in its place, including the orange vase that Olivia insisted had to go.

I weave my hand in both of his and he clasps it tight, his

gaze linked to mine, unwavering. Gone are the days of living on a bubble. He's not that guy. He likely never was. He just lacked the right woman to believe in him. At least, that's the version I'll be sure to tell our kids one day.

"Buffalo, you are on the clock," the commissioner says on the screen.

Someone cranks the volume up, and Logan stares at his cell phone on the well-polished coffee table. His palms rub my hand raw, working back and forth, his doubt threatening his faith that this life he wants is within reach.

The more seconds that tick by, the more my own certainty threatens to wane.

But then the phone rings, the Tiff fight song blaring as his ringtone. The live stream light switches to green, and the twenty-plus bodies sitting in this tight, warm living room freeze. We hold our collective breaths.

"Hello," Logan says, the phone pressed to his ear. I told him not to answer on speaker. I didn't want him to mishear a word. And I wanted this moment to be private, for him and nobody else.

His eyes flit to mine, and his mouth inches up on the right.

"Yeah?" I mouth.

His small nod is all this room needs. Everyone erupts.

"Yes, that sounds great. Thank you. I can't wait. I'm really excited to get started."

There's another pause, but the celebration is already unleashed, and there's no quieting this room now. With one finger in his open ear, Logan bends down and says, "Yes," and then, "Yes, sir. Thank you."

And with that, the call is done. Fifteen seconds. Maybe less. And Logan's life is changed forever. He stands up and pulls off his sweatshirt, revealing his jersey, his brand new and not-so-distant future home. One of his uncles fishes the hat from behind the sofa pillow and tosses it to him. It's on his head before the stream shuts off.

His hands are visibly trembling, and he seems unsteady on his legs. It's an awesome sight, especially for a man who has made a name for himself simply by being so sure on his feet. In six months, he's become this massive man, his beard thicker when he lets it grow out, and his muscles like rock.

He holds his mom in an embrace and promises he'll be safe and will come home all the time as tears fill her eyes. His dad hugs him next, his father's large palm patting his back while he sniffles away the tears in his eyes. Pride shown in so many ways, but all so real, running so deep. The line of family members filters by, like a roundabout forming around the coffee table, and when everyone's had their chance to congratulate him, he sinks down to the sofa, next to me, and holds my heart in his hands.

Our eyes meet. Everything else disappears. It's like this. Every. Single. Time. In him, I'm lost. Then I'm found.

epilogue

Logan

five years later

IT NEVER GETS old seeing little kids wearing my name and number. Their parents usually recognize me first. Sometimes they'll nod toward their son or daughter, just to make sure I see them—the young fandom.

"You can have my ice cream if you want," the kid whose jersey I'm currently signing says. He's maybe ten. I recap the pen and hold it over his shoulder, my full name now scribbled next to the stitched letters spelling FORD across his back.

"Thanks, man. But it's hot out. You deserve that ice cream. Maybe share with your sister over there." I point toward the splash pad in the park beside Columbia University.

"No way! She's a pain!" he protests, rushing away to get back to playing with his friends. I laugh at how some things never change. I have a vague memory of a similar scene playing out with me and my sister, and I still have that Emmitt Smith jersey sealed in a glass case. He was retired when I met him, but the fact I was still rocking his jersey years after his prime moved him. He signed my shirt for me, then gave me the hat off his head and signed that too. I swore I'd never get rid of either. Never will.

That jersey I just signed would sell for four hundred bucks online, but I know, without even asking, that this kid would never give it up. Not even for a thousand. He's me, two decades ago. Full of dreams and energy. He told me I was his favorite player, and that he pretends he's me when he plays touch football at school. That's how I know that jersey is never going in the wash again. I just became a part of his story.

The kids are special, and I take their time and attention seriously. They mean more to me than some guy stopping me in an airport to give me his input on what I'm doing wrong with my run game. I am usually polite and thank them, but sometimes I get grumpy and let my poise slip.

"I'm sure you're an expert. I'll see if we can get you on staff." That was my favorite comeback I dished this season.

Putting up with criticism is part of the gig, but I don't think I'll ever get used to it. It's football. And yeah, I want to win as much as, if not more than anyone, but at the end of the day, it's a game. The science is pretty basic. Work my ass off. Get big. Get faster. Grind and often bleed. Score more than the other guy, and don't fall apart. I do all of that right with a focused group of guys and we might just come away with a title. Regardless, we're paid millions.

Meanwhile, the love of my life is inventing new ways to cure depression and treat migraines with a subtle change in the way a room smells. And her paycheck? *Pffft*, she's still paying for the pleasure of doing it.

But not for long. Rachel's one week away from defending

her thesis, which should be a walk in the park now that she's presented her research to dozens of renowned chemists around the world, today's talk to a group of professors at Columbia included.

I had a little time to kill before she presents her latest research findings on the communication link between fragrance and our sense of smell. What started as a whim—a deep dive into human pheromones—manifested into a passion project to find ways to aid various forms of mental health through chemical compounds and their ultimate scent. She has the attention of all the major fragrance companies, and the people who bottle those essential oils have been after her for months. But rather than selling her data to the highest bidder, Rachel wants to treat it like an open source community farm. The good, she says, is simply too massive to let greed get in the way.

Sorta makes me feel like a chump holding out for four million more in my first contract negotiation. Not *that* big of a chump, but a little one. Tiny. Sliver of a chump. A chump worth a hundred million over the next four years.

I like to think the universe balances out, however. At least, I'm hoping Rachel sees it that way when she gets to that last slide on her presentation. I spent hours making it just right, drawing the perfect graphic, then double-checking my facts. It's been a while since I've had to put my chemistry knowledge into practice. I just hope my tutor takes it easy on me when she sees the intent.

My phone buzzes in my pocket, so I check to make sure I don't miss my own surprise.

RACHEL: It's about to start.

ME: Be right there.

This is the sixth time I've seen her deliver this presentation, so I know the places where I can slip into the back unnoticed. I wait outside the lecture hall door, listening for the group laughter over her covalent bond joke. Smart people jokes are strange, but they sure are predictable. Like the six times before, the room erupts into laughter the second she delivers her line.

"His name is Bond, hydrogen bond."

It kills. Every time. Without fail. Rolling on the floor laughing hysteria. I don't get it.

I slide into the back row amid the laughter and the door falls shut without drawing anyone's eyes to me. I always try to sit near the back when I watch Rachel speak. She's the star in any chemistry room, but I still get attention. I don't want the eyes moving away from her. They'll miss something amazing.

Most people in her circle know we're dating. Actually, most people on the planet know. We've shown up in our fair share of tabloid stories. Never the main feature, but we've been the small inset photo on the cover once or twice. The headline is usually more insulting to me, something to the effect of *Football Star Scores Scientist*. I'm fine with it. In my mind that headline should read *Jock Scores Smartest Woman in the World and Holds on for Dear Life*.

"She's killing it," says Bryan, the Columbia dean who has been pushing Rachel to publish her work. He wants her to serve as a fellow for a new division in their STEM program. She's thinking about it. Especially now that we know Upstate New York is likely to be home for the next four years.

The slides are nearing the end, and she's starting to move

around the stage. She's gotten comfortable talking in front of crowds. No longer the girl in the wings, she's always in the center. It never gets old watching people twice her age hang on the edges of their seats while she tells them what her science makes possible.

I'm on the edge of my seat, but for an entirely different reason. My hands are sunk in the front pocket of my hoodie, my palm wrapped around the small green box. I keep rotating it, my thumb rubbing raw from fidgeting with the tiny hinge on one side.

She's on her last slide before she switches to her bio and contact information, so I get to my feet, but hang back for the right moment.

"And that is how each covalent bond forms a sequence that builds these new diffused aromas. It's science at its best."

Here goes nothing.

The applause begins as she flips to her bio, only . . . I replaced it with something else.

"Thank you for joining me today. I hope you learned some—"

She glances over her shoulder and sees. It's a pretty lame drawing now that I see it blown up on a screen in an Ivy League institution. But I hope she sees past that and thinks it's sweet. Because that's what it's supposed to be. Sweet. Meaningful. Singular.

"Uh, sorry. I don't know what this is. I mean, yeah. I *know* what it is. It's the structure of carbon atoms for a diamond. What I mean is, I don't know why—"

She freezes, her hand still outstretched with her gesture toward the screen. It's hitting her. It's time.

I begin my slow walk down the steps between the two

halves of the room, and the gasps begin when the last few rows spot me and realize just as she has. I'm all in on this. And if she shoots me down in front of a room filled with the smartest people in New York, I might die. But I feel pretty solid about what her answer will be. I feel solid about us.

Rachel turns slowly, her mouth still frozen with the broken words she never finished. Her eyebrows dart to her hairline the moment she spots me, and her hands fly to her mouth, cupping it. All that's left for me to read is her eyes, and I think the fact they are welling up with tears is a good sign. This is a good cry. I'm fairly certain of it.

"Carbon," I say. She nods, her shoulders quaking. I'm not sure if it's from happy sobs or laughter. Knowing Rachel, it's probably both.

I glance to my side as I take the stage; almost everyone in the lecture hall is on their feet. A few people have covered their mouths just like my girl. Several others have their phones out, recording. Good to know I'm building a memory. That was the intent.

"Shortcake," I begin, her shoulders lifting as she laughs behind her hands. Her smile has filled her face, pushing up her eyes and dimpling her cheeks. Her hands can't hide that.

I drop to my knee and pull out the green box, flipping it open, and the audience whistles and catcalls.

"You are the best teacher I have ever had. I may be a C chemistry student, but I think I earned an A in life. And that's because you taught me the right way to live. You showed me how to take things slow, and how to face adversity. You taught me what it means to have a real partner in this world, to have someone's back, and to be loyal. Not a single day goes by that I don't wake up and thank God for you. That I don't go about my day and feel your support holding me up. That I don't come home and wish it was the off-season so I could come home to you.

"I know your life is, well, worldwide. You're meant to be a changemaker. And I'm meant to give the city of Buffalo some hope. I bring people together for a few hours of joy. You change lives everywhere. And I want to be the one standing behind you when you need it. Whatever your dream is, I want to make it happen for you. I want to stand in the back and clap with tears in my eyes while you get the accolades. I want to be known as the football player who scored a scientist—for life. So, what do you say? Rachel Edwards, Shortcake . . . will you marry me?"

My body is buzzing. I'm so nervous that sweat is pouring down my back, and it's not because of the lights on the stage. It's nerves. I see my life with her, our life together, so plainly. It's all I want.

"Yes," she says, through her hands, which still have not left her face.

I stand, and the cheers start.

"I'm sorry, but can you—" I reach for her palms and peel them away, "One more time?"

"Yes," she says, the tears flowing now as she nods along with the word.

"Yes?" I don't know why the hell I'm confirming but it suddenly feels unreal. This is happening!

"Yes!" she laughs out, stretching her hand toward me.

I had this made especially for her. It's an emerald swirl set in platinum, a two karat diamond set in the center. Her birthstones around her favorite element, carbon. I had the formula for emeralds memorized but all that's out the window now. I'm lucky I can remember my name.

"It's perfect," she says, attempting to hold her left hand

still with jittery right one. I embrace them both and help, running my thumb over the place where her ring now resides.

"You're perfect," I say.

Her hands fly to my face and she steps up on her toes, kissing me. I wrap my arms around her and hold her to me, then lift her up and swirl her around while the room fills with more whistling and shouts.

I drop her back to earth, her body sliding along mine until her feet hit the floor, and she wipes away the happy tears collecting on her cheeks.

"I'm not perfect. I'm Bond, hydrogen bond," she says. My head falls back with momentary laughter, but I right my view back on her and shake my head.

"No. You're mine. All mine."

Bonded. Forever.

THE END

Book 3: The Best Friend and the Shortstop

They grew up together and their families are friends, but each of them has been keeping a secret.

Fake dating situation, Friends to lovers, Baseball, College

Coming Summer 2024

if you enjoyed this book, you might also like:

The Varsity Series

A New Adult Sports Romance Trilogy

Begin Your Binge with Varsity Heartbreaker

Lucas Fuller is a lot of things.

He's the boy next door.

He's the first crush I ever had.

He was my first kiss.

He's also the only person who has ever broken my heart.

For two years, I've wondered what happened to the us I used to know.

We were best friends, and then suddenly…we weren't.

I tried to run away from it. I even changed schools just to make the hurt disappear.

But no matter how hard I tried to not think about Lucas, I just couldn't stay away from the high school quarterback with perfect blue eyes and so many secrets.

I'm back. We're seniors now. We've grown—all of us. And Lucas Fuller might be different, but I'm different too.

This is my time to take risks, to experience life and to fall in love for real.

I want Lucas Fuller to be a part of my story, but I know for that to happen, I need to know the truth about our past.

acknowledgments

So many to thank again for helping me to bring this book and series to you. As always, I'm nothing without my wing woman Autumn at Wordsmith Publicity, and Brenda Letendre, my patient and miracle editor. Enormous thanks to my mom and my boys. And of course, again, a shoutout to the incredibly talented Katy Mendoza, who drew Rachel to perfection! The glasses! Chef's kiss!

I am so honored to be able to do the job I do. It's my dream, and the only reason I'm able to keep pouring time and passion into stories is because of you—my readers. You make this possible, and I am forever grateful. If you've enjoyed this book, please consider sharing your excitement with others. Posts, reviews, comments, recommendations, videos, BookToks, inspiration images, photos—all of it! Every little thing helps an author to keep going. We're an anxious bunch, and we dwell in imposter syndrome more often than we care to admit. You are the life rafts that pull us out. At least for me you do. So thank you! And get ready for the last book in the Final Score series. Best friends to lovers and baseball—you know I'm going to make this one special!

about the author

Ginger Scott is a *USA Today, Wall Street Journal* and Amazon-bestselling author from Peoria, Arizona. She has also been nominated for the Goodreads Choice and RWA Rita Awards. She is the author of several young and new adult romances, including bestsellers Waiting on the Sidelines, The Hard Count, A Boy Like You, This Is Falling and Wild Reckless.

A sucker for a good romance, Ginger's other passion is sports, and she often blends the two in her stories. When she's not writing, the odds are high that she's somewhere near a baseball diamond, either watching her son swing for the fences or cheering on her favorite baseball team, the Arizona Diamondbacks. Ginger lives in Arizona and is married to her college sweetheart whom she met at ASU (fork 'em, Devils).

FIND GINGER ONLINE: www.littlemisswrite.com

facebook.com/GingerScottAuthor

instagram.com/authorgingerscott

tiktok.com/@authorgingerscott

also by ginger scott

Final Score Series

The Tomboy & The Captain

The Wallflower & The Running Back

The Best Friend & The Short Stop

The Boys of Welles

Loner

Rebel

Habit

The Fuel Series

Shift

Wreck

Burn

The Varsity Series

Varsity Heartbreaker

Varsity Tiebreaker

Varsity Rule breaker

Varsity Captain

The Waiting Series

Waiting on the Sidelines

Going Long

The Hail Mary

Like Us Duet

A Boy Like You

A Girl Like Me

The Falling Series

This Is Falling

You And Everything After

The Girl I Was Before
In Your Dreams

The Harper Boys

Wild Reckless

Wicked Restless

Standalone Reads

The Moon and Back

Southpaw

Candy Colored Sky

Cowboy Villain Damsel Duel

Drummer Girl

BRED

The Hard Count

Memphis

Hold My Breath

Blindness

How We Deal With Gravity